Public Service

By
Colin Knight

Copyright 2014 by: Colin Knight

All rights reserved

ISBN: 978-0-9940219-0-8

This is a work of fiction. The characters, names, events, views, and subject matter of this book either are the author's imagination or are used fictitiously. Any similarity or resemblance to any real people, real situations or actual events is purely coincidental and not intended to portray and person, place, or event in a false, disparaging or negative light.

The scanning, uploading and distribution of this book via the Internet or via any other means without the permission of the publisher is illegal and punishable by law. Please purchase only authorized electronic editions, and do not participate in or encourage electronic piracy of copyright materials.

Dedication

For my wife, children, family and friends: Thanks.

Prologue

EMAIL

To: Canadian Inland Security Secretariat Mail Group; PCO Media Mail Group
Subject: My Public Service

The Canadian Public Service is diseased. Too many public servants provide for themselves before the citizens they serve.

I joined the public service to serve. I was proud, motivated, and sincere.

However, inside the public service, I discovered a self-propagating, self-defeating machine, mired in bias and cronyism. A service led by narcissists and sycophants: a cadre of people motivated by personal gain, unaccountable, out of touch, insular, ignorant and self-important.

I tried to serve, but I couldn't. They were too strong, too many.

In the Canadian Inland Security Secretariat, I discovered a microcosm of the public service. Rena Kingsmore, Prudence Medowcroft, Cale Lamkin, Dudley Hobbs and Amy Hurley epitomized the diseased bureaucracy.

I couldn't beat them, join them, or change them. Then I understood. My greatest public service would be to cleanse the public service of this microcosm.

Therefore, I killed them.
I hope you understand.
I hope you like my public service.
Rory O'Grady
A true public servant

One

Stapleton & Muddle Murder Room, Ottawa Police HQ

Un-dead eyes, six of them, three pairs, drawn by the photographer, some unseen person, or a distant object, stared in three different directions. Two more un-dead eyes, moist and wide, fixed on the six. Detective Sergeant Muddle did not know the people in the three photographs, fixed by thumbtacks to the worn cork of the homicide department's "murder board." Muddle was glad he didn't. In his ten-year police career, death had not been personal. He hoped it never would.

Social media had provided Sergeant Aaron Muddle the photographs. Each photograph was recent, less than a year old. A testament to the quality of modern photography and digital printing, the eyes conveyed life and vitality. That explained the invigorated life-hue of each person; no one posted shitty photos of himself or herself on Facebook or LinkedIn.

Muddle, and his boss, Detective Inspector William Stapleton, had arrived at seven-thirty a.m. to begin the Saturday to Sunday eight a.m. to eight p.m. shift. Stapleton and Muddle were one-quarter of the Ottawa Police Department's eight person Homicide Squad. With four inspectors and four sergeants, duty called one weekend in four.

Eight a.m. had yielded an empty inbox for Muddle: a worst-case scenario for the ambitious sergeant. Restless, Muddle surfed local media and quickly discovered reports of three fatal accidents. A thread in media reports and a few Tweets that noted how each accident victim worked in the same office alerted Muddle's "coincidence antenna." By nine a.m., Muddle's training and personality compelled him to print the photographs of the dead and pin them to the murder board.

The murder board, fixed by eight flat-head screws to the pale blue wall of the murder room, had hung in the same spot since the building opened in 1983. The pin-holed and peeling board had survived the periodic updates to desks, chairs, phones, and waste bins, as well as the addition of modern desktop computers and laptops. On the far side of the large open-concept room, a modern electronic board, with the latest graphics, display functions, and integrated file sharing capabilities, stood wrapped and unused. Muddle had tried several times to bring the Homicide Squad into the twenty-first century, but the four detective inspectors, all within five years of retirement, disliked change.

Behind the sergeant, feet perched on the edge of a grey metal desk, Detective Inspector Stapleton ate the uneventful morning with a methodical attack on the Ottawa *Citizen's* weekend crossword puzzle. Without lifting his eyes from the puzzle, Stapleton blurted at Muddle.

"Six letters, a pilgrimage goal?"

"Shrine, sir."

"Thank you, sergeant."

Stubby fingers pushed the nib of the pen into the small square boxes of the puzzle as Stapleton inserted the six-letter answer. The pen drifted to the next clue and circled the number four. When the circle was thick and dark, Stapleton challenged his sergeant again.

"Three accidental deaths all connected to each other. Is it a six-letter word beginning with M, sergeant, or an eleven letter word beginning with C?"

Muddle turned from the murder board and faced Stapleton.

"Both are P, possible, sir."

"What have you discovered, sergeant?"

"The F, first, died in an automobile accident, the second drowned in the river, and the third died in a gas explosion in her home. Each one a commonplace accident, yet all the accidents occurred in five days, and all of them worked in the same P, place."

Stapleton had stopped circling the number four and moved on to filling random blank crossword boxes with the number three. Still inserting threes, Stapleton said: "Evidence, sergeant?"

"That's the P, problem, sir. There is no evidence yet, only coincidence. All three deaths are being treated as accidents, and with the third death only twelve hours old, there isn't much to go on."

Detective Inspector Stapleton eyed his young sergeant. Three years they had worked together. Nine murder cases. Seven convictions, one ruled accidental, and one unsolved, a good record. Muddle's assignment to homicide began three months after his third daughter, Alice, provided the inspector and his wife, Kate, with their sixth grandchild. "Muddle is a good kid," Chief White had told him. "I want you to take him under your wing, and make sure Muddle becomes as good a detective as you are, Bill. We will need him to replace you when you finally decide to quit and spoil those grandkids of yours." The reality was different. Muddle, enthusiastic, resourceful and committed, had needed little help.

"Where did they work, sergeant?"

"The federal government; something called the Canadian Inland Security Secretariat. According to the website, the secretariat is part of the government's P, Privy Council Office, whatever that is."

Stapleton's eyes flickered. Kate, a federal government employee for over twenty-five years before her recent retirement, had often explained the structure of the government. Stapleton put aside his crossword puzzle.

"The Privy Council Office, sergeant, is one of three government central agencies that effectively control what happens in the bureaucracy. You said they worked for inland security?"

"Yes, sir."

Stapleton moved his feet from desk to floor and focused on his eager sergeant.

"Well, sergeant, as a reward for your suspicious nature, you had better find out more on the deceased and about where they worked. If your suspicions are accurate, and three bureaucrats employed in the privy council in an area related to inland security have indeed been murdered, I expect a lot of people will soon be asking a lot of questions."

Animated by the prospect of a murder case, Muddle strode to his desk and stabbed the keyboard with his right hand as he dialled an internal phone number with his left. Stapleton, feet back on desk and crossword puzzle in hand, paused and said:

"Sergeant."

"Yes, sir."

"Remember, this is unofficial. The deaths remain accidents until evidence suggests otherwise. We don't want to feed rumours and give the media any pretense to suggest a serial killer is loose in Ottawa."

Jeff Parsons

Through a gap in the curtains, hastily closed less than three hours earlier, weak sunshine cast pale shadows across my bed and up the wall. Moisture, warm and smelly, pooled under my arms and between my shoulder blades. Saturated by death and fatigue, my mind and body craved rest. On the cusp of sleep, urgent sirens pierced my fading consciousness. Polite doorbell chimes, followed by impatient fists on wood, replaced the sirens.

Dishevelled and nervous, I staggered downstairs and opened the front door as my two sons, Michael and Ryan, their sleepiness chased away by apprehension, hovered in the hallway groggy and frightened. On the doorstep, a young police officer, face ruddy from exertion and excitement, blurted my life was in danger. Michael, who had turned thirteen a week earlier, struggled to project a manly tone as he asked why the police were here and what they wanted. To hide my thoughts, I pushed my hand up across my clammy face and through my greasy hair. I had expected the police, only not so soon.

"I don't know, Michael. I don't know what they want."

Beyond the rigid figure of the police officer, my wife's car lurched on to the driveway. Anne, un-fresh from her ten p.m. to six a.m. Sunday evening/Monday morning hospital shift, ran from the car and barged past the officer.

"What the hell's going on, Jeff? Are the kids okay? Is Ryan all right?"

Eyes wide and cheeks flushed, Anne brushed past me into the hallway and embraced Ryan and Michael. A female police officer, trim and focused, trailed Anne and squeezed uninvited into the narrow entrance. She steered Anne and the kids into the living room. Through the open doorway, I strained to hear quiet words counter my family's anxious questions.

The male police officer, still perched on the doorstep, asked me to get dressed. I hesitated. Images of death clawed for acknowledgment in my mind as I strived to convey ignorance.

"Look, what's this all about, officer? What the hell is going on?"

The officer stepped back off the doorstep and gained some composure before answering my demand.

"I'm sorry, sir. I don't know all the details, but it has something to do with the deaths of people you work with. My instructions are to secure you at Police Headquarters as soon as possible."

"What about my wife and kids? Are they safe?"

"Yes. A police officer will remain with them."

Movement behind me broke the standoff as Anne, her youthful skin corrupted by worry lines, bustled from the living room and hugged me. My kids, not understanding, cried. I dressed quickly and let the officer escort me from my home to a waiting police car.

Next door, Anthony Williams, a long-time neighbour and friend, stared in disbelief as the officer touched the top of my head to guide me into the backseat of the car. I felt like a criminal. Across the street, other neighbours, awake to begin their day, or woken early by the commotion, spied through closed windows and half open doors. Disbelief and uncertainty clear under their creased brows; was I a victim or a suspect? The car departed fast. In the back of the car, a different police officer sat beside me. Shielded by his uniform, the officer remained unresponsive to my questions about what the fuck was going on.

#

Eight kilometres and fourteen minutes later, the car entered the secure parking lot of the Ottawa Police Headquarters on the corner of Elgin and Gloucester in downtown Ottawa. The Ottawa Police Department had served Ottawa citizenry for a hundred and fifty-two years, but the HQ building had served less than fifty. Built in 1982, and formally opened by the Prince and Princess of Wales in 1983, the building design and construction reflected the cold "Brutalist" architectural style of the 1950s. Linear, fortress-like, and blockish, with lots of concrete and few windows, it projected a foreboding malevolence rather than the motto "Our Community, Our Inspiration" that adorned Ottawa's police vehicles and posters. The car stopped. The building threatened, and I didn't want to go in. I remained in my seat, unwilling to relinquish the safety of the car. A long night with little sleep had left me vulnerable and fragile.

Sensitive to my reluctance, the officer beside me said, "I'm sorry, sir. All I can tell you is three people from your office were found dead over the weekend, which, added to the three accidental deaths during the week, makes six deaths in seven days. As a precaution, all employees from your workplace are being secured for their safety."

I feigned ignorance and blurted appropriate questions and statements.

"What are you talking about? Who is dead? I know about the three last week. They were accidents. They were my friends. Don't tell me there have been more accidents! Who else is dead? What do you mean secured for my safety? I don't understand."

Rigid in his starched uniform, the officer opened the car door to its maximum and inclined his head toward the building.

"Sir, we must go inside."

My right leg had involuntarily swung off the vinyl seat and out of the car, but the rest of me wanted more information before moving.

"Why am I here? What have accidents to do with me?"

Discomfort and uncertainty clouded the officer's face as he weighed what he knew and what he should divulge.

"Sir, recent information suggests last week's deaths, and the three this weekend, might not have been accidental."

Unsure about how I should react, I remained half in and half out of the car. Confused by my lack of movement, the officer said, "I don't know the facts, but it is suspected that a Mr. Rory O'Grady killed five of your co-workers and then killed himself. He was found dead at his home early this morning."

Fear of a mistake hurled doubt and questions inside my head. How had they found Rory so soon? Had I left something? What did they want? What did they know? Why was I here? I stared at the officer and challenged.

"What? What are you talking about? Rory killed people and killed himself. I don't believe it. There must be a mistake. It can't be. I mean, I saw Rory last week. He is on holiday. Who is saying all this crap?"

Uncomfortable with my protests, but sympathetic to my confused and indignant condition, the officer lightly touched my arm. Reluctantly, I accepted the prompt and wriggled out of the car.

Remnants of the previous night's rain had pooled in the numerous depressions and potholes that characterized the over-used and under-maintained "police vehicles only" parking lot. Marked and unmarked vehicles clustered together close to the building, as though seeking protection and warmth. Bending, sitting, and exiting the car had pulled my hastily tucked shirt from my jeans. Moisture, cold and textured, crept into the space and onto my exposed flesh. Exhaust fumes, trapped by the wet air, hung at nostril height. I shivered, drew a shallow breath, and accepted the firm touch of the officer's hand on my arm.

"This way, please, sir."

He steered me around irregular shaped puddles to a windowless, steel door. A card swipe and pushed keypad buttons released a lock and the door opened. We entered a narrow corridor. Swish, scrape, and click. The door closed. My running shoes, the first footwear I had found by the front door, squelched on the painted, concrete floor. Dirty parking lot water left increasingly faint and imperfect tread marks as I walked, huddled and cold, into the bowels of the unfriendly building.

Eyes and judgment followed my progress along the hallway. Suspects, some with handcuffs, conveyed sympathy while police officers and victims threw suspicion. My escort halted in front of another metal door. Thick, unbreakable glass formed an eye-level, thirty by thirty centimetre square window. A second card swipe and keypad entry permitted access. Stairs downward beckoned uninviting beyond the door.

"Down the stairs please, sir, and then to your left."

Two flights down, another concrete-floored corridor waited. A third of the way down the corridor, a uniformed officer waited beside an open door. The officer motioned me inside. A stark, windowless room with a plain, metal table and four matching steel chairs greeted me. I stopped dead in the doorway, and my escort bumped into me. Anguish and uncertainty swamped me, and I turned around and shouted at the officer.

"I'm not going in there. Why are you putting me in here? Am I under arrest?"

The officer backed away, and held his hands palm

open and arms wide, as though implementing a learned technique to calm an agitated person.

"I'm sorry, sir. It is all we have available now. It's for your own safety, Mr. Parsons. We are taking the same precautions with everyone who works in your office. A detective will be down shortly to explain everything."

Calmed by the officer's tactics, I shuffled into the room and thought about the word safety. Steel door, plain grey walls, steel furniture, and security cameras; secure yes, safe no. Still cold, but not shivering, I flinched as the door closed. Apprehension-induced sweat beaded on my forehead. I sat on one of the uninviting chairs. Exhausted, I bent toward the table and rested my forehead on the cold steel, and thoughts of death claimed my consciousness.

Most people believe they could kill. Everyone has thoughts about killing someone. Many people talk about it: over beers, by the campfire, fishing, hunting, or even golfing. Some express vigilante dismay at the judicial punishment system and, like *Death Wish* One through Five, advocate direct action. In university, I participated in abstract, pseudo-intellectual talk about killing people: the annoying roommate or the professor who bored the crap out of everyone. Many people say they would kill pedophiles, rapists, or losers who prey on old people. Just talk; attempts to combat impotency; misplaced anger; bullshit.

Except, as I later told the detective who interviewed me, Rory O'Grady was one person I believed when he said he would "kill for the right reason." Of course, I said I thought he had meant the same reasons most people usually use to justify killing someone: the person had killed a member of their family; entered their house at night; was attacking someone else, or in self-defence; in service of one's country and situations like that. However, Rory, according to the police, had other reasons to justify killing people. Not only that, but they said he killed them all in one week, but did they believe it?

#

Stapleton & Muddle - Rorke's Drift

The body, cut down and covered, greeted Detective Inspector Stapleton and Sergeant Muddle when they arrived at Rorke's Drift. A length of coarse rope stuck out from the tarp, its unseen end leading to the unmistakable lump that denoted the head of a corpse. Four cats, corralled in a large cardboard box, mewed and pawed as their innate senses told them something was wrong.

Gloved and booted, Stapleton lifted the head end of the tarp. A black tipped tongue protruded between pale lips and bloodless, sagging facial skin. An odour of urine and feces, expelled as the body died, wafted past the head and into Stapleton's nostrils. Death by hanging wasn't new to the detective, and he didn't linger. He could wait for the forensic results. Sergeant Muddle, tasked upon arrival to gather the facts, reported.

"Deceased has been confirmed as P, Prudence Medowcroft. Body discovered hanging in tree this morning at approx. 9 a.m. by Mr. Manuel Cortes, her gardener. Mr. Cortes cut her down with his trimming sheers and said he used the chair over there to reach the rope. Medowcroft lived alone with three cats. There is no sign of a struggle inside or out. Patio door found open. There is evidence of alcohol and marijuana consumption inside, but no indications of other persons. It could be a suicide, sir."

Stapleton, hands stuffed in the pockets of his raincoat, surveyed the scene. A rope tossed over a tree branch and tied off around the tree trunk; a chair, alcohol, drugs, no struggle or forced entry; a lonely woman in a secluded lakeside cottage. Without speaking, Stapleton walked toward the lake. Muddle caught up to Stapleton who said: "Not an accident then, sergeant?"

Muddle didn't respond. It wasn't a question. He knew what the inspector meant.

Before leaving Police Headquarters, an email informed the detectives that Medowcroft was a director at the Canadian Inland Security Secretariat. She had been direct boss of the three accidental death victims pinned to the sergeant's murder board. Close to the lake, Stapleton became more direct.

"Now we have four deaths in six days, all federal government employees, all worked in the same area, and the first three reported to this latest victim, who appears to have committed suicide. What do you make of it, sergeant?"

Brown lake water ended the police officers' march, and Muddle considered the inspector's question. The obvious conclusion, the one to "jump to," as the media would undoubtedly do, was that the boss, Medowcroft, had killed her subordinates and then killed herself. Three years ago, when Muddle joined Stapleton as a rookie homicide investigator, he would have jumped to the obvious. Three years had taught him a lot: especially about his inspector.

Out of sight on the lake, a loon warbled for its mate as water frothed against the sergeant's polished, black leather shoes. Stepping back to save his shoes, Muddle said: "Medowcroft's death is convenient, sir, very convenient."

"And?"

"Well, it's also rare, sir. Female serial killers are extremely rare. Also for a woman to kill three people in such a short time is even rarer plus the fact the nature of the other deaths, by car, river and explosion, don't fit with a female killer."

"Is there anything else, sergeant?"

Muddle scanned the scene, checked his notes, but came up empty.

"Sir?"

"Cats, sergeant, there are too many cats. You said Medowcroft lived alone with three cats. There are four in the box. Three are old, and one is a kitten. Ask the gardener about the kitten. I want to know where it came from and when."

As Muddle strode to find the gardener, Stapleton called after him.

"Sergeant, you had better get me a list of the remaining employees, their addresses, and home phone numbers. I want this to be a suicide, but I don't think it is."

#

Jeff Parsons

My forehead ached. I sat up, rubbed my brow with the sleeve on my jacket, and swivelled my head to view the room. The ceiling was high, about fourteen feet rather than eight. Attached to the ceiling, in opposite corners, small cameras clung to metal brackets. Each camera had a red light on top, indicating, I assumed, invasive watchfulness. I searched the walls expecting the staple two-way mirror of police movies. Instead, where a mirror should logically have been, a grey metal cover, like the metal roller doors used at night on storefronts in fragile urban areas, hung, padlocked to a bracket a quarter of the way up the wall. No plug sockets, or light switch, occupied the walls. The door had no handle. I inclined forward and pushed back on the chair to stand. The chair didn't give. Like the table, the chair stuck to the floor: an unpleasant room for unpleasant business. Hemmed in by the chair, I returned my head to the table and waited as thoughts and images of my victims sparred with the need for focus and consistency.

#

Stapleton & Muddle - Kingsmore's House

Vomit floated on the surface of the brown and yellowed hot water. Undigested yellow corn kernels swirled among cubed orange carrots, green peas, and chewed French fries. Bobbing above and beneath the water, partially obscured by food and bubbles, the body of a woman twisted gently, as though a child in an enormous womb. Clutched in her hands, a distorted image of some sort of speaker system flickered under the ripples. Stapleton, peering into the hot tub, raised an eyebrow to his sergeant.

"The husband, Ted Kingsmore, discovered the body at eleven-thirty p.m. when he came home. He had been at the pub with his curling team and had a pie with fries to soak up the beer. He lost the lot when he found his wife floating in the hot tub."

Steam rose and swirled from the open tub as the heater and pumps struggled to maintain the set temperature. A uniformed officer, hovering by the patio door, responded to Stapleton's nod. He joined the detective and his sergeant by the hot tub.

"Officer Davies, isn't it?"

"Yes, inspector."

"Tell us what you know, officer."

Head down, straining in the poor light, Officer Davies consulted his notebook before speaking.

"Husband, Ted Kingsmore, called 911 at eleven-thirty-four p.m. and reported an accident. Said his wife was dead in the hot tub. I was first on scene. By the time the paramedics arrived, Mr. Kingsmore had told me his wife was the boss at the Canadian Inland Security Secretariat. I recalled there had been three other deaths linked to the secretariat last week and chatter earlier today mentioned a fourth death at Lake Phillip, so I told the paramedics to leave the body in place and await your arrival."

"Good work, Davies. What else have you observed?"

Officer Davies relaxed at the inspector's praise and became less formal.

"Well, as you can see, an electrical cord is attached to the iPod speaker in her hands. The cord runs to a socket in the house. When I unplugged the cord, I noticed the socket is not GFI rated, although there is a GFI socket outside on the wall a few feet past the patio door. Her husband confirmed that his wife regularly took a hot tub with wine and music, but the iPod was always used with the battery, never with a power cord."

"Are there any signs of an intruder?"

"Not so far, sir. Mr. Kingsmore indicated that when he arrived home, all the doors and gates were closed and locked. I did take a quick look in the back by the pool. The bushes are dense, but a section appears disturbed, and a person could get through. It's hard to tell in the dark."

"Did you or anyone else touch or move anything, officer?"

"Besides unplugging the power cord for safety, nothing has been touched or moved since I arrived."

"Thank you, Officer Davies. Please keep the scene secure until forensics arrives. They might be a while as they were still processing the scene of one of Mrs. Kingsmore's colleagues."

Officer Davies left to direct others, and Stapleton

spoke to Muddle.

"Davies is a good officer, sergeant. You might keep him in mind when you are looking for your own sergeant, eh?"

"Yes, sir."

Stapleton, his face moist from the hot tub steam, turned three hundred and sixty degrees, before addressing Muddle again.

"I don't think four apparent accidental deaths and one possible suicide in six days for people who all work together is credible, sergeant. At six a.m. today, I want every employee of the Canadian Inland Security Secretariat brought downtown for questioning and for safety."

"Yes, sir."

"And, sergeant, get some help to gather the reports on the other deaths. There is a killer in Ottawa."

Two

Cale Lamkin - Alive

Cale Lamkin was born blue; blue collar. His family lived somewhere in the Ottawa Valley. His father worked odd jobs while his mother endured fifteen years of childbearing labour for five live births. Since his first awareness of his humble beginnings, Cale had strived to "change colour," rise above, and forget his origins.

As a boy, Cale found order, discipline, and hope in the local Cubs, Scouts, and Air Cadets. In adulthood, he turned to Canada's Army Reserve, where he cemented his compulsion for rules, control, and order.

Cale's average height provided a decent frame for his solid, fit, muscular torso. Short, light brown hair capped an always-close shaved face, clear blue eyes, white teeth and blemish-free skin. Cale was handsome, rugged, and proper in his shiny shoes and crisp pressed clothes. He was also a dickhead and loud: he shouted rather than spoke to convey his inflexible, conservative views. Constantly interrupting to explain how he had always done more, or better, or more extreme, than the other person, Lamkin was a competitive, controlled rule follower, who craved leadership and played martyr-like roles.

University educated, thanks to a government-funded scholarship for underprivileged children, and blue collar, street smart, Cale talked overly loud on the phone in his office, so he could be overheard expressing the importance of his work. Cale wanted, and expected, to be the boss and in control, despite the fact he couldn't function without established rules and clear direction. He was a solider, not a general.

Cale irritated most of his peers. It was both his personality and management's perceptions of him that annoyed people. To his detractors, Cale was a coarse self-promoter, whose narrow-minded and rule-bounded approach to policy development typified the stale Canadian Inland Security Secretariat policies in particular and policy development in the public service in general. His self-righteous, hypocritical elitism, that oozed from every pore and infused his every comment, and his denial of his humble, blue-collar origins revealed Cale's real character; denial of facts, either by commission of outright falsehoods or omission through selective stories, was no more than deceitful lies.

Management, who had their own share of sanctimony, thought of Cale differently. To management, Cale Lamkin epitomized "Mister Reliable." An employee who would always do the right thing, say the right thing, and do as directed with few, if any, awkward questions. Clean-cut, handsome, forthright within understood boundaries, and always the first to volunteer, Cale was loved by management.

Once, when Rena Kingsmore, the Assistant Deputy Minister of the Canadian Inland Security Secretariat, called Cale "the salt of the earth" during a meeting, colleagues smirked. They asked one another if Kingsmore had meant salt of the earth in the biblical sense or in a Middle Ages sense when peasants used salt to poison the land as punishment to landowners who had offended society in some way. Cale wasn't peer-popular.

#

Fitness was Cale's opium: biking, squash, tennis, soccer, climbing, basketball, and Ultimate Frisbee. Cale did every mainstream sport, except swimming, which he said was too slow for him. In support of these activities, Cale ran to work three days a week, forty weeks or so of the year. Only in the worst weather would Cale substitute the treadmill for the sidewalk or river trail.

A classic overachiever, Cale didn't just run to work in shorts, shirt, and shoes. Neither, like others, did he carry the minimum needed for a quick shower and change of clothes. Cale, true to his Air Cadet and Army Reserves training, packed extra weight into his backpack to keep himself in shape and ready for anything. Cale repeatedly pontificated about his running system, especially about his Monday, Wednesday, and Friday runs to work. On Mondays, he packed an extra forty pounds in his backpack, on Wednesday twenty pounds, and on Fridays, he joked that he only had an extra ten pounds. His route was 14.3 kilometres each way, and he ran on the soft gravel by the river to make it a little more difficult. On Mondays, his slow day, Lamkin carried extra towels and clothes for the week to allow lighter and faster runs on Wednesdays and Fridays.

He explained and described his running route and weight system in a superior tone, challenging others to match his physical abilities or doubt his claims. No one did either. His physique confirmed Cale's fitness and abilities.

Cale was also an equipment snob. Every item of sports' related equipment or apparel was, according to Cale, the best, most proven, and most used by the world's leading athletes. His feet pounded the gravel in the latest running shoes, most recently the Mizuno Wave Creation, which retailed for around two hundred dollars. Synthetic, quick dry, stay cool shirts covered Cale's torso, and Max Cool shorts, with dual holsters for energy gel drinks, covered front and back private parts. Ray Ban Sport sunglasses protected his eyes, no matter the weather.

In addition, Cale ran with a heart monitor, a GPS watch, a Bluetooth system for his cell phone and BlackBerry, and an iPod for music. Finally, Cale never left home without his prized Special Ops Black Hawk military watch. All these monitors, communication, entertainment, and time and location tellers, hung securely attached and strapped to appropriate parts of Cale's anatomy.

Dudley Hobbs, another analyst in the secretariat, joked one day that if Cale carried a rifle along with all the other equipment, he would look like Claude van Dam in *Universal Soldier*. Cale had preened at this suggestion, oblivious to the possible duality of the comment in relation to the character and personality of both the actor and the movie's protagonist. Under his breath, another colleague, Rory O'Grady, commented how Cale was more like Dennis in *Run, Fat Boy, Run*, but without the fat.

Often Cale would challenge others in the office to join him on one of his morning runs, adding there was no need for others to carry extra weight! Ever helpful, Cale posted a map of his route in case anyone wanted to join up with him, halfway maybe. Of course, the map included a statistics box indicating Cale's most recent time, heart rate, calories used and distance. Cale was such a prick.

#

Stapleton & Muddle
Rory O'Grady's House
Old Barrhaven

The morning was cool. Steam condensed on the windshield and side windows of their unmarked police sedan. Stapleton and Muddle sipped coffee and chewed Tim Horton's breakfast sandwiches. It was five-thirty a.m. Monday. An hour had passed since the coroner had pronounced on Rena Kingsmore's death and allowed her body out of the hot tub. The detectives, exhausted yet stimulated, had sought substance at Tim's twenty-four seven drive thru on Alta Vista Drive. Stapleton reached for the vibrating phone on the dashboard. After a few grunts and two questions, Stapleton ended the call. In response to Muddle's inquisitive expression, weary words slipped by Stapleton's food-laden teeth.

"We have another dead government worker: Rory O'Grady, 223 Shauna Street in Old Barrhaven. When uniform responded to the 911 call, they recognized the victim's name and address from the list of employees they were to bring to the station this morning."

Muddle pushed the car into drive and stomped the accelerator. Coffee escaped Stapleton's lid and dripped unnoticed on to his right thigh. Both men munched and sipped slowly as they reflected on another death.

Twenty-five minutes later, Muddle eased their car beside an assortment of emergency vehicles, bystanders, and a local cable TV network SUV. With no fire to extinguish, and no body to revive, fire crews repacked hoses and breathing apparatus as ambulance crews mingled and waited for direction.

The detectives passed under the improvised grey duct tape a resourceful uniformed officer had strung from bush to tree to garage. On the ground, twenty feet from the open garage door, a thin blanket conformed to the contours of the body it covered. A uniformed officer greeted the inspector and nodded at the sergeant. Unbidden, the officer withdrew his notebook, took a breath, and began.

"A 911 call was received at 3:58 a.m. Mr. Gordon Bertrand, a retired bus driver, was out with his dog when he saw smoke coming from the garage door. Mr. Bertrand is disabled and has a motorized wheelchair. The garage door is stiff, and he couldn't open it. Fire crews were first on scene at 4:18 a.m. and entered the garage. The smoke was exhaust fumes. They pulled an unconscious male from the backseat of a car. Paramedics and fire crew attempted resuscitation, but the man was dead. The deceased is Mr. Rory O'Grady. After the body was retrieved, and the fire crews gave the all clear, the scene was cordoned off."

"Thank you, officer," said Stapleton. "Could you expand the crime scene to a one hundred and fifty feet perimeter around the house and all the way to the end of the driveway? Also, see if you can locate a crime scene tent and have it placed in front of the garage. I want to keep the TV cameras from zooming inside." With the officer dismissed, Stapleton turned to Muddle.

"What did O'Grady do at the Canadian Inland Security Secretariat?"

"P, Policy analyst: same as Dudley Hobbs and Cale Lamkin."

"Did O'Grady work for Medowcroft?"

"Yes."

"Forensics will be a while at Kingsmore's hot tub. We had better look inside the garage. Bring the boots and gloves, sergeant."

"Do you want to view the body first, sir?"

"No, not now, sergeant. I've seen enough death

this weekend."

Stapleton shuffled his feet as he waited for Muddle and ignored shouted questions from reporters hemmed in by the police cordon. The questions were all the same: Is there a serial killer on the loose in Ottawa? Stapleton was in no doubt, but it wasn't his place to tell them. Muddle returned and, booted and gloved, they approached the garage.

A black SUV occupied most of the single car garage, and the odour of exhaust fumes remained heavy in the air. Muddle squeezed left and driver's side, while Stapleton eased right and passenger side. They had to close the rear doors, opened by the fire crew, to extract the body, before meeting, leaning head and torso, in the front of the car. Silence accompanied their assessment. Muddle exited first and closed the driver side door. He slid sideways to the front of the SUV and bent down to examine the front bumper. A grunt preceded his call to Stapleton.

"Sir. Over here."

Stapleton edged backward out of the front seat and stumbled on the recycling bins that crowded the doorway to the house.

"What is it, sergeant?"

"Hard to tell in this light, but it looks like a narrow scuff mark with a very F, faint imprint of a tire tread. I'm guessing, of course, but the mark could be F, from a bicycle tire. The height is about right, and reports on Dudley Hobbs's accident included sightings of a large black SUV."

Stapleton leaned and strained between the car and wall to view the scuffmark and nodded for Muddle to exit the garage. Outside, Stapleton sucked air and said to Muddle: "So, sergeant, another apparent suicide and perhaps a convenient suggestion that O'Grady, or at least his car, was involved in the death of Dudley

Hobbs."

Muddle bounced on his toes, eager to enter the house.

"Yes, sir, we should get inside the house. There might be another body or…"

Stapleton held a hand up to his eager sergeant. "I don't think so, sergeant. Let forensics go first. I have a feeling this is the last one. We need to talk to someone from the Canadian Inland Security Secretariat who is still alive."

Three

Interview - Room 5, Ottawa Police HQ

The cell door squeaked open. I peeled my forehead, numbed by hard cold steel, from the table and pushed the palms of my hands into my eye sockets to massage blood and warmth up to my head and brain. Between my fingers, distorted images of two men entered the room. One, small, dishevelled, and maverick, took the chair opposite mine. The other, tall, tidy, and professional, stood behind the sitter: Opposites. Good cop, bad cop. Which was which?

"Good morning, Mr. Parsons," said the short one. "I'm Detective Inspector Stapleton. This is Detective Sergeant Muddle. First, let me apologize for the room. It's all we have available right now. We will find something more suitable soon. Meanwhile, is there anything you need?"

Confidence bypassed the unkempt clothes and Colombo-like appearance. Good cop. Without a strategy or a plan, I demanded an explanation of what was going on, coffee, and something to eat.

"Coffee and food are on the way. As to what is going on, I understand our uniformed officer provided some preliminary information."

"Kind of, but it didn't make sense. He said something about three people found dead on the weekend and that the other deaths last week, of people at my office, might not have been accidents." I hunched my shoulders, shook my head left to right, and quietly asked, "What's he talking about?"

Stapleton, the inspector, held a silver pen between thumb and forefinger; its tip hovered a millimetre above the steel table as though he was about to write or draw something.

"I don't want to alarm you, Mr. Parsons, but on Saturday night, Prudence Medowcroft was discovered hanging outside her cottage. On Sunday night, Rena Kingsmore was found floating in her hot tub, and early this morning, police officers discovered Rory O'Grady's body at his home in Barrhaven."

I pushed my eyes wide, threw my shoulders back, and tried to push away from the table. Frustrated by the immovable chair and table, I shook my head and stammered.

"Jesus. What the hell is going on? This is crazy. Why? What does it mean? Are you sure?"

Cool, pensive eyes followed my movements. I imagined the detective evaluating my body language as he placed marks and numbers against some personal measure that indicated a person's guilt or innocence.

"Unfortunately, Mr. Parsons, we are sure. We have reason to believe these deaths, as well as the deaths last week of Cale Lamkin, Dudley Hobbs, and Amy Hurley, may not have been accidents."

I wriggled, uncomfortable, under the detective's scrutiny.

"Come on. You can't be serious. I don't believe it."

"Oh, but we are serious, Mr. Parsons, which is why you are here."

I sensed the implied link between non-accidental

deaths and my presence at the police station had been deliberate. Afraid I might be a suspect, I went on the offensive.

"What? What do I have to do with it? Hold on a minute. The police officer, the one who sat next to me in the car, he said Rory killed them and then killed himself. What am I doing here? What's all this about my safety if Rory killed them, and he's dead?"

Leaning back and opening his arms, Stapleton eased away from his overt approach.

"I'm sorry, Mr. Parsons. That was a bit of a communication mixup. When we discovered the bodies of Rena Kingsmore, and Prudence Medowcroft, we decided five deaths in six days of people who all worked together was too much of a coincidence. Therefore, to be prudent, we decided to secure all other immediate members of your work group. But in between sending officers to collect you and the others, we found Mr. O'Grady's body, as well as some incriminating evidence."

I copied the detective and tried to relax against the hard chair.

"I'm not in any danger then?"

"We don't believe so."

"Good. Can I go home?"

The detective paused. We locked eyes. I should have left, insisted I be taken home, but while I hesitated the inspector spoke.

"Well, Mr. Parsons, you are certainly free to go; however, we would appreciate your help to understand Mr. O'Grady. Some of your colleagues indicated you knew O'Grady better than anyone."

An impulse to flight lifted my heels from the floor. My legs bounced on the balls of my toes. Damn.

"Er, yes, I guess I did know him pretty well. But I don't know anything about him killing people, for

Christ's sake."

"I don't expect you do, but you might be able to help us understand him. Get to know what he was like perhaps?"

I was about to protest when a knock at the door preceded a tray-bearing police officer. He was the same officer who shared the backseat of the unmarked police car. Motioned by Detective Sergeant Muddle, the officer placed the tray on the cold table. Detective Stapleton nodded, and the officer withdrew. A Tim Horton's coffee cup, sugar with milk and cream, along with what I recognized as Tim Horton's breakfast sandwiches, occupied the tray.

The detective motioned to the tray. "Coffee and sandwiches, Mr. Parsons. Sergeant Muddle and I will give you a few minutes to eat, and then perhaps we can get started."

Stapleton paused at the doorway. He turned and asked with surprising casualness, "Mr. Parsons, where were you on Monday morning between seven and eight a.m.?"

Focused on the breakfast in front of me, I was caught off guard by the detective's question. I pried the lid off the coffee cup to buy time before I answered.

"I was probably on my way to work. I usually leave around seven-fifteen and get to work at eight depending on traffic."

"Do you drive to work or take the bus?"

"Drive, why?"

"Some people car pool, Mr. Parsons. Do you?"

"No, I tried once, but my wife's schedule at the hospital and helping my kids get ready for school make it difficult for me to commit to carpooling."

"I see. So, you travel to work by car and alone?"

I fixed the detective with an annoyed expression and raised my voice to challenge the obvious implication.

"Yes. Why, what the hell are you getting at, detective?"

Indifferent to my expression, he continued his poorly veiled accusation.

"Cale Lamkin's death occurred by the Rideau River not far from where you live. Based on your home address, I expect your drive to work would take you part way along the river. I wondered if you recall anything from Monday's drive to work."

I thought about the drive to work that Monday. I recalled a lot, but nothing I wanted to share with the detective.

"No, it was just another Monday morning. I don't remember anything unusual."

Stapleton nodded in response to my answer, his expression blank and unreadable. When the detectives had left, I added cream and milk - half-and-half - to my coffee and inspected the two English muffin sandwiches. One held egg, bacon, and cheese, the other, egg, sausage, and cheese. I ate both. I didn't recollect saying I wanted to get started, but it didn't seem as though I had a choice. Invigorated by coffee and grease, I thought about Stapleton and Muddle.

My first thought was Muddle was a hell of a name for a detective. Not that he looked muddled. On the contrary, Muddle was clean-shaved and well dressed. His pants and shirt well pressed, his tie was straight, and his jacket hung well. Un-scuffed shoes, short-cropped hair, and a bland but tidy face, completed the immaculate picture: a walking, talking mannequin. At least, I assumed he talked.

Detective Inspector Stapleton was an older, more used mannequin. His clothes, the same ensemble as Muddle, except worn around the edges, rumpled in the middle and stained in the usual places. Stapleton's face resembled his clothes: experienced, used, comfortable. Except his eyes: they were bright, clear, and insightful. His nonchalant question about my whereabouts on Monday morning when Cale Lamkin died had been sly. I would have to be careful about what I said to Detective Stapleton. He was no slouch.

Four

Cale Lamkin - Dead

Cale Lamkin dumped his gym bag and squash racket on the hallway floor before the front door had closed behind him. Hesitant, for fear of pulling a muscle, Cale lifted his body up and down on the balls of his feet to ease the tightness in his calves before he climbed the stairs to bed. Cale's last conscious thought before he slept had been to reaffirm to himself how the pain and exhaustion was always worth the result.

A buzz, loud and insistent, dragged Cale from contented slumber. He cursed the radio alarm clock as he stabbed at the off switch. Cale wasn't married, but his long-time girlfriend, Rhonda, stayed over most weekends, and she stirred beside him at the sound of the alarm.

Cale was exhausted. A weekend filled with sports had left him drained and sluggish. Basketball on Saturday afternoon and soccer on Sunday morning would have been no problem, but the squash club round robin competition on Sunday night, and the fact that he kept winning until he lost a grueling three-match final to the club champion, had left his legs throbbing and jumpy. His run to work would be difficult and slower than usual, but with the possibility someone from the office might accept his challenge and unexpectedly join him,

Public Service

he had no choice but to slog his way through. He couldn't take the chance. He would never hear the end of it.

Rhonda also exercised constantly to maintain her lean body to match Cale's physique and the stamina his exercise regime gave him in bed, and for that matter all over the house. Similar personalities, they both counted the number of thrusts per minute and calculated how many calories they used. Rhonda reached for Cale, caressed his inner thigh, and used her fingers to cup Cale's testicles as expectation and desire mounted. Workday mornings allowed little time for foreplay, but if they rutted, more than made love, at least they had plenty of it, unlike many of Rhonda's friends who complained of three-minute fucks, three times a week. Like this morning, for example, twenty-eight minutes and thirty-six seconds: God, how they had fucked. Distracted by leaden legs, Cale's stamina had more to do with an inability to maintain the peak rhythm needed to achieve orgasm than sexual prowess. Three times, he had come close before a final fourth attempt released him to a mix of relief and dehydration.

By seven thirty-five a.m., Cale was dressed, packed, cinched, secured, electronically activated and ready to begin his 14.3 kilometre run to work. The townhouse he called home backed onto the Rideau River. A gravel path abutted the river for eleven kilometres until it changed into a paved footpath for the last three kilometres into the downtown core. The gravel path was about one hundred fifty metres from the backyard fence and Cale, against city rules, had installed a gate from which he could access the path without having to use the official public access point.

When Cale reached the gravel path at seven forty-one, he set the GPS, the MapMyRun software, activated his heart monitor, checked his BlackBerry was on and the Bluetooth enabled. Then he inserted his iPod earphones, set the volume to sixty per cent, and selected his Monday playlist. After checking his Black Hawk watch, he donned his Ray Ban sunglasses, despite an early morning mist, and placed one heavy leg in front of the other.

Six steps into his run, *We Built This City* by Starship pulsated into Cale's ears. Three minutes and eighteen seconds later, *Photograph* by Def Leppard took up the beat until seven minutes and 1.2 kilometres into his run, Abba's *Does Your Mother Know?* brought a smile to his face as the memory of sixteen-year-old Alison Scott floated into his mind. Alison Scott hadn't been his first, but she had been the first one to use music as an accompaniment to sex, and in her particular case, as a way to mock her mother. *Does Your Mother Know?* had been their favourite fuck song. Not for the first time, Cale asked himself where she was now. Was she a mother? Maybe Alison's influence had drawn him to 1970s and 1980s music for running.

As Cale reached the 3.7 kilometre mark, and rounded a gradual bend where the gravel path ran less than ten feet from the bank of the Rideau River, the music's tempo changed to *What I Like About You*, a classic Romantics song from the eighties.

Twenty metres into the bend, Cale slowed. Turned earth, piles of gravel, and a large drainage tube ready for installation under the gravel path, blocked his route. Maintenance work had begun on the shore side of the path, and bright orange cones marked a temporary grass path closer to the river's edge. Three point seven kilometres had loosened Cale's leg muscles, and Cale sprung toward the temporary path, imagining the grass path was a Special Forces test that he had to cross quickly without leaving a mark. Had it been a Special Forces test, Cale would have failed because he didn't cross the path, although he didn't leave much of a mark.

So focused on his Special Forces fantasy, lulled by the rhythm and words of *What I Like About You*, and processing images through mist-covered sunglasses, Cale's first sensory signal of something, or someone, hurtling toward him from the shore side of the path was a blurred image of a large, solid figure wearing an oddly familiar flat cap style hat. The image solidified and made contact. The impact shunted Cale off the gravel path toward the river like a locomotive shunting a freight car onto a siding, and Cale's right arm wind-milled in a desperate and ineffective effort to prevent his plunge into the indifferent water.

Two hours later, at nine forty-five a.m., numerous unanswered emails and calls to Cale's BlackBerry prompted Cale's boss, Prudence Medowcroft, to tell Amy Hurley to call Cale's home. Unanswered phone calls to his home provoked a search of his personnel file for emergency contact numbers. Calls to his parent's home in the Ottawa Valley revealed they hadn't seen or heard from Cale since the spring when he had come home for the funeral of a former leader of the local Air Cadets Squadron.

At ten-fifty, a group discussion led to Rhonda's name, and the recollection she worked for the Department of Fisheries and Oceans. A search on the Government Electronic Directory Service provided Rhonda's phone number, and a quick discussion with Rhonda confirmed Cale had left for work as usual around seven-thirty a.m.

At eleven-thirty, a call to the local police elicited a calm but firm response that four hours did not constitute a missing person. A second call, this time from Rena Kingsmore, the Assistant Deputy Minister of the Canadian Inland Security Secretariat, hinting how Cale's employment included access to top secret and classified government documents, stimulated the local police into action. Officers on bicycle and foot followed Cale's running route but found nothing.

In late afternoon, a police dog, its nose filled with scent from one of Cale's gym bags, set off from Cale's home toward the riverside trail. Thirteen minutes later, the dog ran circles around several City of Ottawa Parks and Recreation workers who were shovelling dirt and gravel on top of a drainage pipe they had earlier laid under the path. After a few false steps, the dog ran toward the river and stopped at the top of the embankment. Police officers, city workers, and the dog stared into the water.

Cale's weighted backpack, combined with the river's slow current, hadn't moved the body far. Shortly before midnight, police divers found his body close to where the dog's sniffing had ended. Initial consensus concluded accidental death due to drowning, and nobody suggested the need for a criminal investigation.

Cale's parents collected his body and took him back to their small, blue-collar town in the Ottawa Valley for burial. They held a memorial at the local Legion, and Air Cadets dressed up and paid tribute to a former comrade. The paper ran an obituary entitled "Local Boy Made Good Comes Home." Despite all his efforts, Cale died as blue as he was born.

Several days after Cale's burial, Ottawa city officials announced they had begun an investigation into the City of Ottawa's policies and procedures concerning the fencing and marking of temporary paths, but no one ever recalled or asked for a report. Media investigators reported on Cale's fitness but noted that despite his athletic abilities, he had not been able to swim. They also mentioned his weekend activities and Rhonda's assertion that Cale had been tired that morning, although she made no mention of the twenty-eight minute, thirty-six second body fluid exchange that preceded his departure. The media made much of the quantity and variety of Cale's equipment, and, of course, how his backpack contained an extra forty pounds. Although media reports didn't explicitly say it, unspoken common sense concluded Cale had been foolish to run along a slippery riverbank, loaded down with a weighted pack, wrapped up in "God knows" how many electrical devices, and wearing sunglasses on a dark, misty morning! Common sense and compassion seemingly had no time for each other.

Five

Interview - Room 5, Ottawa Police HQ

Breakfast sandwiches consumed, and coffee down past halfway, the handle-less door opened. Muddle entered first and held the door for Detective Stapleton. Pecking order affirmed.

Sergeant Muddle strode with purpose to the far wall and made a sharp parade ground turn. He parted his legs, placed his hands behind his back, and leaned lightly against the wall. Sergeant Muddle's position against the far wall placed him directly behind the chair affixed to the floor on the opposite side of the table from my own chair. When Detective Stapleton sat in the other chair, as he had during his earlier visit, it would be impossible, unless I dropped my chin on my chest, or turned completely around, to avoid observation by at least one pair of eyes. Coincidence perhaps, strategy probably, unnerving certainly.

Detective Stapleton spread himself into the other chair and haphazardly deposited his detective wares on the table: notebook, pencil, several manila folders, cell phone, and a glasses case. Last, he removed his gold wristwatch and placed it, facing himself, among the other detective equipment. The detective wriggled in a fruitless attempt to find comfort on the steel seat. I could have told him, and he should have known, that no amount of wriggling would have made these steel chairs comfortable. With his ritual complete, Stapleton scratched three lines on his pad to check the pen had ink and said: "Ah, Mr. Parsons, are you feeling better? How were the sandwiches? Do you need more coffee?"

"Sandwiches were great. I'm good for coffee, thanks."

"Right, let's get started, shall we? First, thank you for agreeing to help us with our investigation. You are, of course, under no obligation to remain and can leave any time. However, as I said earlier, I believe your knowledge of Mr. O'Grady, and the inner workings of your office, will provide valuable information as we begin to build a picture of Mr. O'Grady and try to understand his alleged actions."

Stapleton peered at me, pen poised and expectant. I had heard his words but didn't quite grasp what he meant.

"Okay, but what do you mean by the inner workings of the office?"

"Well, Mr. Parsons, all the deaths were co-workers. Logic suggests there may be a link between their deaths and the work environment. Of course, something else might account for Mr. O'Grady's actions, but at this time, I plan to focus on the work environment."

I nodded. He was right: more right than he thought. Detective Stapleton and Sergeant Muddle stared at me. Two heads, four eyes. Unfair odds. Stapleton asked if I knew of anything about Rory, or the work environment, that might have caused Rory to what he did. They waited expectantly. I let the four eyes merge and blur as I thought about all the things I did know about Rory O'Grady and what went on at work. After a decent thinking period, I said, "I don't think so. What reason could anyone have for killing five people?"

Detective Stapleton waited, silent. I soon learned silence was one of Stapleton's interview techniques. The other was the use of his eyebrow. Finally, unnerved by the silence, I said I couldn't think of any big event or anything that would make anyone crazy enough to kill someone, let alone five people. Pushed by the detective's silence, I suggested perhaps an accumulation of little things juxtaposed against perceptions, conjecture, and maybe Rory's own personality traits, might explain something. Ink from Stapleton's pen created algebra on the page as the equation $X+Y+W=R$ appeared from underneath the detective's hand. When his pen stopped, Stapleton spoke.

"What do you mean, Mr. Parsons?"

I asked the detective if he remembered the character Michael Douglas played in the movie, *Falling Down*.

"You know, the scene where the man was driving home on the highway and got gridlocked and people were blaring horns, shouting, and cursing. The guy snapped. He got out of the car, and left it right on the highway. He just walked away. Turned out the man had a shitty life, lost his job, his wife left him, and lots of everyday things had piled up, one after another, until their combined weight got too heavy, and well, he sort of went nuts. Then he went on a kind of rampage and… "

Detective Stapleton's eyebrow lifted slightly. "No, Mr. Parsons, I'm not familiar with that movie or the character. And I don't think comparisons to Hollywood movies are helpful at this point."

Rebuked, I stopped rambling. Within the silence, I sensed another question coming from the detective. Knuckles on steel interrupted the detective's thoughts, and the formulated question remained behind his halted lips.

Public Service

A uniformed officer, different from the earlier one, entered the room and handed a note to the detective. Detective Stapleton read the note. Irritated, he handed the note to Sergeant Muddle, who read it and shrugged.

"I'm sorry for the interruption, Mr. Parsons. We will be back shortly."

I wasn't sorry. I needed more time to compose myself.

Six
Dudley Hobbs - Alive

Dudley Hobbs entered the world into a middle, middle-class family in 1978. He had remained in the middle ever since. In 1999, less than a month after graduating from the University of Ottawa with a mediocre Bachelor's degree in history, Dudley joined the bloated ranks of the Canadian Public Service. Thirteen years later, Dudley, like so many other bureaucrats, shaped public policy without ever having been, or having experienced, Joe Public.

His career choice mirrored that of his father who, after devoting thirty-seven years to public service, retired at a respectable mid-management level. Like his father, Dudley was a plain, uninspiring, unimaginative man. With a slim, girl-like figure, contradicted by the kind of full, wide bottom that women hide with long un-tucked shirts, he had never been a man's man. His dry, brown hair was a permanent home for dandruff, and his round shoulders led down to small hands that proffered damp, towel-like handshakes. Round, wire-rimmed glasses sat on a narrow, pointed nose, reminding people around him of Waldo from the children's book, *Where's Waldo?*

Despite his appearance and mannerisms, Dudley managed to marry his high school sweetheart, but after ten years of cohabitation, no children cluttered their tidy suburban home. Insecure, and afraid of conflict, Dudley arrived at the office a little late every day, and began work even later. He rode a bicycle to work, brought little lunches, didn't swear, never got drunk, stole office supplies and tattled on his co-workers.

His late arrival, late work commencement, and tendency toward procrastination, resulted in Dudley remaining at work long after other analysts had gone home. Management viewed his inherent inefficiencies as signs of a dedicated and committed employee who embraced and exemplified, by virtue of staying after working hours, the dogma of putting work first. This contradiction formed a cornerstone of his peer's underlying dislike of Dudley. The perverse management view that because Dudley stayed late most evenings, he was justified in coming in a little late each morning, pissed people off even more.

Dudley didn't own a car. Instead, he rode a European style city bike to work from the first day of spring to the last day of fall. His cycling route was a short, 4.3 kilometre ride, over flat ground along a city maintained public cycle path that ran nine kilometres east to west across the city. This allowed Dudley a leisurely twenty-minute commute from his home in the near-East End to the downtown office of the secretariat.

In winter, when average daily temperatures ranged from minus five Celsius to minus twenty Celsius, snow fell regularly, and ice covered every surface, Dudley had to ride the city's ineffectual and subsidized bus system.

East to west city buses ran on a transitway adjacent to the cycle path up to a point one kilometre from the city centre. Here the buses turned south and passed through Ottawa's main downtown mall, depositing and collecting well-bundled and ill-tempered commuters. According to the bus schedule, the southern detour added six minutes to Dudley's winter bus journey. In practice, the detour added eleven minutes due to the inevitable congestion caused by the volume of buses and people. With winter weather, the southern detour, and the pressures of mass transit, Dudley's winter bus journey lasted between twenty-one and thirty-six minutes. Dudley loved his bike and hated the bus.

Dudley's father was born in London, England, and like many expatriates, he held romanticized memories of his homeland, which he had passed on to his son. One such romanticization was a distorted memory of how his own father, who had been a city clerk in the forgettable London borough of Croydon, had ridden an English Roadster bicycle to work each day. Dudley, having heard the story throughout his childhood, had gushed ecstatically when his wife, Beth, presented him with an English Roadster bicycle for his twenty-ninth birthday.

The English Roadster sits high and upright. Standard versions come complete with an enclosed chain case, skirt guard, O-lock, hub gearing, manually operated steel warning bell, and simple, dynamo-powered, built-in lights. Beth had opted for the three-speed geared hub version with a black, steel frame, front suspension fork, suspension seat post, rear basket and an adjustable kickstand. Sometimes, while winding his way along the paved cycle path to and from work, Dudley mused how riding his bike was his only real pleasure.

There was one blot on Dudley's cycling commute to work: his house was located one hundred and fifty metres south of the public cycle path, and Dudley had to cross the busy Millwood Road to access the path. Eastern housing developments had increased traffic on Millwood Road over the previous five years, especially during morning and evening rush hours: a fact acknowledged by the installation, just prior to Dudley receiving his English Roadster bicycle, of a light-controlled pedestrian crossing.

Much to Dudley's irritation, the crossing was located two hundred metres to the east of the point at which he could logically enter the public cycle path. For these reasons, Dudley had a habit of crossing Millwood Road without the benefit and safety of using the crossing. His wife, who often watched him head off on his roadster to work, worried about Millwood Road and repeatedly asked her husband to use the crossing. Dudley, in a misplaced attempt at masculinity, ignored his wife and scurried apprehensively across Millwood Road each day. Another misguided attempt at masculine bravado was his refusal to wear a helmet. Dudley's father, who asserted that neither he nor his father had ever worn one, perversely supported this refusal. The success of using seat belts in automobiles had apparently not occurred to Dudley and his father.

On Wednesday, October 14th, at 9:03 a.m., Dudley Hobbs placed his small, box-shaped briefcase on the steel rack mounted above the rear wheel of his beloved bicycle. The last of the leftovers from the Sunday roast dinner formed Wednesday's lunch. He always worried the gravy might spill inside his briefcase, and he made sure his wife used spill-proof containers to secure the roast beef, vegetables, potatoes and gravy.

Lunch secured, Dudley used the heel of his left shoe and deftly pushed the kickstand into place. Then, after pushing the bike to the end of his short driveway, he stepped, due to the low angle of the frame, ladylike into the bike rather than swinging his leg high, wide, and over the seat. With a thin smile and a curt nod, Dudley placed his brown shoes on the pedals and headed north toward Millwood Road.

#

Stapleton & Muddle
Ottawa Police HQ

Stapleton did not like to interrupt an interview, but the note handed to him by the uniformed officer indicated that new information had arrived. Forensic details, witness memories, and tidbits from other employees ebbed and flowed to Stapleton and Muddle. Established methodology between the two investigators had refined itself into a process in which Muddle provided facts for Stapleton to digest and extrapolate into questions and observations. The system worked well. Stepping briefly into the corridor outside the cell, Muddle, who had taken hold of a folder from the uniformed office, got to the point.

"Sir."

"Yes, sergeant."

"Two new facts."

Stapleton nodded.

Consulting the folder, Muddle conveyed the new information.

"First, the fourth cat, the kitten. Medowcroft's gardener, Mr. Cortes, confirmed the kitten was not at the cottage on Friday afternoon when he left. However, he did say that stray cats are not uncommon, but he could not recall Medowcroft ever taking one in."

"I'm not surprised there is no evidence Medowcroft had taken the kitten in, sergeant. I'm more interested in how Medowcroft would react to a lost or stray kitten. My impression of cat lovers is their first reaction would be to help a kitten. Is there anything else on the kitten?"

Muddle flipped through the notes and continued.

"Forensics noted small abrasions around the kitten's neck consistent with straining against a leash or restraint of some kind."

Public Service

"Which, sergeant, may imply an inconsistency with the kitten being a stray that wandered onto the victim's property at or near the time of the victim's death. Has a leash or collar been found near the scene?"

"No."

"What else do you have?"

"Mr. Parsons arrived more than two hours late for work on Wednesday. He told colleagues that he had taken his car for an oil change."

"Two hours is a long time for an oil change, sergeant. What time was Dudley Hobbs knocked off his bicycle?"

"Approximately 9:15 a.m."

"I want you to check what kind of car Mr. Parsons drives."

Muddle folded the paper and picked up on Stapleton's implication.

"Do you suspect Parsons, sir?"

Fingering his pen, Stapleton held Muddle's gaze.

"Anyone still alive from that office is a suspect, sergeant."

Seven

Interview - Room 5, Ottawa Police HQ

Detective Stapleton interviewed me a lot. Probably because I was one of the few left alive, and because I was the only one who had spent any non-office time with Rory O'Grady. He wanted me to explain Rory. What made him tick? He especially wanted to know about our work, our office, and who was friends with whom, as well as any gossip or rumours. Stapleton and Muddle had only been gone for a few moments. When they returned, Stapleton began.

"Could you give me a little context about the people, the place, and any situations or events you think might have prompted the killings? Maybe you could begin with an overview of your dead colleagues, where you all worked, and what you did?"

Stapleton's questions seemed to presume Rory's guilt. I considered protesting Rory's innocence, but when I thought about it, I judged silence was my best option, and I focused on the detective's question.

"Okay, but it's not that exciting, you know."

Stapleton pursed his lips and stifled what I thought might be another rebuke at my flippancy.

"Many people think their jobs are unexciting or

boring, but I'm not here in search of entertainment, Mr. Parsons. I simply want to know the facts about where Mr. O'Grady worked and if there were any issues or events that might help us understand what happened."

I decided to take the detective at his word. I thought about the Government of Canada website and paraphrased the official jargon.

"Our office is a small part of the Canadian Government's Privy Council Office, or PCO. PCO employs about a thousand public servants to provide non-partisan advice and administrative support to the prime minister, and its decision-making structures, such as cabinet committees, and other senior executives including the national security adviser, the clerk of the privy council, and ministers.

"We work in the Canadian Inland Security Secretariat. A secretariat is an office responsible for the secretarial, clerical, and administrative affairs of a legislative body, executive council, or international organization. In our case, the combined secretariat and PCO function made us responsible for providing advice and support to the minister of national security on inland security issues related to national policy, coordination, intelligence and response."

Even upside down, I could see that Detective Stapleton had written the letters CISS and a question mark three times on his notepad. He interrupted me and said, "I know about the Canadian Security Intelligence Service, the Canadian Security Establishment, and the Department of Public Safety, but I haven't heard much about the Canadian Inland Security Secretariat. Where does the secretariat fit in?"

I wasn't surprised Stapleton didn't know much about the secretariat. While we have a presence on the government website, our public profile is low because we are concerned more with policy and politics than the more functional aspect of security. In addition, the secretariat had only been around for twelve years.

"Terror and death brought the secretariat to life, detective. In January 2002, in response to the September 11, 2001, terror attacks in the US, the Government of Canada, desperate to neuter American right-wing claims that the Al Qaeda terrorists had been able to enter the US because of inefficient and uncoordinated Canadian security and intelligence policies, established the secretariat."

"How many people work in the secretariat?"

"Thirty-five: an assistant deputy minister occupies the top of the pyramid. A director general is next, and then there are two directors. More hierarchy follows with senior analysts, ordinary analysts, and junior analysts providing the analytical function. An office manager runs the shop, and the cheap seats are occupied by administrative assistants and general office support staff: a typical, generic, and unimaginative government office."

Stapleton shifted in his seat at my irreverent description, and I began to enjoy the opportunity to tell someone about the reality of the Inland Security Secretariat. I spread myself in the chair and launched into a caustic and oft repeated description of the secretariat and the public service bureaucracy in general.

"We conduct our work in a modern, overpriced, downtown office edifice that conforms to all government regulations concerning square footage per person, cubical size, desk size, number of chairs, window proximity, lighting, and access to hand sanitation stations and chilled water fountains. The floor plan is a designer blend of cookie-cutter cubicles, shared spaces, and passageways that allow us to produce in a soft, pastel coloured, light sensitive, and scent free environment. A perfect climate controlled, sterile, one-size fits all atmospheres, in which non-tangible work products materialize harmoniously out of sight and scrutiny of the taxpayer. Perfect, except for the humans who mess the place up."

While I spoke, the detective drew. I paused at the sight of rectangles and squares linked by rail track passageways punctuated by water drops. Broken lines depicted doorways and windows. Smiley faces suggested people. The detective looked up from his drawing. A soft grin pulled his face apart.

"Oh, don't mind me, Mr. Parsons. It's just my way of making a few notes."

I tried not to "mind" him, but his note-taking method made me itch. I continued.

"As federal government employees, our jobs are safe, secure, and soft. We don't produce anything original or particularly tangible. Mostly, we repackage other people's work into short forms, or briefing notes, for government 'decision-makers.' For example, we would receive a twenty to fifty page document from another government department or agency concerning the implementation of X or Y, or the possible consequences of doing, or not doing, something or other."

Muddle, who had thus far snorted or harrumphed about some of my descriptions, smirked widely and shuffled from one foot to another. I ignored him.

"Our value-added job is to reduce the original document down to two or three pages, add an 'informed opinion,' and possibly a 'safe recommendation' at the end, and pass it on up the bureaucratic line for others to render more creative reductionism. All the while, veteran employees, with decades of bureaucratic experience, ensure margins, paragraphs, full stops, commas, and the like, are in the right places. More importantly, they ensure nothing written contradicts the established views of the decision-makers and recipients of the briefing note; it's all tidy, circular, safe, and a bit inconsequential."

I glanced at the table separating me from the detective. He had begun a new page. This time, punctuation marks ran from left to right in neat lines. I began to wonder if the detective had some kind of learning disability or obsessive-compulsive problem. I coughed. The detective looked up and nodded for me to carry on.

"In short, detective, we are consummate bureaucrats. We operate in a comfortable world, guided by some well-established mantras about providing advice to the executives: tell the decision-makers what they want to hear; assume they are all idiots and know nothing, and keep it that way; provide only enough information to let them conclude what you want them to think or what conforms to the already established position. We use short, simple sentences, and selective comparisons when available, and above all, provide concluding 'non-opinions.' Finally, we over classify the product as secret or top secret to make the briefing note appear important and help stave off Access to Information requests from inquisitive reporters."

I was out of breath, caught up in my vent. When I paused, the detective, his body rigid and tight, said, "Your description sounds like a right-wing, anti-big government rant about bureaucracies filled with incompetent, overpaid, and under-worked bureaucrats. This is a serious matter, Mr. Parsons."

His reaction was typical. I was tired of people taking offence at the truth, and I jutted my chin and head toward him.

"Look, detective, you asked me. It's not my problem if you don't like the answer. Have you ever watched the old *Yes Minister* shows from the UK or the 2010 *SNL* skit, 'Public Employee of the Year Awards' or looked at any news medium for an update on the latest bureaucratic fiasco or scandal? You might not like to hear it, but sometimes even a comparison to *Seinfeld* might be appropriate, as it is a show about nothing! That's kind of what we do."

The detective flushed red at the mention of *Seinfeld*, and wary of creating an enemy, I softened my voice and qualified my statements.

"Listen, detective, I don't want you to misunderstand me. Inland security is important. Terrorists, both international and domestic, are a real threat. Everyone felt the horror of the Twin Towers, the bombs on trains in Madrid in 2004, and the underground train bombings in London in 2005. Do you remember the Toronto 18 in 2006, the Glasgow airport car bomb in 2007, and the jihadist gunman in 2012 in Toulouse, France? The task and objective of inland security is vital to lives, property, and the economy. When I say the secretariat does nothing, I'm talking about the confluence of two things: intangible products and piss poor management."

Temporarily placated, but not convinced, the detective sat back and crossed his arms. In the silence, Sergeant Muddle grunted a prompt to the detective, who pulled his arms tighter across his chest and asked me about Wednesday.

"Mr. Parsons, I understand you arrived late for work on Wednesday morning, which, as you may know, was when Dudley Hobbs became the victim of an unfortunate accident. Can you tell me where you were on Wednesday and why you were late for work?"

I forced indignation into my posture and voice and spat back at the detective.

"I don't like what you're implying, detective. I had nothing to do with Dudley's accident. I was nowhere near Millwood Road. You said yourself that my drive to work takes me down by the Rideau River, not out east where Hobbs lives."

Stapleton unfolded his arms and leaned forward as though he would scoop me up.

"I'm not implying anything, Mr. Parsons. Everyone connected to the case will have to provide information about their movements when each of the deaths occurred. Now could you please confirm where you were on Wednesday morning until your arrival at work at ten-fifteen?"

Mention of my late arrival at work on Wednesday left me flustered for a moment. I fussed with my wedding ring as I wondered who had told them and how they had found out so soon. I knew Wednesday's alibi was weak, but it was all I had.

"I took my car for an oil change."

Muddle let another snort escape. My irritation with Muddle grew, which I think was the point. I blocked Muddle out and repeated my statement.

"I took my car for an oil change."

Stapleton didn't snort, and he wrote "oil change" on his pad. I half expected him to draw a car hoisted on a ramp next.

"Did you leave for work at your usual time?" asked Stapleton.

"Yes, I think so, sometime between seven and seven-thirty."

A slight glint entered the detective's eyes as he leaned his elbows on the steel desk.

"If you left home at your regular time, that would mean your oil change took between two and a half to three hours. That is a long time for an oil change, Mr. Parsons."

I resisted the temptation to be glib and tell him the oil change only lasted twelve minutes. I also didn't explain how, because of a long lineup, I had grabbed a coffee and read the newspaper in the car outside Tim

Horton's for an hour or so. I did not want to appear rehearsed. Instead, I simply said, "Well, I went to Pennzoil on Bank Street. You can check if you want."

The detective inclined his chin at the sergeant, who nodded and pushed himself off the wall. He left, I presumed, to conduct the required check.

Eight
Dudley Hobbs - Dead

Early fall leaves clogged the roadside forcing Dudley Hobbs to ride a little more into the road and away from the curb. Dudley liked the fall: the leaves, the pungent air, and the slight discomfort the cool breeze brought to his face and hands. Yet he resented the way the beautiful fall scene signalled the end of his daily cycle and the beginning of the dreaded city bus ride to work. Another month at most, thought Dudley sadly, as he approached Millwood Road.

Millwood Road. Why hadn't he thought more about the road when he and Beth bought their house ten years ago? They should have brought one of the houses north of Millwood instead of south. Yes, they were a bit more expensive, but now he knew why. Millwood Road. More traffic every year. So much traffic the city had to install a pedestrian crossing. Moreover, the crossing spanned Millwood Road east of where he wanted it to be. Why should he have to go the opposite way to his destination to cross the damn road? Moreover, why did the crossing need to be equipped with one of those annoying beeping sounds for the blind? His bedroom was on the east side of his house. In the middle of the night, the faint beep, beep, beep of the crossing interrupted Dudley's sleep. Dudley remonstrated with his wife about who crossed the road in the middle of the night anyway. Not blind people, surely. Then Dudley had laughed to himself at the thought of blind people: How would they know if it was day or night?

Dudley, distracted by his disparate and selfish thoughts, slowed his approach to the Millwood Road intersection. A battered Toyota Corolla sped by Dudley and turned onto Millwood without stopping. Dudley followed the Toyota's example and made lazy, casual checks on the flow and speed of the traffic on Millwood Road. In the distance, Dudley registered a large, black vehicle. Moments before his death, Dudley would wrestle with his assessment that the large, black car travelling west to east had seemed far away. He was sure he had plenty of time to cross the road before the car reached him, especially because he had only to cross one lane, as the far lane was clear of traffic. Focusing on the need to pull his front wheel up the small curb on the far side of the road, Dudley pushed his pedals firmly and set off to cross Millwood Road.

When Dudley made his first casual left to right scan of the road, the large, black car had indeed been quite far away, but when Dudley failed to look left again, as he and millions of others had been taught, the car's four hundred and sixty-five horsepower engine snarled and the car jerked purposely forward. The back wheel of the English Roadster crossed the Millwood Road centreline and began to slow. Dudley braced for the approaching sidewalk and gripped the handlebars to jerk the front wheel up in time to clear the curb. He needn't have bothered.

Plenty of witnesses came forward: too many. Differing witness accounts were expected, but the accident investigators were baffled at how contradictory the statements were. Some claimed Dudley neither stopped nor looked before he rode right into Millwood Road. Others thought Dudley had looked but not stopped. Everyone said Millwood was very busy, and he should have used the crossing and have worn a helmet.

Unanimity, for those witnesses who recalled seeing a car, described a big, black vehicle with shiny chrome wheels. Witnesses were uncertain whether the driver was a man or a woman, but several said the driver was wearing a funny-looking hat. Forensic examiners confirmed no skid marks, but could not establish with any certainty the location of the bicycle when the car struck. Officers checked the few traffic cameras in the vicinity, recorded the presence of several large, black vehicles in the area around the time of the incident, and began to trace and interview all identified drivers. In the meantime, the coroner recorded an initial verdict of suspected accidental death, and the police launched an investigation.

Nine

Interview - Room 5, Ottawa Police HQ

Sergeant Muddle did not actually leave the room to conduct the required check on my claim about going to Pennzoil for an oil change on Wednesday morning. Instead, Muddle leaned through the doorway and into the corridor. After some mumbled instructions to an unseen minion, Muddle returned to his perch against the wall behind Detective Stapleton. While Muddle directed someone to check on my oil change, Stapleton busied himself drawing cats. Three cats, each with a different pose, surrounded a fourth smaller cat. As Muddle resumed his place, Stapleton drew a thick, black circle around the smaller cat.

"Do you like cats, Mr. Parsons?"

Images of the kitten raced through my mind: Had I taken off the leash?

"Mr. Parsons."

Knife, leash, and cat. Fear nibbled me. I was certain I looked frightened, but I couldn't change that.

"Er, no, I mean neither do or don't. We don't have one. Why? What is this about cats?"

"Your boss, Prudence Medowcroft, had cats. Did you know?"

"Yes. Everyone knew about her cats. She talked about them all the time."

"Apparently, her four cats were all quite old, you know?"

Stapleton held a steady stare. I stared back. Medowcroft had three cats.

"Four, I thought it was three, but I could be wrong. Like I said, I don't really care for cats one way or the other."

"You are correct, Mr. Parsons. Ms. Medowcroft had three cats, but four were discovered at her cottage."

I had involuntarily rubbed my left wrist, and a small scratch I hadn't noticed began to smart.

"Your wrist seems a little swollen, Mr. Parsons. I could have it looked at if you want."

"No, no thanks. It's just an itch or something."

The detective eyed me expectantly. I shrugged and sipped cold coffee. The detective let the silence hang way past decency. It wasn't easy, but I waited him out until he switched back to ask questions about the secretariat.

"Mr. Parsons, you stated that what you called 'piss poor management' was responsible for the secretariat doing as you said 'nothing.' What do you mean by 'piss poor'?"

Instinct told me to sweep my arms back in dramatic fashion and pronounce with an exaggerated flourish that I knew not where to begin. However, heeding earlier signals of Detective Stapleton's disapproval of the dramatic, I proceeded with bland bureaucratese.

"The first problem, detective, is that the secretariat produces nothing that can be touched, crouched behind, or erected to protect or prevent. We produce paper. And the paper production is so ineffective, inefficient, and self-serving that the inland security policies, which the papers contain, or refer to, are often many steps behind the threat.

"The second problem begins at the macro level. Management and non-management in the federal government follow an eighty/twenty rule: eighty per cent of those in management in federal government are narcissistic, incompetent, and possess lousy leadership skills. Twenty per cent are decent, hardworking, dedicated professionals, who hold the bureaucracy together despite the eighty per cent."

Muddle, consistent with earlier behaviour, interjected an unintelligible sound. This time the sound fell somewhere between a snort and a chuckle. I peered at Stapleton for a reaction, but he either had failed to hear his sergeant or had chosen to ignore the unintended comment.

"Workers, or non-management, follow the same mathematical split but with different characteristics. Eighty per cent share some or all of the following: kowtowing yes people; uninterested freeloaders; people promoted to levels far beyond their competence due to long years of service rather than ability; and unoriginal, uncreative, and dour individuals who bring little to the workplace except their warm and often lazy carcasses. The remaining twenty per cent, like the twenty per cent in management, work hard, challenge the status quo, ask creative questions, provide stimulating ideas, and pursue their responsibilities with professionalism and dedication, and like the twenty per cent of dedicated management, they enable the public service to function despite the vast majority. In essence, twenty per cent of good workers toil under eighty per cent bad management.

"In the secretariat, at the micro level, the problem is compounded and the rule is more ninety/ten: with ninety per cent of management being incompetent narcissists leading ninety per cent of kowtowing, uninterested workers, the reality of the secretariat's concrete contribution to Canada's Inland Security is clear: Self-interested, paper-pushing bureaucrats do not stop terrorists or bombs."

Carried away with my tirade, I hadn't noticed how Stapleton had stopped writing, placed his pen on his notepad, and sat staring fixedly at me. I got the message, ended my harsh critique, and returned to the point.

"Anyway, Rory O'Grady, like me, is a policy analyst in the secretariat. We are neither senior nor junior, just analysts. Other key people are Rena Kingsmore, the assistant deputy minister, Sherwood Rosborough, the director general, and Prudence Medowcroft, who is one of two directors. Dudley Hobbs and Cale Lamkin are senior policy analysts. Lastly, Amy Hurley is the office clerk. There are other workers, of course. More analysts, clerks, bosses and executives, but the ones I mentioned are the core of the secretariat function."

I sat back, exhausted. I hadn't meant to rant and rave, but an event in the office a few months ago had changed my perspective about the secretariat and some of the people who worked there. I guess I had some pent-up frustrations, and the detective caught me at a bad time. I reflected on my candid and jaded assessment of the secretariat as Stapleton inked more notes on his pad and underlined others.

Spurred by the detective's silence, I asked, "Is that all? Can I go now?"

Stapleton's pen rotated slowly between his wrinkled fingers as he spoke softly to me.

"Yes, Mr. Parsons, you can go if you want, but I could still use your help. Your description of the secretariat is helpful and enables me to build a picture of Mr. O'Grady's work environment and the pressures he may have experienced. Nevertheless, I still need details and

Public Service

information about Mr. O'Grady himself to help me place him in the context of his work. I understand you and he were good friends. Perhaps you could provide more personal insight into Mr. O'Grady, something to understand how the pressures of his work might have caused him to do the things of which he is accused."

I thought about what the detective said. Who had told him about my friendship with Rory? I mean, we were friends. Sort of. We did share a bad habit once a week, but we had never told anyone about it. Funny thing was, the nature of the shared habit enabled me to learn all about Rory O'Grady. Much more than Rory would have wanted anyone to know. Marijuana does that to some people: They just want to talk. And Rory had talked. I realized the detective had offered me an opportunity to portray Rory any way I chose, as no one was available to contradict me. I hesitated, stuck between quitting while I was ahead or using the opportunity to paint Rory O'Grady as the killer I hoped they thought he was.

"Mr. Parsons?"

"Yes, all right. I can probably help you understand Rory a little better. He kind of told me his life story over a couple of beers at his house one night."

Back on track, the detective wasted no time.

"Did you often go to Rory's house, Mr. Parsons?"

"Yes. About two or three time a month on Fridays after work."

"So, you were good friends then?"

"Yes, I suppose so."

"Go ahead, Mr. Parsons. Tell me about Mr. Rory O'Grady."

Before I could begin, a ringtone echoed off the sterile walls. Stapleton inclined his head toward his sergeant and raised an eyebrow as Muddle withdrew a cell phone. Between Muddle's ear and the phone sound seeped into the room. Poker faced, Muddle spoke to his boss.

"We need to talk, sir. F, forensics, has some information"

Muddle's neck and lower cheeks coloured light red. His eyes avoided mine for the first time. I didn't smirk at the sergeant's slight stutter with the word forensic, but it felt good to know that his silence was attributable to a speech impediment rather than some mind-reading skill or awesome deductive reasoning ability.

Stapleton led the way out of the door.

#

Stapleton and Muddle
Ottawa Police HQ

Stapleton, eager for information, asked Muddle for details.

"What do forensics have so soon, sergeant? We only left the O'Grady house two hours ago."

Muddle, excited by the prospect of tangible evidence, bounced as he recounted the forensic report.

"Inside O'Grady's house, they discovered a hot tub manual. The manual was open to the electrical section, which had yellow highlight and pencil marks around the warnings about the use of electrical appliances, such as radios or iPod systems plugged into electrical sockets. One of the technicians had attended the hot tub scene at the Kingsmore house earlier and made the connection between hot tub and the manual."

"What else?"

"Forensics also found documents and publications about the Irish Republican Army showing how to make bombs, hand to hand combat, and the use of guerrilla tactics."

"The IRA," said Stapleton. "That adds a twist to things, sergeant, especially when you consider that O'Grady worked for Canada's Inland Security Secretariat."

A crease crossed Muddle's face at Stapleton's connection and he said, "Sir, does this mean the case is a national security issue and the RCMP will take over?"

Stapleton, half-smiling at Muddle's concern about the possibility of losing a serial killer case, assured his sergeant.

"No, not yet, sergeant; possession of terrorist-related instruction manuals and propaganda might indicate a degree of awareness, but by itself, it does not indicate intent and capability. We need more information before we open the national security box; besides, my gut tells me this is a basic murder case. Albeit, a complicated one."

Relieved, Muddle opened the door, and the two detectives returned to the interview room.

Ten

Interview - Room 5, Ottawa Police HQ

Stapleton and Muddle hustled through the door and took their positions with purpose. Their enthusiasm made me cautious, and I sighed inwardly and wondered how I had gotten myself into this. I should have said Rory and I shared a few beers sometimes, and I didn't know him well. I took a moment to compose myself to figure out how to tell the detective all about Rory when an image of Rory, half drunk, loosened by a quality joint and babbling about his boyhood troubles, came to mind. I decided to beat the detective to the punch, and I shouted Rory's own words at the detective.

"Hey, ya little Bog Trotter. Get the fuck over there, and pick up the garbage like I told you before."

I must have been louder than intended because Stapleton pushed back into his chair and dragged his pen across his notepad as Muddle took a step toward me. Stapleton recovered first and said, "Pardon me, Mr. Parsons?"

"Oh, I'm sorry, detective. Rory used that line once when he told me about his life and how he grew up. I remembered and thought of it as a way to start."

Stapleton settled and cancelled out the line his

sudden movement had caused on his notepad by adding a wiggly line atop the length of the first line. With his notepad restored to order, Stapleton frowned and said, "Mm, I see. Perhaps you could be a little less dramatic."

"Yes, all right. Anyway, Rory didn't have a happy childhood. He often told me boys would yell racial slurs at him as they shoved him to the ground. He also mentioned Mr. Miller, his crass grade four teacher, who used to call Rory either Mick or Paddy but never Rory. Rory said everyone called him names like Leprechaun, Cat-lick, and Potato Head. Every day in school, in the street, even on the way to and from church, people muttered under their breath as he and his family passed by."

A slight smirk flit between Muddle's eyes and lips, and I wondered if Muddle wasn't quite as proper as he appeared.

"Rory said his father, Mick, didn't help things by teaching Rory to call his tormentors Polacks, Jews, Canucks, Chinks, Dyke-Jumpers, Ragus, Sheep fuckers or fucking Brits."

For the first time I noticed that Stapleton's pen was still. He hadn't tried to draw a Polack, Dyke-Jumper, or a Sheep fucker. I suppressed a smile and continued.

"Rory told me he had been named in memory of Ruaidri Ua Conchobair, who reigned as the king of Connacht in the eleven hundreds and something and was the last high king of Ireland before the Norman invasion changed Ireland forever. "Remember and be proud," Rory's father had told him. "They can't take away a man's pride. A man can only give it away."

A Norman helmet and a large cross flowed from Stapleton's pen as he said, "You seem to remember the details well, Mr. Parsons."

"Yes, I have a good memory. One time my school thought I had an eidetic memory; you know, like a photographic memory. My mom even got me tested, but I didn't have one. I'm just good at recollecting things. Is it a problem?"

"No, not at all. Your recollection of details surprised me. In fact, your memory will likely be quite helpful. Please continue."

"Well, Rory said he never felt proud or like a king. One of his grandfathers, Rory couldn't remember which one, fled Ireland for Canada in 1847 to escape the Irish Potato famine. His grandfather came to Ottawa, by steamship via Quebec, and found farming and logging work in the surrounding area.

"According to Rory, generations of O'Gradys endured endless social and economic upheavals. You know, things like the Fenian raids, Confederation, the anti-Catholic Orange Order, WW1, the Great Depression, and WWII. In the late 1960s, his father, Michael Seamus O'Grady, moved Rory, his three older siblings, and his mother to a cramped, three bedroom, semi-detached house in Cabbagetown in the centre of Toronto."

The letters IRA appeared on the detective's notepad and a question I expected followed.

"Did Rory ever mention the Irish Republican Army or talk about Irish independence?"

I knew why the detective asked, and I fed the myth.

"Once in a while, when Rory became riled up about something or other, he would mention how the Irish had been treated badly by everyone. I think he owned some flags or books about the IRA. He seemed interested in his Irish heritage for sure and occasionally talked about going back to his roots or something. I don't think he was serious about it, though."

"Okay, thanks."

I expected Stapleton to ask more questions about the IRA, but he seemed content to add question marks around the letters IRA and remained silent. I filled the silence with more about Rory.

"Rory's father, an unskilled labourer, found work in the booming Toronto construction industry. When Rory was eighteen, he and his three older brothers had grown like his father: lean, six foot four or six inches, well-built, with bright red hair. Despite their size and fiery hair, though, Rory said his father and siblings were mild mannered men, who would talk and drink their way out of disagreements, shrug off racial slurs and slights, and avoid physical conflict."

Stapleton glanced up from his notes and said: "Would you say Rory was like his father and brothers?"

"I don't know. I mean I never met any of his family, but Rory said he was different from his father or brothers. He didn't like to admit it, but I got the impression Rory had more of a brooding temperament laced with resentment and loathing for people who demeaned him, his family, and the Irish."

"You mean Rory was more of a fighter?"

"Maybe, I'm not sure. He did tell me a few stories about when he was a kid. Like, when he was in grade five and how, because of his size, the taunts and insults became less frequent. In grade six, Rory said he beat the crap out of three boys for calling him a Leprechaun, shagging turf-cutter. After beating the three boys, Rory said things really improved."

Stapleton, who had been busy scratching point form notes on his pad, stopped writing and tapped his pen on the desk.

"Tell me, Mr. Parsons, would you consider Rory violent?"

Despite a clear opportunity to portray Rory in a

bad light, I said, "No, I don't think so. I mean, the stories he told me came from grade six. I never saw him violent with anyone."

"Okay. What else did Rory tell you about his life?"

"Well, he said he was smarter than his brothers and the other kids in his neighbourhood. Actually, Rory told me he graduated in 1987 and that he was accepted to several universities. Rory was proud to tell me how in 1987, with government loans and bursaries, he, Rory Michael Ethan O'Grady, became the first O'Grady to enter a university. Four years later, Rory graduated from the University of Toronto with a BA honors degree in political science and economics. From there, Rory said he attended Dalhousie University in Halifax, Nova Scotia, for two years until 1993 when he graduated with a Master's degree in public administration."

Stapleton interrupted my flow with an observation.

"Ah, I guess the combination of political science and public administration degrees would explain how Rory became a federal government employee."

"Yes, that's right. Although Rory did seem a bit funny about how he got started in government. I remember him being a little bitter and cynical about his first few years."

"How so? Can you recall what he said?"

"Well, not exactly, but he did talk about how he came to Ottawa with his educational credentials, and how he was full of that positive, liberal optimism which attaches itself to new university graduates. He said he had wanted to search for a job and change the world. In Ottawa, the federal government, which was then a few years away from one of its many cyclical downsizing exercises, readily provided new university graduates with entry-level positions. Rory, with six years of formal education, and empirical observation of Canada's political and bureaucratic system, had been convinced of the

Public Service

need for change and improvement. Rory believed he possessed the knowledge and the grit to make change and all he needed, he told me, was a foot in the door and revolution would follow."

Revolution appeared in big letters on the detective's pad next to the letters IRA. The detective pounced.

"Revolution, are you sure Rory said revolution?"

"Well, yes, but I doubt he intended to start a revolution or anything. It was an expression. He wanted to change things for the better."

Seemingly disappointed at my inability to assert Rory had singlehandedly begun a revolution in Canada's political system, the detective settled back and let me continue.

"Rory also told me he experienced a sense of historical fate when his father reminded him how his great-great-great-great-grandfather, Michael Patrick O'Grady, landed in Ottawa in 1847 as a penniless refugee from Ireland. 'Yes, Rory, you've done us all proud,' Rory's father had told him."

"You said a few moments ago Rory had been a little bitter about his first few years with the government. What did you mean?"

"Well, Rory said he had been euphoric about securing a job with the Department of Foreign Affairs on his first try and had been full of hope and determination. He told me he had been so high with optimism that it was perhaps predictable that his first reality check had been so utterly crushing."

"Utterly crushing, what happened?"

"Well, the way I remember it, Rory said he began as a junior political affairs officer in the Western European section with a job that focused on Ireland's role in the European Union. After preliminary identification card and general orientation business, Rory said he met his immediate boss, the deputy director of the European division. Three minutes into their first meeting, the deputy director said to Rory, 'Rory Michael Ethan O'Grady. Well, you shouldn't have any problem understanding the bogtrotters then. I can't understand a fucking word they say. Every time I call Dublin, it's after lunch, and I swear they've all been at the Guinness. Drink is all those bloody paddies do all day. I don't understand how their economy is doing so well.'

"Rory told me he couldn't believe what the guy had said, and he had wanted to rip his head off. Luckily, for Rory, and more so perhaps for the deputy director, a third party joined them, and her presence caused the deputy director to turn away from Rory. The distraction allowed Rory time to suppress his emotions.

"Rory said hearing the deputy director made him think back to his childhood and the racial and discriminatory injustices he successfully buried, first with his fists in high school, then through the acceptance and tolerance of university life. This is where Rory's story got a bit funny. He told me the deputy director never let up on the insults and he - Rory - was about to quit his job until, on his way home from a post-work drink at the Earl of Sussex on Rideau Street, the deputy director was inexplicably assaulted and beaten unrecognizable by an unknown assailant. Rory said the deputy director never returned to work and spent years on long-term disability until depression and loneliness gave way to suicide."

The detective straightened and pushed his chin toward me when I mentioned the assault on the deputy director, and he said excitedly, "So, Rory beat the deputy director half to death?"

"What? I don't know. Rory never said he did it. Just that it happened. Rory did seem a bit coy when he told me about it, though. Like I said, Rory's story was a bit funny."

What I didn't tell the detective was Rory told me he was glad the deputy director suffered, but he knew he couldn't count on that happening to everyone who offended him, so Rory built little cupboards in his mind where he placed people like the deputy director.

#

Rory's story spilled out of me in a rush, and Stapleton scratched a mixture of jumbled letters, numbers, symbols and arrows on his notepad. The end of my narrative heightened the silence of the sterile room, and my eyes followed the detective's pen as it continued to transpose my words into a written form only the detective could understand.

When Detective Stapleton finished spreading ink on paper, he pressed me to describe Rory and consider what might have caused him to murder his colleagues. He suggested I take it month by month, "Say, for the six months or so leading up to the murders. The investigation," said Stapleton "needs to establish a motive."

I said I didn't want to get involved, but the detective again explained that there were few colleagues left alive who knew Rory. He said my knowledge of events before the deaths would be crucial in enabling them to envision what happened. He didn't say it, but I sensed he also wanted to understand why I hadn't been on Rory's death list.

So, duly pressed, I thought about March 2012. Not so much because Stapleton wanted me to but because March had been a bad month for my family, and it had also been the time when I had come to my own decisions about work and life and, ultimately, death.

I stared past Stapleton at the cold, grey wall and tried to recall March and anything relevant concerning Rory. But the wall, sterile and functional like the wall in the waiting room at the Children's Hospital of Eastern Ontario, pushed my thoughts toward my son Ryan instead of toward Rory as the detective wanted.

March had been a difficult month for my family. During the first week, Anne and I miscommunicated about who was checking Ryan's blood glucose levels to ensure Ryan took his insulin injections. Anne was on the last of her five back-to-back night shifts, and I was busy at work covering Dudley Hobbs's files because he was off sick with a stomach bug. Most of the time Ryan, who was only seven, had a pretty good awareness of how he felt and would tell me or Anne if he began to feel sick or tired. However, in March, Ryan was determined to play competitive soccer, and he had three indoor tryouts that week.

Anne, tired from night shifts, and me, distracted with handling unfamiliar files at work, both thought the other person would keep a close watch on Ryan as he pushed himself to do well in the soccer tryouts. Anyway, Ryan, focused on playing soccer, forgot to snack before practice, and I forgot to give him a shot of insulin. Predictably, Ryan had a serious hypoglycemia event in the gym, collapsed, and paramedics took him to hospital. Even worse, I had left the tryout to get a coffee from Tim Horton's, and Ryan's insulin shot was in my pocket. When I got to the hospital, Ryan was stable, but I was frightened, especially when the doctors told me how low his blood sugar levels had become and how close Ryan had been to sustaining permanent kidney damage.

Anne, sensitized to medical issues due to her profession, worried continually about Ryan, and had rightly laid into me for "putting a cup of fucking coffee before Ryan's health." Ryan, who couldn't complete the tryouts, placed in the developmental instead of competitive soccer stream and became depressed and sullen about his condition.

Added to all this Michael, who is very protective of Ryan, broke the nose of a boy who had ridiculed and teased Ryan about his condition and what happened at the soccer tryout. I sighed heavily as the thought of Ryan's vulnerability washed over me.

Detective Stapleton nudged my consciousness back to the police interview room with a soft, dry cough and said with some sincerity, "Mr. Parsons. Are you all right? I realize this must be difficult for you, but you can really help us figure all this out."

In the rush to get dressed, I had forgotten to put my watch on. I craned my neck and eyeballs to read the fingers of the detective's inverted watch on the table: eight forty-five a.m. I had been in the room for about an hour and a half. My arse was numb. My back ached from the cold metal chair and the awkward distance that separated the fixed chair and table from each other and forced the chair's occupant to strain ever so slightly to rest elbows or arms on the table. I sat up, reached behind, and kneaded my lower back with my knuckles.

"Okay, you want some context and anything that happened to do with Rory in March, right?"

"Yes, if you could please, Mr. Parsons."

I hated March. Accumulated procrastination, endemic in the public service, combined with a self-aggrandizing political frenzy to squeeze short-term policies and populist imperatives through government and public service structures before the end of the fiscal year. March was madness, and I told the detective so.

"Every March is frantic for federal government departments, detective. March is the last month of the fiscal year. Eager elected officials return from March break, and the implications of the government's February budget become more apparent. There is an increased focus on completing legislative bills before the government recesses in mid-June for the summer break. The government makes reams of announcements concerning near-term trade, policy, security and cooperation initiatives designed to signal the proletariat their government has returned and has begun working harder than ever to make Canada and their lives better. These big picture issues always impact the secretariat and stimulate a flurry of analytical activity as we try to understand the government's latest policy directions and how best to ensure we position ourselves to, as our Assistant Deputy Minister Rena Kingsmore often said, 'support and promote any policy shifts or new directions.'"

I watched Stapleton reduce my ramble to two terse words: "March busy" headed a new page on his pad. Undeterred, I continued.

"I always wondered how Kingsmore's declaration of support and promotion reconciled with our stated and published mandate to provide non-partisan, unbiased, and impartial advice to the government which, because the secretariat is part of the government's Privy Council Office, applied to us more than most."

The detective, scratching notes, focused my ramblings.

"So, March is always a busy time for the secretariat. How did it affect Rory?"

"Rory said many times that he believed the core mandate. According to Rory, we had to achieve the highest professional ethics and standards in the federal public service. When his attempts to provide non-partisan analysis and advice concerning inland security-related issues was viewed by higher ups as confrontational or contrary to established positions, he would become upset. He would often rant about people being more concerned with their next promotion than about good policy."

Public Service

"Are you saying Rory thought senior people lied or misled elected officials by obscuring facts or through omission of details?"

"No, no. Well, not exactly. I mean, I can't say for sure what he thought, but let me give you some idea of what I mean. The most important part of the product an analyst like Rory would produce is the recommendations section, which comes at the end of every briefing note. The recommendation, based on the preceding analysis, is the meat of our responsibility to provide advice to decision-makers."

"Do you have an example?"

"I can't provide any specific examples because all our work is classified, but I can give you an idea of how Rory's recommendations, or concluding statements, might have been viewed and changed."

"Okay."

"Often, Rory's recommendation section would request a definite answer. For example, asking for a decision on an issue; seeking direction on something; or requesting agreement on a course of action. Rory objected to the way his clear, direct, and as far as he said, non-partisan, requests changed to less direct, softer, and often useless statements."

Stapleton had drawn a vertical rectangle box and filled it, left to right, with squiggly lines. The box was headed with the words "briefing note", and the letters T or F had been placed at the bottom right. Holding his pen still but without looking at me, Stapleton said, "What do you mean by 'useless statements'"?

"Well, asking for a decision on an issue might be changed to sensitizing the official to the issue. Seeking direction changed to seeking consideration of the problem. A request for an agreement on a course of action would become recognizing the situation. In Rory's mind, at least how he told it to me when he vented, his

77

valuable and direct requests were reduced to meaningless platitudes. No wonder, he said, the government views the public service with contempt."

"So, Rory would get upset if the director changed his work?"

"Yes. We all do to some degree. The difference is Rory actually seemed to care. He either hadn't been worn down enough or didn't learn how to, or want to, play the game."

"What do you mean by play the game?"

"Wiggle room."

"What?"

I was enjoying the detective's puzzled expression and disdainful frown. When the detective drew a three dimensional room with wiggly stick figures in it, I almost forgot why I was there.

"Wiggle room. Rory called the changes to his work meaningless platitudes, but for bureaucrats, the changes to less forthright wording allows wiggle room. Depending on the decision-makers' views, the 'wiggle room' wording can be explained with either more, or less, emphasis in relation to the decision-maker's position on the issue at the time. That's playing the game. Instead of boxing yourself in with a direct and honest recommendation, toss an ambiguity and modify as needed. Here, I will give you some more examples."

Seeming uncertain if he wanted more or not, the detective mumbled a reluctant, almost sarcastic, "Yes, please do."

"Recommend might become suggest; will cost X dollars would change to costs between X and Y dollars; clear becomes to be determined; contradicts becomes uncertain; assured becomes inconclusive, and words like definite, precise, exact, or certain, are never used and would be struck out of a briefing note."

"Did this happen to Rory often?"

"Yes, all the time. He seemed to want to challenge them. See how far they would go."

"Who do you mean by them?"

"Prudence Medowcroft and Rena Kingsmore; Medowcroft is, was, our direct boss, and Kingsmore was Medowcroft's boss."

"Well, I suppose having your work changed might bother a person, but it doesn't seem like a good reason to kill someone."

"Well, no, but the other part bothered Rory even more."

"What other part?"

"Oh, when his name was left on the documents. The name has to be there, so people can identify the analyst responsible for the file. That really pushed his button."

Stapleton tensed up and said, "So, you are telling me that in the public service, if someone disagrees with the recommendation on the briefing note, the person who has prepared the note still has his or her name left on the note?"

"Yep. That's how it works."

"That doesn't sound very democratic."

"Funny, Rory said that once, too."

Eleven

Amy Hurley - Alive

Amy Hurley was a sexually experienced twenty-five year old. Her blond, short hair, green eyes, slim figure, perky breasts and tight, apple-like bottom had drawn male attention since her tenth year. Under her mother's guidance, Amy became skilled with makeup to lengthen eyelashes and accentuate lips. Dress sense, to emphasis her figure without being slutty, came easily to Amy. Combined with permanently manicured nails, excellent white teeth, and a complete absence of facial hair, Amy had been a natural for the high school cheerleading team. Inside, though, Amy was insecure and shallow. She flirted and spoke loudly and often to compensate for her insecurities. Since the death of her father at age twelve, Amy had tried hard to please anyone and everyone who gave her attention. The only child of a working-class family, Amy had managed to complete high school and two years of college. While Amy was smart, she didn't have the skills or self-esteem to manage the double edge of her good looks and perfect body. Instead of becoming a successful model, as many people resentfully thought she would, her youth, innocence, and beauty elicited attention from older, manipulative, and selfish men: men who used Amy for their short-term needs until they got bored. Each experience left Amy more insecure and vulnerable.

Recently, since joining the secretariat, life had improved for Amy. She was proud of herself. So was her mother, kind of. After only eighteen months, Amy gained promotion from general helper, to office assistant, to senior office assistant, and just two months ago, she became the assistant office manager. Her mother's question about which and how many guys Amy had fucked or blown to get her promotions still hurt, as did Amy's suspicion her mother did not believe she had earned her promotions with hard work. Well, that was the truth. Except maybe the time she let Sherwood Rosborough, the director general of the secretariat, fondle her tits, or the time she sat on his lap and felt his dick harden. However, she had not fucked or blown anyone for a promotion, and that was the goddamn truth.

Oh, Amy flirted all right. That was easy and fun. Men were so predictable. Did they really think she didn't notice how they peered down her shirt to catch a glimpse of her firm tits? Before every staff meeting, Amy would go to the bathroom to pinch and squeeze her nipples until they hardened and caused little crease marks to radiate out from her aureole on her slim-fitting, white blouse. Amy loved how men did fake stretches, yawns, and neck cracks, to obtain a better and longer look at her tits.

Amy played a similar flirting game with her butt. Seven years of high school cheerleader performances had given Amy an awesome butt. Small, tight, firm, and accentuated by slender legs, Amy felt every fixed stare as she crisscrossed the main office or exited the office of senior executives. G-strings were Amy's choice for accentuating her curves and firmness. She also performed an occasional dip or bend to allow the top of the G-string to show above the line of her skirt, or on casual Fridays, her jeans. Nothing too trashy; after all, she was no slut.

Not that she didn't want to fuck one or two of the people she worked with. Cale Lamkin was attractive, and his body was fantastic. Amy had dreamed many times of Cale pounding away at her from behind. Even though he was a loud mouth and a poser, she didn't want him for his voice and clothes. Kind of how men thought of her, she supposed.

Then there was Dudley Hobbs. Poor Dudley. Amy wasn't sure why she sometimes wanted him. He was such a dweeb, but his softness and vulnerability drew her to him. She knew doing Dudley would be a sympathy fuck. He would probably do something stupid and say he loved her and promise to leave his wife. Rory O'Grady could be a candidate, too, even though he frightened her a little. Rory's body was tough and hard like Cale's, but something about him, his brooding and calculating manner, made Amy shiver with mixed emotions. Anyway, she had promised herself that this time, she would not fuck anyone she worked with. She had been down that road many times, and it always ended badly. No fucking, just flirting, especially with the older guys, but she shouldn't let that randy old creep Sherwood grabs her tits anymore. Well, maybe one more time, just to keep him on her side.

Amy wished she could flirt with the women also. She had never been with a woman, but she had thought about it a few times, mostly when she was in high school. Half of the cheerleading team had tried it with each other or with girls from other teams. Once, Amy had watched two of her teammates kiss and fondle in the locker room and had become aroused, but when they had seen her, and invited her to join, she ran away. Since high school, and especially in the public service, other women were more hostile toward her than friendly. Her mother said they were jealous of Amy's beauty and figure and worried their men might wander. That could be true, Amy had thought. In the secretariat, many women were older, frumpy, and married, but Amy had never met any of their spouses. This is why she couldn't understand their frequent hostility to her and their snootiness. If only one or two of them were lesbians, or bi, thought Amy.

Friday was Amy's favourite day, especially this Friday because, after work, Amy would be meeting up with her three best friends from high school. They had all been cheerleaders, and like Amy, they all still looked good and liked to party. Especially Debbie, who was addicted to dick and loved playing one man off against another until she chose a man to take her home. F.F.F. - "Fresh Fuck Friday" - was Debbie's joke reference for the first Friday of every month. And this Friday was the first. Even though Stella and Maria were married, they flirted just as well as Amy and Debbie and played supporting roles well. Amy and her friends always had fun together, and this Friday would be the same.

Actually, it had been a fun Friday already. Kingsmore and Medowcroft had been in meetings all day, and little work had come her way. She had plenty of time for coffees, lunch, and a forty-five minute facial at a nearby spa. There had also been time to apply fresh makeup and change into designer jeans, shirt, and shoes more suitable for a night out with her best friends.

By five o'clock, the last of the analysts had scurried out for the weekend. Even dull Dudley had left. Only Sherwood remained in the office, and Amy thought mischievously about giving him a little titillation to help him through the weekend. The vibration of her cell phone interrupted her thoughts:

"Hi, Amy, it's Debbie. You ready for tonight? I'm

all done at work. Let's meet at the Oak in fifteen and get an early start."

"What about Stella and Maria? Where are they?"

"They called earlier. They will be downtown around six-thirty. Something about dropping cars off and getting Stella's husband to drive them back. Come on, Amy. You know it's F.F.F., and I want to play."

"All right, Debbie. It's good that you called because I was about to do something naughty. See you in fifteen."

As Amy hung up and squeezed her phone into the front pocket of her Victoria Secret Hipster Boot Cut Jeans, she turned to meet the yearning eyes of Sherwood. Amy's conversation with Debbie had energized her, and she thought it would be fun to start the night by telling Debbie how naughty she had been.

Amy beckoned the director general over with her index finger. She directed him to sit on her armless chair before loosening her shirt and straddling him. Unbeknown to Amy and Sherwood, not everyone had left the office. Seething eyes watched Sherwood grope and pant toward another unfulfilled fantasy.

If Sherwood hadn't grunted and huffed so much, Amy might have heard the faint click of a cell phone camera. Instead, the director general's stiffness approached the point of no return, and Amy got off before things got messy. Later, Amy admitted to Debbie how the old guy had aroused her, and she almost let herself go. Debbie laughed and said Amy had better watch herself if she was to keep her promise not to fuck anyone at work.

Leaving Sherwood to relieve himself in the men's washroom, as she knew he had done before, Amy left the office for the last time at five thirty-five p.m. Debbie was waiting for her with a martini, bought for them by a rugged guy Debbie had met at the bar. Stella and

Maria joined them at six-thirty, and the four of them set off for a raucous, booze filled night, where numerous egos and hearts waited to be frivolously bruised and broken as the promise of sex drew men like moths.

Twelve

Stapleton & Muddle Murder Room

Stapleton leaned back to tilt his chair on its rear legs as he held his phone at arm's length to focus the text message words. Muddle, energized by the flow and quantity of facts, stabbed a finger at the photograph of Rory O'Grady pinned above the other five victims on the homicide board and said to Stapleton, "Evidence is mounting that O'Grady is our killer, sir."

Stapleton, still straining to read a text message, grunted, his open expression suggesting skepticism. Muddle, well attuned to the inspector's face, pressed on.

"Sir, we have the hot tub manual, the IRA, a history of violence, drug use, lots of P, problems with the victims, and the scuff mark on the F, front of his car. Plus, O'Grady was unaccounted for the entire week. No one can confirm he was at home. He could have gone out anytime and gone anywhere. He has no alibis!"

Muddle turned from the board as Stapleton brought the chair down on four legs and clicked off his cell phone.

"Sir?" said Muddle, desperate for some confirmation of his analysis and conclusion.

"Yes, sergeant, the evidence appears overwhelming. In fact, there is more. A message from the officers interviewing witnesses report that the old lady who lives next door to Amy Hurley has remembered seeing a man in a car driving slowly by the Hurley house a week or so before the explosion. Also, Debbie Ross, a friend of Hurley's who was out with Hurley the night she died, mentioned that she thought a man had followed them for a while early in the evening."

Muddle waited. Stapleton had told him many times to resist the impulse to judge or comment before he had all the information. Sighting of men was unremarkable unless something connected them. Pleased with his sergeant's patience, Stapleton continued.

"Both accounts mentioned that the man wore an odd or funny cap or hat."

Muddle connected the dots and said, "Same then as the witnesses to the death of Dudley Hobbes, who said the driver of the car wore an odd hat or F, flat cap."

"Yes, sergeant, so all we need…"

"All we need, sir," said Muddle, "is to find a hat at O'Grady's house and confirm that it belonged to him."

An insightful grin spread Stapleton's face and eyes as he spoke.

"Oh, I have no doubt a hat will be found, sergeant. You can be sure of that."

"Sir, am I missing something?"

"We may both be missing something, sergeant, or at least we might be unable to prove something. Each of the three sightings of a man with a hat coincides with a slight weakness in the whereabouts of Jeff Parsons. Also, sergeant, if you were going to kill someone, would you wear a hat that people would remember? Surely, a generic baseball cap would be a better choice for a disguise. On the other hand, if I were the killer, and I wanted to direct suspicion at another person, I would certainly wear something distinguishable and attributable to the other person. Hence the odd hat, sergeant."

Muddle mused for a moment and then bubbled with a counter.

"Yes, sir, but if I were the killer and I P, planned to commit suicide after I had killed everyone, then wearing my own hat would be normal. It's the same as using my own car to knock someone off a bike or not caring if I had credible alibis. I agree that one or two of Parson's alibis have weaknesses, but the evidence is mounting against O'Grady."

Stapleton, his face contracted with thought, drew the only conclusion available before sharing it with his sergeant.

"Unless, sergeant," said Stapleton, "O'Grady and Parsons were working together."

Thirteen

Interview - Room 5, Ottawa Police HQ

Fatigue weighed me. I had zoned out. Contradicting science, lightness in the top of my skull made my head drop forward. I came back as Stapleton and Muddle strode in, brisk and purposeful. If Stapleton thought I was tired, he ignored it and pushed on.

"Mr. Parsons, we were talking about March. Did something happen in March? Something significant?"

"Er, yes. Sorry. I just got carried away. I remember Rory was very pissed off about the promotions."

"Promotions?"

"Actually, I should say competitions not promotions, although from the way Rory told me about them they were the same thing."

"Okay. You've lost me, Jeff; competitions or promotions?"

Jeff. Detective Stapleton had called me Jeff. A subtle change from formal to friendly, designed to disarm and sedate. I needed to be careful.

"Sorry, competitions for promotions. That's what I meant. In March, the secretariat posted competitions for senior analyst positions. Competitions and promotions have two things in common: winners and losers.

During Rory's four years with the secretariat, he entered six promotion competitions and lost every time, which is a lot of losing.

"I'm pretty sure... no, I'm certain, Rory agreed, or accepted, that three of the losses and the competitions had been fair and that the best, or at least as good as, candidates had received a promotion."

"Why are you so sure? You said you don't know what Rory thought."

"Well, don't take this the wrong way, but I'm certain because three of the six are still alive."

Large, looping 6-3=3 filled half a page of Stapleton's notepads.

"Okay. Go on," said Stapleton. Then he added, "Which three promotions did Rory disagree with?"

"The first was Dudley Hobbs's promotion to senior policy analyst. The promotion did not provide much of a title change and only about ten thousand dollars more in income. The title and the money didn't bother Rory, though."

Stapleton added more to his math: 6-3=3+10,000.

"Why? Aren't money and title important?"

"They are, but more importantly, promotion to senior policy analyst places one foot on the executive ladder, provides access to higher level meetings, and signals to the community you had been identified as up and coming. Missing out on title, money, and status did give Rory angst, but it was the behind-the-scenes actions that pushed Rory to the edge."

Saying Rory was pushed to the edge seemed to galvanize the detective, and he edged forward in his seat as though readying for a meal. I almost flinched when his arms animated as he extended and flexed them in preparation for serious note taking.

"This might be significant, Jeff. What do you mean when you say 'behind-the-scenes actions' pushed Rory to the edge? What did he say or do? Did he have an argument with someone or threaten anyone?"

The detective seemed eager, almost desperate, and I began to wonder about what I was saying and how it might influence the detective's conclusions about Rory. How far should I go? I decided less would be more.

"Urm, no. I mean I didn't see Rory do anything crazy, if that's what you mean. He was pissed off at people. Upset. That's all."

Stapleton's body sagged when I didn't have some conclusive, rage-filled anecdote to provide, and he sighed and said, "Why don't you just tell me what happened?"

"First, Rory claimed Dudley had been advised of the competition in advance. Second, Rory believed the 'in basket' of questions used in the written exam had been skewed toward the type of long-term, slow-moving, single-policy focus files Dudley worked on as opposed to Rory's multiple, short-term, fast-moving files.

"Third, Rory did some snooping on the shared computer drive system and found single page summaries of issues directly linked to the exam questions. Dudley had written the summaries, and they predated the exam by a week. Proof, maintained Rory, that Dudley already had the questions.

"Fourth, Rory said he had seen a new draft organizational chart on the copy machine showing Dudley's pre-competition 'box' blank of his name. Another assurance, said Rory, Dudley would win the competition.

"Last, according to Rory, if these incidents had not been enough, one look at Dudley's work ethic, personality, and general dweebness was enough to show there was no way Dudley Hobbs, rather than Rory O'Grady, should have received the promotion. A winner and a loser."

Stapleton divided 6-3=3+10,000 by 5, and I became distracted by trying to work out the answer. Stapleton's voice interrupted my calculations.

"So, Rory thought the competition for the senior position had been rigged in Dudley Hobbs's favour?"

"Yes. And he didn't like it."

"Did he talk to anyone, make a complaint or anything?"

"No. The secretariat doesn't encourage complaints. If the competition was rigged, the people in charge did the rigging. No use complaining to them."

"What about the union or some kind of complaints body or something?"

"Well, you're right. We do have a union with a complaints or grievance procedure, but once you start a complaint, you're future in government becomes limited. You get labelled as a trouble-maker, and no one will hire you."

"I'm surprised. Isn't personal information confidential?"

"Is anything in government confidential? Anyway, Rory didn't believe in the system."

"Do you believe in the system, Jeff?"

"No more or less than anyone else, detective. It's not perfect."

"Tell me about the other promotion or competition Rory didn't like."

"Cale Lamkin. He also moved from policy analyst to senior policy analyst. This time though, according to what Rory told me, the evidence was more personal than a collection of questionable clues and suppositions. Rory claimed he overheard Cale on the phone saying he had been guaranteed the promotion because he had threatened to leave the secretariat."

"Is it usual for people to threaten to leave in order to get a promotion? I would have thought that a risky tactic."

"Yes, normally a person would be crazy to threaten to leave, but Cale had been on a complex file for three years. No one could take over the file quickly, and it was a hot file at the time for the government. According to Rory, Cale also said there was no real competition either - which probably pissed Rory off more than Cale's claim he had been guaranteed the promotion."

"What did you make of Rory's claims?"

"Well, the part about overhearing Cale Lamkin is believable because Cale was always overheard on account of his loud voice. Whether the content was true, I don't know. Of course, the rumours about Cale being Rena Kingsmore's favourite didn't help. Either way, Cale got the promotion; Rory didn't. Like I said, a winner and a loser."

"What did you think about the promotions? Did they bother you?"

"With Dudley Hobbs and Cale Lamkin, I would probably meet Rory halfway. I'm sure they were the preferred candidates. Tweaking the competitive process to favour preferred candidates is not unheard of in government."

"Is that what happened?"

"I don't know. Maybe advanced notice of the competition? Questions given ahead of time? Assurances? Guarantees? There are so many ways to glean, misunderstand, or intimate actions or overheard conversations. Anything is possible, but it would all be subject to contextual interpretation. Rory ranted and raved about the promotions for weeks and left no doubt that, from his perspective and context, these events happened. Hobbs and Lamkin received promotions. He didn't."

"Did you apply for the promotions, Jeff?"

"Oh, no. They were bilingual positions. I don't

speak French well enough."

"You said Rory wasn't happy with three promotions, but you only mentioned two."

"Yes, that's right. The other happened in July, and I thought you wanted things by month."

"Okay. Was there anything else in March?"

"No, not really."

Stapleton had stopped taking notes about halfway through my description of March, and for a moment I had the perverse thought that I had somehow let him down. The detective's arms had relaxed, and he sat back in his chair. I couldn't determine if the detective's intensity, when I had first mentioned Rory being on edge, had been real or a feint to tempt me to say something to incriminate Rory. Mimicking the detective, I also sat back, hoping he was done. He wasn't.

"Amy Hurley was a very attractive woman, wouldn't you say, Mr. Parsons?"

Stapleton's sudden change of tack didn't faze me this time. He had already asked me to account for my whereabouts when Lamkin and Hobbs had died, and I was ready for him.

"Yes, she was."

"Rumours suggest she was a bit of a flirt and perhaps more."

An image of Amy's nakedness flashed into my mind, and I beat down the urge to smile.

"Yes, Amy flirted a bit, but that was all. If she did, I know nothing about it."

"Did she flirt with Rory?"

"Pretty much everyone, I'd say. She was like that."

"What do you mean 'like that'?"

"Oh, you know, happy, outgoing, and casual."

"I see. Did she flirt with you, Mr. Parsons?"

"A little, I guess, yes. Nothing serious, though."

Stapleton drew a short breath and paused as

though ready to implement a prepared move. I was getting the hang of his tactics, and as I expected, Stapleton got to the point.

"Amy Hurley died on Friday night. Where were you, Mr. Parsons?"

I didn't bother with indignation this time and provided my alibi tersely.

"After work, I had a few beers with some friends from my soccer team. Then I went home."

"What time did you get home?"

"I don't recall exactly, around eleven. You could ask my wife."

I watched as eleven p.m., home, wife, check appeared on his notepad.

Suddenly curious, and a little concerned about the need to account for Friday night, I said, "Why do you want to know where I was on Friday night? I thought the fire happened on Saturday morning, not Friday night."

"Oh, it may be nothing, but a neighbour reported seeing someone in the area on Friday evening and early Saturday morning."

I was a little unnerved. The nearest neighbour to Amy's house was eight hundred feet away. She was old, half-blind, and lived alone. I doubted if she had seen anything. I wondered what the detective was doing. Was there really a witness, or was he testing me, and if so, why?

Fourteen

Amy Hurley - Dead

Desire and lust sparred with contempt and disdain as calm eyes, hidden by the shadow cast by the brim of a flat cap, watched and judged the women as they tramped across town from one trendy bar to another. Signs of inebriation became apparent around eleven-thirty, as vulgar talk, shrill giggles, and loud laughs accompanied the click of high-heeled shoes. At eleven forty-five, Amy Hurley and her friends, skirts hitched up, and mouths pouting, bypassed the lineup and descended steep steps in to Club Vibe, the latest meat-market dance club to arrive on the Ottawa scene. Confident of the likely outcome, the man pulled his cap down and went to find his car. Another woman, much less attractive, needed watching.

#

By one a.m., Debbie had chosen a mate for the night: tall, muscular, handsome, shallow, vain and drunk. "A perfect F.F.F.," Debbie said to Amy as she led her prey to the slaughter. "He'll go all night and be gone in the morning."

Stella and Maria lived close by each other in the West End and shared a cab home. Amy, drunk, but not falling down, hailed her own cab for the twelve kilometre, forty-dollar ride home.

The backseat was vinyl. Amy, tired and drunk, slid left and right as the cab sped and lurched around corners, eager to get another fare. Frustrated, Amy placed a leg on the rear of each front seat, her legs parted invitingly. The driver, aware of his charge, angled his head to better view the tight lines of inner thigh and crotch. Distracted and aroused, he drove more erratically, forcing Amy to brace herself harder. Her knees rose, and her butt slid to the edge of the seat, poised and accessible. Unaware of the driver's rising pulse, Amy thought about the man whom she had seen several times that night. Amy hadn't seen his face, but she knew the hat. Had it been coincidence? Had Rory followed her?

The cab's brakes squeezed the wheel disks hard, and the cab rocked forward and bounced back to stop on the curved driveway of Amy's semi-rural house. The cab driver, perspiring as imagination-fed fantasy, suggested a "free ride for a free ride, if you know what I mean." Tired of flirting, and beginning to experience some post-binge loneliness and depression, Amy said she didn't know what he meant, and threw a fifty dollar note into the front of the cab. Without waiting for change, she hurried from the cab and slammed the door.

Amy's semi-rural home belonged to her mother. Semi-rural meant it was located on the edge of South Ottawa on a half-acre lot, set back from the road and about eight hundred feet from the nearest neighbour. Her mother had bought the house thirteen years earlier with the money she received from the local poultry plant where Amy's father had worked before his accidental death. Buying the house outright was the only good decision Amy's mother ever made.

Amy's father, Bill, had fallen from a ladder while doing maintenance work, at the plant, for which he was untrained. After first denying responsibility, the company offered Amy's mother four hundred thousand dollars cash if she gave up any right to sue. Amy's mother, herself an epitome of the hot, blond, small-town chick, pounced on the four hundred thousand dollars before she even considered any advice, legal or otherwise. For a short while after, many people said she had been crazy for taking the money, and should have sued the company for millions. Eight months later, the company went out of business because the owners had siphoned off millions of dollars while under-declaring profits and tax liability. The owners, who had lived in the area for thirty years, disappeared into the night.

Amy's mother had been twenty when Amy was born, a widow at thirty-two, and chasing "toy boys" at forty. The house, a one-level, three bedroom bungalow built in the 1970s, had seen better days, especially since Amy's mother started drinking heavily and smoking marijuana joints as though they were cigarettes. The heavy drinking and marijuana began shortly after her fortieth birthday and coincided with a wild relationship with a man twenty years her junior. The relationship ended badly when the man/boy told her mother he was only fucking her because he wanted to get to Amy.

The drinking, smoking, and man chasing had been ongoing since then, and the last five years had added fifteen years to her mother's appearance and health. The house had suffered the same fate. Outside and in, the theme was neglect. Faded, peeling, temporary fixes, doing without, unkempt, and increasingly dirty were all words that came to mind if Amy let herself fall into a melancholy mood thinking about the house. Nevertheless, it was home, it was cheap, and, well, Amy loved her mother.

Sweet marijuana and stale booze hung in the air as Amy stepped over empty beer bottles and cans, toward

Public Service

the kitchen. Discarded jeans and shirts lay across disturbed sofa cushions, suggestive of torrid, frenzied, and passionate activity. Surprised to find a clean glass, Amy drank some water while sucking back her last cigarette of the night, or the first of the day, depending on how one counts two a.m.

Amy locked the front door and walked wearily down the hall to the bedrooms. Amy's room was at the end of the hallway, and she stopped and glanced in on her mother. Amy wasn't concerned about a guest being with her mother. The men never stayed. Her mother was alone, alone in a sordid sort of way, as an odour, not fragrance, but an odour, of sex crept into Amy's nostrils.

The condition of her mother was the reason Amy did not follow Debbie's lead and find a F.F.F man. She wanted someone who loved her, not someone who would simply fuck her for his own satisfaction and then leave. The irony that her persona signalled the opposite never occurred to her. After peeling off her Victoria's Secret jeans and pulling off her G-string, shirt, and push-up bra, Amy fell exhausted to her bed. Her hand slipped between her legs, and a few strokes, murmurs, and twitches later Amy slept.

During the night, annoyed at being woken by a swollen bladder, and disappointed at the loss of the warmth and comfort of her self-induced orgasm, Amy scampered to the bathroom. Hunched over the toilet bowl, intent on emptying her bladder as quickly as possible, Amy did not grasp the significance of the rotten egg smell that mingled with the odour emitted from her urine, concentrated by alcohol, cigarettes, and perspiration. Empty and chilled, from the cold toilet seat and her nakedness, Amy hurried back to her bed and pulled the blankets over her head, ending her nasal sensors' efforts to alert the brain that a bad egg smell could mean more than rotten eggs.

#

Amy's mother regained consciousness at eight forty-four a.m. Despite drink, drugs, and the emotional strain of another loveless fuck, Amy's mother had survived the sordid encounter. Frank, a beer-bellied, bearded, motorcycle gang member, in town from Toronto to conduct business with local gang members, had bought her drinks all night. They hadn't spoken much or danced or much of anything, really. She had hung around until he crooked his finger and said it was time to go. Helmet-less, they had ridden to her home. Inside, he commanded, she complied. Mouth, vagina, and anus: rough and functional. Finished, he zipped his pants and left. Abandoned, she smoked marijuana until, numb, she had stumbled to bed.

Blurry eyed, Amy's mother reached for the nicotine that beckoned from the bedside table. Caught in the smoker's compulsion, she grasped the cigarette and lighter with unsteady fingers. She drew a breath before she placed cigarette to lips and lighter to cigarette. Her calloused thumb stroked the wheel of the lighter. No spark. No flame. Frustrated and desperate, she shook the lighter and blew rancid breath into the mechanism. She gripped the lighter, positioned her thumb, and pressed hard on the wheel and pulled her thumb backward. Metal crunched on flint. A spark ignited the butane gas, and blue yellow flame illuminated her cracked and wrinkled hand. Her last breath seared her throat and scalded her lungs.

Eight hundred feet away, Amy's neighbour sat on her covered veranda with her second morning coffee. Her eyesight had deteriorated recently, and her flinch was more intuitive than reactive. She needed whooshes and bangs to locate the source of the explosion, but she knew the sounds had come from Amy's house. Frightened and disoriented, the seventy-five-year-old retired schoolteacher allowed several minutes to elapse before she was able to compose herself enough to make a coherent 911 call.

Firefighters, ambulance, and police arrived without effect: no building to save, no humans to rescue, and no one to arrest. Only the media found something useful; charred human remains made good pictures.

Amy's mother's reputation for alcohol and marijuana consumption, together with the fire marshal's preliminary assessment that the explosion and fire had resulted from the ignition of gas, precluded any serious thought of criminal activity, and consequently, any effort to conduct much of an investigation.

The media conducted biased interviews with local bar patrons and painted a picture of a woman well known for booze and drugs and loose morality. Without pity or compassion, Amy and her mother died a cruel and painful death.

Fifteen

Interview - Room 5, Ottawa Police HQ

Detective Stapleton turned a page on his notepad. He wrote April 2012 in large, bold letters at the top of the blank page and underlined the word and numbers twice. The detective's tactics concerning March still bothered me, and again I wondered about his intentions. Was I a suspect? Did I need a lawyer? Only guilty people asked for lawyers. Among these thoughts, Stapleton inserted an unexpected question.

"Jeff, I understand you like soccer."

"Er, yes. How do you know?"

"The scarf you were wearing when the officer brought you in. I noticed the scarf had a Chelsea crest and name on it. I follow European soccer also. I guess Chelsea is your favourite team?"

Stapleton's switch to something personal and unrelated to Rory confused me for a moment, and I floundered as I tried to figure out the detective's angle. I decided he might just have a friendly streak, so I responded in kind.

"Yes, I've followed them since I was a teenager. I grew up in London and moved to Canada almost thirty years ago. Who do you support?"

"Oh, I like Barcelona and Dortmund. There is some Spanish and German in my heritage, and I was hooked on the teams through my grandfather. I've never been to a game, though. I guess you have?"

"Yes, lots of times."

"Did Rory like soccer, Jeff?"

Well, so much for Mr. Friendly, I thought.

"Not that I remember. Why?"

"No reason," replied Stapleton as he flipped a page or two back on his pad and consulted his previous notes. After a few moments, he asked me to repeat or clarify a few points about the promotions. He wanted to be sure that I hadn't heard Rory make any specific threats either to, or about, Dudley Hobbs or Cale Lamkin.

"No. Rory hadn't threatened anyone. He was pissed all right, but that's all."

I received the raised eyebrow and silent treatment again. I didn't fall for it. Instead, Tim Horton's coffee, renowned for its strength, had penetrated my bladder, and my bowels signalled their need for immediate evacuation. Before I could ask to go to the bathroom, Detective Stapleton, seemingly done with March, put down his pen and said, "How about April, Mr. Parsons? Did anything happen with Rory at work you want to tell us about?"

"Not really. March madness had ended, and we had figured out where the chips would fall for the next few months."

"What do you mean by March madness?"

"Well, like I said earlier about March. The government had made statements about inland security-related issues, budgets, priorities, etc., so we had a good idea what would most likely be the hot topics for the minister and the public."

"Like what?"

"Like the announcement the prime minister would meet the US president in July to discuss North American security issues. A US/Canada meeting would mean we would have to produce lots of briefing notes and paper to support the meeting."

"Did Rory have anything to do with preparations for the meeting?"

"Well, some of his files would certainly be on the agenda, but I don't recall a specific issue. I mean, everyone would be involved to coordinate and produce briefing notes and background material for the prime minister. The only thing I can think of would be the brainstorming session in early April. The minister of inland security wanted some update or other on security and Prudence Medowcroft, the director, called a brainstorming session."

"Brainstorming?"

"Yeah, you know. Everyone gets together, brings creative ideas, shares opinions, and solutions to come up with a plan to address a problem."

"Ah, yes. Why did Rory have a problem?"

My gut churned as coffee asserted its dominance. I had to go.

"Can I go to the bathroom first? Tim's coffee is, well, you know…"

"Yes, certainly. Sergeant Muddle will show you the way."

Sergeant Muddle stepped smartly toward the door. I wondered how he would open it without a handle. In answer to my unspoken question, the door opened before the sergeant reached it. I guessed someone monitored the cameras. A uniformed officer stood framed by the doorway, and he gave way when the sergeant reached him. I followed the sergeant out of the sterile room and into the narrow, bright corridor. Ten steps down the corridor, Sergeant Muddle stopped and pointed to a plain door. No washroom sign. No men sign, no women sign. My puzzled expression prompted mannequin Muddle, as I had begun to think of him, to utter his first words directly to me. "Unisex. No need for signs."

I pushed on the door and saw Muddle smile. The door didn't budge. Muddle spoke for a second time. "Opens outward, prevents barricading." I thought about asking who would want to barricade themselves in a bathroom, but my bowels had no interest in that information.

Cold steel greeted me. Urinal, toilet, sink, mirror, even the toilet seat was steel. A steel half wall, with no door, provided a bare minimum of privacy for bodily function number two. I turned to lock the washroom door: no lock, no handle. I had the quickest, most uncomfortable shit of my life.

Mannequin Muddle smiled when I exited the bathroom. Bad cop. I disliked the sergeant. We walked wordlessly back to my safe room. I was surprised at how warm and comfortable the steel chairs felt after the muscle tensing experience of the bathroom.

"Feeling better, Mr. Parsons?" asked Detective Stapleton.

Sensing no amusement, unlike the sarcasm in Sergeant Muddle's comments, I said, "Yes, thanks, although I don't care much for the facilities."

"Ah, yes, not our best location. Perhaps next time, Sergeant Muddle will take you upstairs to the officers' washroom, eh, sergeant?"

"Yes, sir."

I got the feeling the ~detective and the sergeant had played this routine out many times before. I wondered why people with power or authority over others needed such petty affirmations of their positions.

I hoped my visit to the bathroom might allow Detective Stapleton time to conclude the uselessness of my boring and irreverent description of the secretariat and realize he might obtain better investigative results elsewhere. I was wrong.

"So, Mr. Parsons, are you ready to explain how brainstorming bothered Mr. O'Grady?"

"Rejection," I said.

Confusion leaked from Stapleton's eyes, and he said, "Rejection?"

"Yeah, rejection. First, though, you need to understand how brainstorming works in the federal government."

This time, skepticism dominated the detective's face.

"Doesn't it work like everywhere else? People get together and talk out a problem until a solution is found?"

I sighed inward and outward. I wanted to shake the detective. We were talking about the public service bureaucracy. Allowing some exasperation to creep into my voice, I said, "Not exactly, detective. Everything is different in government. Yes, people are called together to deal with a problem, or as we call them 'the challenging issue of the day.'"

Substituting the perfectly good word "problem" for the pretentious and bureaucratic phrase "challenging issue of the day" caused an involuntary twitch of Detective Stapleton's eyebrow and elicited a quiet sigh from mannequin Muddle. I threw my hands up in mock surrender and smirked.

"Hey, I don't make these names up. That's what we call brainstorming problems."

Silence.

"Okay, look, these issues of the day, or problems if you prefer, usually result from one or a combination of several things: senior management could no longer ig-

Public Service

nore the elephant in the room, or senior management had provided ambiguous or contradictory positions over a protracted period. A policy analyst exercised indifference or poor judgment concerning the importance of the issue, or political or media attention wagged the dog. There was concern about a real, or imminent, inland security event, and on the rare occasion, there was a desire to conduct proactive, forward thinking, strategic consideration of policy options and implications."

Unimpressed, Detective Stapleton tersely summarized my bureaucratizing.

"So, a problem needed a solution?"

"Yes. Anyway, no matter the reason, the format is always the same: the director would call in the senior and non-senior policy analysts directly responsible for the issue. Other experienced analysts joined the mix, as well as other directors, and on occasion, a subject matter expert from another area of government with related responsibilities for inland security.

"Due to the relatively small size of our core analytical group, most policy analysts attended these ad hoc brainstorming sessions. Once assembled, the director would iterate the issue and invite options and ideas from the assembled brains to address the problem."

"Seems like a normal approach to problem solving. What's so different?"

"Yes, the theory was sound; however, the practice was different."

"How so?"

"Well, the exchange was predictable. Senior policy analysts would use different words to reiterate the issue to show the director, and everyone else, their awareness and understanding of the problem. Junior policy analysts would do the same but with less confidence and detail. The subject matter expert would reiterate, in detail, the issue, and add more problems the director and policy analysts had not been aware of, or discovered, in their analytical capacity.

"Then, with the problem and issue thoroughly articulated in several different ways, by several different people, the director would summarize the dialogue, and remind the group of the need to provide options and ideas on a solution to the problem. Back to square one. Full circle. Navel-gazing would follow as people waited for the director to offer a solution for them to endorse. You see, detective, the real objective of the brainstorming session was to legitimize whatever solution or recommendation the director wanted."

"And Rory?" said Stapleton as he populated a page of his notebook with a square in a circle surrounded by empty "idea bubbles."

"Rory wanted none of this. In the ensuing vacuum, he would weigh in with a selection of options and ideas ranging from radical to extreme. First, Rory would suggest a need to revisit the problem itself to challenge and validate the claims, predictions, and conclusions everyone around the table had so willingly, and repeatedly, reinforced like head-bobbing decorations on the back of those old, pastel coloured sedans driven by older, pastel coloured people. Then Rory would show how a small invalidation of the stated problem might enable different approaches to possible solutions."

"How did the group and the director respond?"

"She was shell-shocked. No matter how many times Rory challenged, the director always acted like a deer in the headlights. In response, the director would tell the assembled Rory's ideas were impractical, untried, and were too difficult, too risky, too out there. The head bobbing would start again, and the group would discount Rory's approach to the problem without serious consideration, evaluation, or reasonable discussion. In short, he was rejected."

Public Service

An "R" landed in Stapleton's idea bubbles.

"What next?" said the detective.

"Well, sensing the need to show some kind of leadership, the director, or senior policy analyst, would trot out the four mainstays of public service problem-solving solutions."

Stapleton's pen stopped mid "R." I thought I had finally stumped his crazy note-taking methodology until he simply wrote 4M and asked, "The what?"

"Okay, there is no official name, but I call them the four mainstays. You know, like the four mainstays of therapy, or the four mainstays of cooking, or sailing, or anything: four generic ways to address any situation or problem in a given topic area. Look at it this way: no matter the problem, one of four ways can always be used to address it."

"And what are these four mainstays, as you call them?"

"The first and most used mainstay of public service brainstorming sessions is to agree the session had been useful in articulating the issue more thoroughly, and everyone should take a day to think about the issue. A second meeting for those interested would follow. Of course, this was code for, 'we will convene a group of likeminded people to address the issue, as a wider, diverse group like this one isn't working.'

"A second mainstay was to decide to write a briefing note to senior management describing the issue and advising how, after group evaluation, 'the issue should be placed on a more senior level management committee agenda for consideration and direction.' A classic pass the buck option.

"Third, depending on the sensitivity and timing, the public sponsored Committee on Inland Security, comprised of private sector business people and academic subject matter experts, could be tasked to consider the problem.

"Fourth, a consultant, preferably a retired senior public servant, might be engaged to provide recommendations. When the group agreed on one of those four options, the head bobbing would recommence, everyone would give a sigh of relief, engage in self-congratulations, and group-delusion on a job well done, and go for a well-earned coffee."

Out of breath, I paused and Stapleton filled the space with a terse, "What about Rory?"

"Rory seethed. I asked him twice why he continued to attend these sessions as they obviously frustrated him."

"What did he say?"

"He said he couldn't stop himself, and he couldn't sit by and let them be so useless. I told him they ignored him anyway, so why bother? They didn't give a fuck what he said, even when he made sense, which in fairness, he did some of the time. I guess I didn't realize how my comments, which I had meant to soften the tension, only infuriated Rory even more."

Done, I exhaled and spread my arms wide.

"So, Mr. Parsons, that's brainstorming in the secretariat, is it?"

"Yes, sad but true."

Stapleton, shoulders sagging, pushed on.

"Okay, what about the actual brainstorming session you referred to? Did it happen in April then or some other month?"

"Oh, yes, I think so. Maybe it was on the last day of April or in early May. Does it matter? What is it with this month thing anyway? Do you expect me to remember everything that happened on each fucking day? Come on!"

"All right, Jeff. Just do your best. Let's assume it was April. If the date becomes important, we can sort out exact dates later."

"Fine, I'll give you the gist of the actual meeting. I don't know when exactly, okay?"

"Yes. Thank you."

"What I remember is the issue of the day, or problem, was the minister of national security wanted a two-page update on our state of readiness to respond to a coordinated, asymmetrical terrorist attack. As usual, we had forty-eight hours to prepare the briefing note. Prudence Medowcroft called for a brainstorming session. The meeting went something like this:

"Medowcroft stated the issue and opened the floor for comments. Lamkin, who was always the one to speak first, restated the problem and said something like, 'We tell the minister the Government Operations Centre is twenty-four seven ready and the Emergency Management Act is up to date. We add that all departments are aware of their responsibilities; the 'Five Eyes' Intelligence Sharing Protocols are established; we have a mechanism to convene the Cabinet Security Committee, and Business Continuity Plans are required of all departments. I can pull the information together by end of day, no problem. We have a good news story all around!'

"Dudley Hobbs followed Lamkin and basically restated the issue with a wishy-washy concurrence about the minster's wants and an agreement with Lamkin's suggestion.

"Next, a junior analyst - I don't remember who - piped up and said department such and such had produced something on this when the prime minister met with the US Homeland Security Director last fall."

Stapleton interjected and said, "I'm no expert, but the proposal sounds appropriate. What bothered Rory?"

"Remember earlier when I told you about wiggle

room? You know how ambiguities and imprecise words are used in briefing notes to allow more, or less, emphasis when challenged, or asked to explain the meaning of something?"

"Yes, I remember. How does wiggle room fit with brainstorming? I don't understand."

"Consider the wording suggested by Lamkin; 'up to date' and 'aware of their responsibilities'; 'protocols established'; 'has been compiled'; and 'are required'.

"None of these actually says anything about effectiveness or real readiness. Words like aware, established, compiled and required don't say anything concrete about readiness. For example, do the 'established' intelligence sharing protocols actually work? Departments may be 'required' to have Business Continuity Plans, but do they actually have plans, and are the plans any good? Etc., etc.

"Okay. I see what you are getting at. What did Rory do next?"

"Rory wanted clarity. He said, 'The minister wants an update on what exactly? What kind of readiness: response, prevention, preparations, crisis management, communications-media, intelligence, allied assistance, expectations, materials, people, or executive readiness? Does the analysis need to be comparative? Since the government took office, since X or Y policy initiative? What does he want to do with the information? Will he use it for a public speech, the House, a committee meeting, or for his own edification?' He also made the same points about the words as I did. He finished by saying, 'Answers to all these would inform the scope and direction of the analysis for the briefing note.'"

"He said all that?"

"Well, maybe not all, but those were the kind of things he would say. Look, I said I would give you the gist. I can't remember word for word."

"Okay, then what happened?"

"This is where the meeting got a bit ugly because Rory asked Medowcroft what she had been told when she asked all these questions to the minister's office. Of course, we all knew she had never asked any of these questions. That was part of the problem. Brain fart, mile-wide questions from the minister or minister's office, would arrive in the secretariat, but no one would ever seek clarification of exactly what the minister wanted. Medowcroft wriggled a bit, became visibly annoyed, and said Rory had overcomplicated things and added something like, 'We don't need to go into all those details, as we all know it's not good news on all fronts.'"

"What did other people do?"

"Oh, Amy Hurley took notes and flirted with Lamkin. Dudley looked out the window. Others treaded water and waited for Medowcroft to do something."

"What about you? What did you say?"

"Me. I agreed with Rory, but I've been through the mill a few times and prefer not to get involved. I nodded non-committedly at all ideas and continued to doodle.

"Anyway, Medowcroft endorsed Lamkin's suggestion and said, 'Write it up. Check and include the material previously prepared for the prime minister last fall, and ensure consistency with any recent government positions on the subject. We are good to go.'"

"Rory didn't let go, though. He pointed out how the prime minister's note they planned to use was almost a year old, etc. Nevertheless, Medowcroft ignored him and said, 'Thank you, everyone. I think we have a way forward. Cale, send a draft to Dudley and me. If we need more input, I will pass the draft around for comments.'"

"That's how we actually brainstorm in the secretariat."

"Did Rory finally give up?"

"Not quite. Cale never circulated the draft-briefing note for comments, so Rory did some snooping on the shared drive. He found the note, and he showed me the concluding comment on our state of readiness for a coordinated, asymmetrical terrorist attack. The conclusion went something like: "'Asymmetrical security threats make static assessments of the government's state of readiness difficult to definitively qualify. However, the monitoring, coordination, and information sharing structures put in place by the government during the past two years have greatly enhanced our state of readiness and are in line with the readiness states of our closest allies.'"

"After I read the conclusion, Rory said, 'More fucking platitudes. All this means is we have no fucking idea how ready we are, what we are supposed to be ready for, or what we would do if anything asymmetrical happened, but hey, don't worry, we are as ready as our allies!'

"I admit I responded mischievously. I said the real meaning was we had done as much as anyone else, but if anything happened, we would have both the plausible deniability of having been as prepared as others, and we would have the means to monitor and coordinate that deniability.

"I even joked how the briefing note reminded me of what the CIA did during the Kennedy administration when they withheld information from senior officials to protect them from repercussions of events, or actions of parts of the government, should they have become public."

"What did Rory say?"

"He said, 'We are not the fucking CIA.'"

Public Service

Detective Stapleton did his eyebrow-raising thing again. I couldn't tell if he was skeptical about the events, amused by my telling, offended by my bit of profanity or exasperated by the inner workings of the secretariat. Somewhere in between my guessing at what the detective's raised eyebrow might mean, I blurted out I could tell him about our staff meetings, too.

"Why?" said the detective.

"Well, they pissed Rory off a lot."

"In April?"

"Every month, sometimes every week."

"Okay, okay, yes I would like to hear about the staff meetings. However, before we begin, I just need a few moments with Sergeant Muddle. Why don't you take a break for a few moments until we come back?"

Sixteen

Stapleton & Muddle Ottawa Police HQ

Stapleton left the room without waiting for Muddle and made for the parking lot. When Muddle caught up, he remained silent while the inspector drew air. Renewed, Stapleton said, "Sorry, sergeant, I needed a break. Mr. Parsons could talk the proverbial leg off the donkey. Let's review what we know. Run me through Parson's alibis again."

"Yes, sir. On Wednesday morning when Hobbes died after being knocked off his bike, Parsons did have an oil change. The time stamp at the garage puts Parsons at the garage at 9:30 a.m. The mechanics confirm that Monday was very busy, there was a long wait, and that many customers go to a nearby Tim Horton's while they wait. Interviews at Tim Horton's can't confirm or discount if Parsons was there or not. In addition, if there were no incidents, the Tim Horton's CTV automatically wipes itself after forty-eight hours. There is simply no way to confirm when Parsons arrived at Pennzoil or how long he waited. All we can confirm is the oil change occurred at 9:30 a.m."

"What about Saturday, sergeant?"

"Things are similar with the Athletic Club on Saturday evening when Medowcroft died. Entrance to the Athletic Club is via swipe card. Entry time establishes that Parsons, or someone with his card, entered the club at 7:04 p.m. However, the club does not require an exit swipe, so there is no record of when he left the club. The next confirmed account of Parsons whereabouts is eleven p.m. when his wife said he came home from the gym. There are four hours between when he entered the gym and when he arrived home. Drive time to Medowcroft's cottage is about thirty-five minutes. If he left the gym right after he arrived, four hours would provide enough time to drive to Medowcroft's cottage, somehow get Medowcroft to hang herself, and then return home."

"I have a theory about how someone might have gotten Medowcroft out of her house. How was Mrs. Parsons about the time her husband arrived home?"

"Very certain, sir. She said she dozed on and off, but when Mr. Parsons arrived home she recalls looking at her watch. She also recalled Mr. Parsons mention that he had walked by the river to cool off after the gym."

"And what night was Parsons out with his soccer team?"

"Friday, sir, the night Amy Hurley died."

"All right, sergeant. What does your gut tell you?"

"Parsons is at the centre of things, all right, and circumstances imply potential involvement in some way for some of the deaths, but the evidence is simply not there. What we do have is circumstantial. Weighed against the concrete evidence we have implicating O'Grady, I just can't see how Parsons is the killer."

"Yes, sergeant, we mustn't make circumstances fit yet. Tell me, what do you think of Parsons's description of his office and co-workers?"

"Kind of thing most people say about government

workers although the details make it far more believable than what you hear in the pub or by the BBQ."

"Why do you think he is telling us all this?"

"Because we asked him, I guess. I mean, if what he says is true, O'Grady has lots of reasons to dislike where he worked and who he worked with and for."

"The same could also apply to Parsons. Many of the circumstances and events affect him also. We only have Parsons's word that he is a cynical, disillusioned, yet benign bureaucrat waiting out his days until retirement.

"What we don't have, sergeant, is the smoking gun, a trigger, something to push a person over the edge. So far we have ongoing small stuff, those kinds of things happen everywhere in all workplaces. No, sergeant, we are missing something. We need to identify a catalyst, something that brought things to a head."

Stapleton began to walk back to the entrance, but he paused at the door and said to Muddle, "I have a feeling that we are losing this one."

Seventeen

Prudence Medowcroft - Alive

Prudence Medowcroft was one of Rena Kingsmore's many disastrous executive recruitments. Medowcroft was the Director of Operational Policy for Inland Security in the Canadian Inland Security Secretariat. She earned between one hundred and thirty-five and one hundred and fifty-five thousand dollars annually, and at age fifty-five had spent more than thirty years as a bureaucrat. Fifteen of those years involved overseas work for the Canadian Government's Foreign Affairs Department. Medowcroft had no private sector experience, was single, had no children, and lived alone with three cats.

Shades of grey were Medowcroft's colour. Lank hair, dry skin, and pale eyes all carried a grey hue. Grey rimmed reading glasses, light grey sensible shoes, and dowdy grey skirts and blouses. Perhaps she was colour blind. Physically, Medowcroft was under-inflated. Stomach, breasts, and shoulders sagged and languished on her tall, awkward frame: a bookish, unattractive, monochrome woman. Yet she was intelligent and analytical in a small-details sort of way. Unfortunately, especially considering her position as director of operational policy, Medowcroft often missed the big picture.

Medowcroft oozed a superior sense of entitlement, born of her colonial-like upbringing and fed by years of witnessing the inability of indigenous populations to grasp the benefits of well-meaning, but ineffectual, Western aid programs and policies. Absolute in her convictions, Medowcroft bossed and micromanaged everything and everyone, except for people of equal or greater stature to herself, such as deputy ministers or ministers. Medowcroft was a snob. A snob who endured her workweek, suffered her employees, and yearned to rule her minions without question.

Saturday was her day. A time to escape the peons who worked for her and the incompetents she toiled under. True, Medowcroft, due to her position, was beholden to the BlackBerry twenty-four seven, but as she had often explained to her boss, Rena Kingsmore, reception in cottage country was patchy in wet, windy, stormy or for some unknown reason, hot, humid weather.

Medowcroft had purposefully covered the majority of weather possibilities, and as a result, often ignored email messages on Saturdays, unless they were from the minister's office. That was different. The minister was a person someone of her calibre and breeding should communicate with, not any of those miscreant policy analysts who thought they were her equal. At least Lamkin and Hobbs knew their place, and most correspondence from them was to alert her to anything that might catch her unaware.

Then there was Rory O'Grady, who constantly challenged her position and decisions concerning inland security policy. She hated that small-minded Irishman. Always the same refrain: revisit the problem, challenge and validate the claims, predictions, and conclusions,

Public Service

look at things differently, understand the broader context. Why could he not understand the system? Do as I tell you, not what you think you should do. In fact, don't think; that's the job of your superiors. O'Grady's tiresome opinions were bad enough, thought Medowcroft, but the man didn't know how to write. Christ, he couldn't even identify a split infinitive, misplaced modifier, or dangling participle, let alone comprehend a compound possession or understand why pleonasms can, in fact, be appropriate. Also, he was of Irish stock, a far more severe deficiency than the inability to use proper grammar.

Oh, how Medowcroft longed for the kind of colonial authority she'd had during her time in Ghana, West Africa, when she had been the head of Canada's Overseas Aid and Development Office for the West Africa Regional Aid Program. There was no need to suffer the likes of O'Grady in Ghana. Yes, ma'am, no, ma'am. That was the way to run an organization. An almost natural order to governance, where the decisions and directions of the right people from the right backgrounds were not challenged by upstart, university-educated socialists who interpreted democracy as providing the right to challenge everything and everybody, irrespective of social status.

Oh, she had been happy in Ghana: a beautiful, peaceful country with a stable democracy and just enough poverty and colonial subservience to nurture and maintain Medowcroft's self-delusional grandeur. She had been an important person in Ghana, often sought out by the highest members of the Ghanaian Government, and invited to all foreign embassy functions and national events. Housed in a former British colonial house, in an exclusive suburb of Accra, and pampered by servants who earned less than three dollars a day for their labour, she had lived a fantasy life in the West African backwater at the Canadian taxpayers' expense. In fact, Medowcroft's happiness had been such that she had made property investment plans with the intention of retiring in Ghana at the end of her diplomatic career. Fortunately, for Ghanaians, a combination of personal and professional events cut short Medowcroft's tenure and stymied her retirement plan.

#

Prudence Medowcroft had been an anachronism in Africa. She had been born to diplomatic parents, who had, during almost forty years as Canadian representatives in British Commonwealth countries, learned and practised many of the worst traits of colonial superiority. They raised their only child on a diet of "white is right," as her mother often said.

Prudence's private girls- and whites-only school education, which at the time still used dogmatic propaganda, like "the sun never sets on the British Empire" and "the white man's burden," complemented and reinforced her superior and pro-white colonialist views. Views reinforced by her literary tastes, which included writers of colonial novels such as H. Rider Haggard, Rudyard Kipling, and Joseph Conrad, especially Haggard's *She* and Kipling's *Kim*. In addition, Medowcroft loved writers like Jane Austen, Charlotte Bronte, Charles Dickens, and George Eliot, who, though focused on domestic British society, used Britain's overseas possessions for significant context and action. These authors, and more of the same, filled her office and home bookshelves.

Together, these literary works formed the spine of Medowcroft's library, and like the authors, she constructed and propagated a colonial ideology by embracing the implicit justification for British imperialism within the novels. This was evident in the way she

Public Service

adopted the idea of the savage nature of natives, and the white man's burden of bringing them civilization. Finally, the existence of such views in renowned and famous literature sanctified, for Medowcroft, the dissemination of racial and colonial ideologies that had provided the conceptual framework for colonialism.

These views and attitudes toward native peoples crept into her daily dealings with Ghanaians until, utterly frustrated with the "wogs," she had unloaded a tirade of inappropriate colonial and racial innuendos toward her staff and members of the host countries bureaucratic establishment. Medowcroft's professional chastisement and subsequent demotion were swift.

#

Personal implosion was no less dramatic: Medowcroft, full of romantic notions fueled by Bronte and Austen, was ill-equipped to deal with the man whose path she walked into so willingly. Brigadier Albert Edward Williams, Distinguished Service Order, had arrived in Ghana, Africa, as part of a British contingent attached to the United Nations Institute for Training and Research, specifically, the Peace, Security, and Diplomacy Unit. Ghana was the brigadier's fifth African deployment, and his reputation as an expert on African affairs was well-founded and well-known. Also well-founded, but much less well-known, was the brigadier's penchant for women. Lots of women.

Prudence Medowcroft was a fish in the proverbial barrel for the brigadier. She was immediately smitten by the brigadier's name, which for Medowcroft conjured images of Victorian monarchy blended with Norman nobility and awakened in her thoughts of the ideal British gentleman portrayed in many of the novels that had shaped her distorted views of the modern world. The brigadier, sensing with ease a vulnerable virgin, plied

Prudence with compliments and old-fashioned courtship from their first meeting at the British ambassador's residence.

Amused by her colonial absurdity, the brigadier drew out the seduction to maximize any intelligence opportunities that might have presented themselves. Canada might well be an erstwhile international friend, but his real job was intelligence gathering, no matter the source. Of course, wooing Prudence Medowcroft did not preclude the brigadier's indulgence in pleasures of the flesh with other women. Before long, he had secured the ample services of local women, who were far more satisfying and accommodating than educated white women.

The undoing of the brigadier would have done Medowcroft's Bronte or Eyre novels proud; one Sunday afternoon, giggling at the prospect of surprising the brigadier with homemade scones and cream, Prudence dropped by his in-town quarters in the expectation she might be invited in for tea, no matter how scandalous that might be. Instead, strange grunting and rhythmic slapping greeted her arrival at the brigadier's door. Curious, and fearful something untoward had happened to him, Prudence cautiously entered the unlocked house. The sound drew her to the backroom parlour.

An incomprehensible sight assaulted her very fabric: facing the door, a young, naked, black woman knelt on all fours as the equally naked brigadier, one hand on the woman's shoulder, and the other clasping her braided hair, thrust his manhood into the woman's anus. Behind the brigadier, another naked woman wielded the brigadier's little wooden baton deftly against his buttocks in perfect rhythm with each carnal thrust.

Scones and fresh cream slipped from Medowcroft's white gloved hands as she tried to stifle the gasp and scream rising in her throat. The brigadier, ejaculation imminent, continued to thrust and grunt. Stunned by tangled, sweat-sheened bodies, and shocked by a swelling arousal, Medowcroft, in good Victorian fashion, swooned and fainted in front of the focused threesome. The brigadier, after a brief struggle to avoid laughing, satisfied his need and embedded his seed into his willing partner.

Medowcroft woke in her own home. Alone. No word of the event ever reached her ears, but she was sure the natives smirked and snickered behind her back. Humiliated, and unable to cleanse her mind of the scene, she avoided the brigadier and retreated into ever-decreasing social circles. No man would ever enter Prudence Medowcroft's heart again.

Incapable of trusting another human with her feelings, Medowcroft sought and found companionship, loyalty, and commitment with cats. Three cats shared her lakeside cottage, and she spared no expense on their care or well-being. The cats even had their own room, which overlooked the lake and basked in sunlight, courtesy of its southern orientation.

Eighteen

Interview - Room 5, Ottawa Police HQ

Stapleton and Muddle were back. Frowns spoiled both faces. Whatever they had left to discuss had not gone well. I decided to go on the offensive.

"'Guidelines for Effective Staff Meetings,' inspector."

"What?" said Stapleton.

"You asked me to tell you about the staff meetings. Well, the government's 'Guidelines for Effective Staff Meetings' were the root of Rory's problem with staff meetings. He once quoted to me how staff meetings 'should be one of the most effective ways to motivate and communicate with your employees.' He even went so far as to hand out the guidelines to everyone and underlined sections on what not to do, what to always do, and emphasized key directives such as 'be upbeat and inspirational, start and finish on time, and end the meeting on a positive note.' He believed proper, professional staff meetings were important and valuable. Unfortunately, our staff meetings fell short of the ideal."

I paused, expecting the detective to say something like "Go on," or "Hmm," or "Okay." However, he had reverted to his silent approach, so, neither encouraged nor discouraged, I continued.

"Staff meetings were scheduled on Tuesday mornings from nine to ten a.m., but in practice, the meetings occurred every two weeks rather than each week. Medowcroft often cancelled the meeting because she had another meeting, or decided she did not want a meeting. Anyway, when they did happen, staff meetings were torture for the majority of attendees."

"Torture? How could a staff meeting be torture, Mr. Parsons?"

"First, there was the venue. A small, cramped room, made worse by a large, oblong table, and oversized chairs, served as the boardroom where we held the meetings. The heavy, wooden table was a holdover from our previous accommodations, which had been in a heritage building where large, wooden tables belonged. Rena Kingsmore, the boss of the secretariat, had insisted the table, which she at one time deemed to be symbolic of steadfast stoicism, be moved to our current, and much smaller, boardroom. The oversized chairs came too. Consequently, every Tuesday, or second Tuesday, twenty-five or so staff squeezed, like economy-class passengers on a charter flight, into the windowless, poorly ventilated, starkly-lit boardroom."

Halfway to drawing a table and chairs, with sitting stick figures, Stapleton stopped drawing and said, "Mr. Parsons, I don't think we need so much detail on the room and table."

Excitement welled up. I fucking hated the table and the staff meetings, and I did not intend to lose my audience.

"Yes, you do. You need to understand how the table and the seating played into the meetings. You see, the short side of the oblong table, nearest the door, was reserved for Director Medowcroft. This had more to do with her habit of arriving last and late, and departing first and early, rather than her being the boss. Taking their cue from her seat, senior, ordinary, and junior analysts would arrange themselves outward in declining seniority, leaving the extremities for lesser mortals, such as administrative support staff, assistants, and technical support staff.

"Two exceptions to this arrangement existed: the office manager and her assistant, Amy Hurley, would sit to the left or right of Medowcroft, enabling them to pass documents, make notes, and remind her of important office management stuff. Rory provided the other exception. He would position himself at the other short side of the oblong, directly facing and confronting Medowcroft."

"Did Rory always sit opposite Medowcroft?"

"Pretty much all the time but more so in recent months, I think."

"Would you say Rory wanted to intimidate Medowcroft?"

"Hmm, yes, I think so, maybe."

"Go on."

"After shoehorning themselves into their desired oversized chairs, individual rituals concerning coffee, BlackBerries, folders, bagels, muffins, notepads, water bottles and photocopied handouts, ensued until everyone sat poised and ready.

"Fifty per cent of the time Medowcroft arrived late, flustered and scowling. She did not like staff meetings either. Her body language conveyed disdain, as though staff meetings were an unavoidable obligation, rather than an opportunity to connect with her employees.

"Without cordiality, Medowcroft would launch into a stale, disjointed ramble about the past week's events, the relevant substance of Monday's executive staff meeting, and indicate what she thought the com-

Public Service

ing week's priorities and issues would, or should, be. The degree of attentiveness the assembled showed mirrored their actual, or perceived, status in the group, and their real, or desired, opinion of the relevance of the information given."

My rendition of the staff meeting wasn't as scintillating as I thought because Stapleton's drawing had become stuck as he repeatedly drew small circles arranged in bigger circles. Perhaps, through his pen, his subconscious was expressing his opinion of my ramblings. Without direction, I continued.

"When her debrief of Monday's executive staff meeting ended, and she had performed her retrospective on the previous week and revealed her clairvoyant abilities for the immediate future, she would instruct one of the analysts to commence the round table component of the staff meeting."

"Round table? I thought it was oblong," said Stapleton as an eyebrow lifted and descended.

"Er, yes, it is oblong. Round table is where everyone gets a turn to say something. Unfortunately, most people think they have to say something."

The detective's eyebrow rose again, but he didn't speak, so I described the staff meeting torture in detail.

"Cale Lamkin, always the analyst sitting closest to Medowcroft and the one to whom she often turned first, would launch into a loud and detailed account of every action he had taken, or would be taking, on his files. He would lay special emphasis on even the most obscure connection between his labours and any details Medowcroft might have provided concerning the executive staff meeting or near-term priorities. Lamkin also stretched the thinnest of threads, to link his work, or area of responsibility, with those of the minister and the government writ large. Finally, in both senses of the word, he would be shameless in his agreement and endorsement of whatever Medowcroft had flagged as priorities for the week.

"Dudley Hobbs followed Lamkin. He also recounted minutiae, except his oratory was even more tedious because he only had two primary files, both of which moved like molasses. Moreover, Hobbs's soft voice was difficult to hear, which prompted less experienced junior staff to ask him to repeat what he had said. Although he didn't take as long as Lamkin, his verbiage seemed longer because of his slow speaking style. When he had finished convincing himself of his importance, and was satisfied he had convinced everyone else, he too would add a few words of flattery to Medowcroft. Then, guided by the senior analysts, the other senior analysts, and the two junior analysts, would adopt the same self-serving strategy and bore the crap out of everyone."

Stapleton's circles had become thick and were close to tearing through the paper as he asked, "What about you and Rory?"

"Well, like in the brainstorming sessions, I doodled a lot and made lists of personal things I had to do that week. Sometimes I would amuse myself by writing down the word said by speakers at every thirty-second point of their monologue. I would make a column for each person, and then compare the columns to discover the most common words."

"Really?"

"Yes. Most used words included: best practices, off-line, parking lot, silo, wordsmith, empower, dashboard, facilitate, toolbox, pros and cons, promote synergy, issue, going forward, touch base, synergies, prioritize, utilize…"

"I meant what, or how, did you and Rory present your reports?"

"Oh, I rambled a bit like the others but much

Public Service

shorter. I didn't believe anyone listened anyway."

"Rory?"

"Rory had a system. He called it his 'gone in sixty seconds' rule. He would make short notes on the three most important things he thought would be of interest and relevance to the wider group. Then he would give himself sixty seconds to convey those things in the fewest and most expressive words."

"That seems efficient and effective."

"Yes and no. I mean, it was efficient, but it wasn't effective."

"Why not?"

"Because of the inherent forces at work within public service staff meetings: first, those who had already spoken would hit the off switch. It's like an automatic defence mechanism that kicks in and closes off audio receptors to save a person from having to listen to the drivel of others. Second, anyone more senior than the speaker automatically adopted the 'What could they possibly have to say that is of importance to me?' posture. Third, the heat, closeness, and staleness of the room would have already made people uncomfortable and eager to depart. Fourth, those who couldn't sit still because of the uncomfortable chairs became functionally comatose by the self-serving rhetoric of previous speakers. Fifth, people had finished their coffees. Sixth, Rory's delivery was so complete and focused that fifty of his sixty seconds would elapse before anyone who was able to combat factors one through five could process such succinct information. When Rory finished, a delay, like the delay between a gunshot and impact, or thunder and lightning, hung in the air until startled by the silence, Medowcroft would cough and harrumph before asking if there was any other business."

"Mmm. Is that all?" said Stapleton as he gave up on circles and flipped to a blank page.

"No, no. Listen, when Medowcroft asked for any other business, she really meant the meeting was over, and indeed everyone would begin gathering up his or her baggage in anticipation of a rapid departure, except, of course, Rory. The invitation to raise any other business provided Rory with an opportunity to bring up what he considered important questions."

"Like what?"

"Oh, links between inland security policies, recent news events, tidbits of intelligence information he had obtained from other government colleagues, any statements by ministers related to policy issues, suggestions for future analytical focus or products, ideas relating to office management, structure, location of amenities. All manner of things which, according to Rory, would provide valuable discussion topics, and generate interest and life into the meetings."

"That sounds reasonable. Did people have a problem with it?"

"In principle, no, but the problems were the one through five I mentioned earlier and, of course, Medowcroft."

"What was her problem?"

"Rory's efforts to open up any other business, and generate meaningful and substantive discussion, made her appear, well, inadequate and dull. She never pursued a policy of actual dialogue with her staff, which Rory's suggestions might have caused to happen. Instead, she preferred to dictate how things would be and what was important. Besides, she gave the impression of suffering through the presence of her employees rather than engaging with them."

"I guess Rory didn't like these meetings."

"That would be an understatement. He loathed them. But, like the brainstorming sessions, he seemed compelled to attend and participate."

Public Service

"From what you describe, it appears Medowcroft wasn't popular."

"Yes, that's right."

"What about you? Did you like Medowcroft?"

I thought for a moment. I could see no advantage to lying, so I said, "I didn't like her at all."

Without warning, Stapleton switched focus, became formal, and punched out a question.

"Did you go out on Saturday night, Mr. Parsons?"

Of course, Medowcroft had died on Saturday night, and I sensed Stapleton already knew the answer to his question.

"Yes, I went to the Athletic Club to work out."

"What time did you go?"

"Seven."

"What time did you return home?"

Here I had a problem. My wife had been home when I arrived at eleven, and a four-hour gym workout wasn't believable. I wrestled with what to tell the detective.

"Mr. Parsons. Is there a problem?"

"No, I'm trying to recall what I did. I remember now. After the gym, I felt energized and hot, so I decided to take a walk by the river. It was a beautiful night, so I walked for an hour or so. I got home around eleven, I think. My wife was home; she will know for sure."

Stapleton, not hiding his skepticism, scratched a smiley face on his notepad. I didn't know if Stapleton's smiley face was an intentional ploy, but the face, and the casual way Stapleton drew it, unnerved me. What, I thought, did the detective have to smile about?

Nineteen
Prudence Medowcroft - Dead

The cottage, named Rorke's Drift by her great-great-grandfather, who, according to Medowcroft, participated in the 1879 defence of Rorke's Drift British mission station in the Anglo-Zulu war, had been in the Medowcroft family for four generations.

The original structure had been no more than a two-room shack suitable for high summer use only, and Medowcroft had lavished several hundred thousand dollars to transform the cottage into a four season, luxury home.

The extensive remodel included a spacious, open-concept design on the main level, complete with vaulted ceilings and skylights for natural light, to complement the floor-to-ceiling windows that looked onto Lake Phillip. The upper level also housed two enormous bedrooms, a four-piece bathroom complete with a jetted tub, a large living room, dining room, and custom kitchen. A wood-burning fireplace dominated the large living room. The walkout lower level included a big entertainment area, with a Napoleon wood stove, a den, a wet bar, and a full three-piece bathroom. Both upper and lower floors had expansive cedar decks, each occupied by six black, wrought-iron patio chairs and matching tables.

An electric forced air furnace, heat pump, and central air conditioning maintained ideal internal temperatures in all seasons. Professionally landscaped grounds included a multitude of interlocking stone in the entry, patio, garden walkway, and functioned as fixed borders for perennial flower beds. Designed and remodelled for peace of mind and maintenance-free living, the cottage made Medowcroft eager to retreat there on weekends.

Transformed from its humble origins, Rorke's Drift was an immaculate residence located on 2.5acres of prime real estate on Lake Phillip in the Gatineau Lakes and River system. With less than a thirty-minute commute to Ottawa, Rorke's Drift was an extremely desirable address.

#

T.G.I.F., Thank God It's Friday, was, in Medowcroft's opinion, a proletariat refrain. T.H.I.S., Thank Heavens It's Saturday, was far more apropos. Medowcroft anticipated all Saturdays, but this week Saturday had not arrived soon enough. An interminable week of policy meetings, document preparation for cabinet committees, and media questions concerning the inland security implications of the recent arrest of a Canadian naval officer for alleged spying, as well as several confrontations with Rory over internal promotions and competitions, had almost pushed her to the breaking point.

Forced, for the first time in months, to go into the office on a Saturday, and then remain there until six-thirty p.m. to fend off more media calls, Medowcroft had gone straight to her three favourite stores: the liquor store, Ottawa's International Cheese, Bread, and Delicatessen, and finally, Herbert Cuthbert's Fine

Meats, the last real butcher in Ottawa. By seven-fifteen p.m., she had gathered three bottles of Old World red wine, a selection of aged European cheeses, a variety of salted and smoked deli meats and fresh bread, and from Cuthbert's, four New Zealand lamb chops and one fresh fillet mignon. She added a few greens from the local market stands, and at seven-thirty p.m., she crossed the Ottawa River Bridge in her AWD Volvo XC90 and headed north to the comfort, safety, and solitude of Rorke's Drift and her beloved cats.

By eight fifteen p.m., Medowcroft had parked the Volvo in the garage, unwrapped several cheeses and meats, so they could reach room temperature and ideal texture, and poured her first glass of red Burgundy. Disciplined enough to let the wine breathe, she fed and watered her three cats, and recounted to them the ills of her day that had made her keep her kitties waiting.

Cats placated, she took the wine to her bedroom and changed from her dour, functional, work attire into her one hundred per cent, long, silk robe and matching slippers. Silk, yet greyish. Comfortable, Medowcroft returned to the kitchen area, poured a second glass of wine, and selected various cheeses, meats, and bread. She placed the provisions, and the open bottle, on a silver tray and took them to the leather chair and matching ottoman beside the fireplace, facing the windows that overlooked Lake Phillip.

A third glass of Burgundy accompanied the sustenance until a relaxed Medowcroft reached for a hand-carved mahogany box on the small side table. From the box, she withdrew papers, a lighter, and a bag of marijuana. Spliff, joint, cone, booner, doobie; Prudence knew all the names. This was the one concession she made to the habits of the unwashed masses. Besides, Queen Victoria had reportedly used opium and cannabis. If drugs were good enough for a queen, then they were right for Prudence Medowcroft.

On Sunday morning, Medowcroft's gardener, a recent immigrant from Mexico, arrived at Rorke's Drift to prune and clear shrubs in preparation for winter. Although a qualified and professional horticulturist, he undertook menial gardening work on weekends to increase his income to send money home to his waiting family. Instead of pruning bushes, he found Medowcroft hanging by the neck from the old Maple in the backyard.

Preliminary police and coroner reports concluded death by suicide: evidence of alcohol and drug use, absence of a struggle and no sign of coercion, rope burns on her hands, and no reports of strange persons in the area, all indicated Prudence Medowcroft had taken her own life. Immediate and poorly researched media stories portrayed Medowcroft as a lonely woman, employed in a highly stressful job who, without any immediate family and few friends, sought solace through drugs and alcohol, and companionship through her cats: a sad, and perhaps predictable, end.

Twenty

Interview - Room 5, Ottawa Police HQ

"Okay, Mr. Parsons," said Stapleton, "let's get back to building a picture of Rory, his relations with the people he worked with, and the office environment. According to your earlier statements, Rory had become upset in March when Cale Lamkin and Dudley Hobbs won job competitions and received promotions to senior policy analysts. In April, you said brainstorming sessions and staff meetings had made Rory feel rejected. Did Rory express any aggression toward anyone in the office during this time? You know, toward Cale or Dudley concerning their promotions?"

"No. I don't recall any. I mean, he didn't walk around saying he would kill them or anything."

A rueful grin stretched the detective's cheeks.

"Well, evidence of a direct threat would be helpful. How about hints he might do something drastic? Any outbursts at all to show Rory was becoming more upset with things? What about May, Jeff? What happened with Rory in May?"

"I don't really recall May. I took two weeks' vacation in May."

"So, nothing?"

"Well, the coffee shop exchange might be something."

"Why, what happened? Did Rory threaten someone?"

"No, not threats. More like a shift in relations among the group."

"A shift in relations sounds interesting. What happened?"

"Are you sure you want to hear about this?"

"Yes, all background is helpful."

"Okay, look. Coffee shops are usually pleasant places to go with friends or alone, right? But it's not always the case for public servants. For us, coffee shops are often centres of sedition and group-think."

"Sedition and group-think? Really, Mr. Parsons, I find 'sedition' a little hard to believe."

"Maybe for you, but from what I've seen and heard, coffee shops are often negative environments. Listen, blue-collar Tim Horton's is across the street from our office. Public servants do a lot of their complaining and plotting at Tim's. I've watched them. Hell, I've been them. Between seven a.m. and four p.m., Monday through Friday, they display their colonial heritage to form orderly lines for Tim Horton's dark, strong coffee. Then, with a donut, breakfast sandwich, or biscuit, they gather around tables, and complain and plot. Not right away, of course. First, they discuss generic subjects, like sports, kids, weekends past and weekends future, but soon talk turns to office politics, gossip, and problems. White-collar types, who prefer to pay more for their dark, strong coffee and donut, sandwich or biscuit, can go to Starbucks three doors down from Tim Horton's. Same conversations, though."

"You're a little disparaging, Jeff."

"Yes, well, I am. Fifteen years in government narrows a person's perspective."

"How does your characterization of public servants' behaviour in coffee shops relate to Rory?"

"Rory participated in these gatherings along with everyone else in our little group. It was as though Rory's antagonistic and confrontational posture toward management and self-superior colleagues hibernated out of reverence for the sanctity of the coffee break. But Rory's involvement changed one day when I sort of jokingly asked what people thought about Medowcroft providing day-old croissants for Thursday's morning coffee."

"What?"

"Oh, yeah, you don't know about morning coffee and cake, do you?"

"I thought we were talking about coffee and cake now."

"Er, we're talking about the coffee shop. Morning coffee and cake is something different. We do morning coffee and cake in the office on Thursdays. Everyone takes a turn to bring cake or something to share, and one day Medowcroft brought old croissants for people and…"

"Hold on. You're in Tim Horton's, and you asked what people thought about old croissants? I am correct. Who were you asking?"

"Yes. I didn't ask anyone in particular. Amy, Dudley, Cale, Rory, William, Philip and a few others had exhausted the usual discussion topics, and in the lull I tossed the question to the crowd."

"And Rory became upset about croissants?"

"Kind of, I can't remember the exact details, but it started with Dudley or Cale saying the croissants hadn't been day-old and asking why I said they were. Then Amy Hurley, you know, the assistant office manager who…"

"Yes. I know who Amy Hurley was."

"Um, anyway, Amy said Medowcroft told her to pick up croissants the night before because they would be cheaper than buying them fresh in the morning. I said they had been day-old stale. Dudley or Cale said no they weren't, and anyway the croissants had been fine with butter on and heated in the microwave for a few seconds. Then Rory launched into a tirade about croissants and…"

"A tirade about stale croissants. Are you remembering correctly, Jeff?"

"Yes, yes, I remember now. Rory got himself all worked up and said something like 'cheap fucker; that's what she is. She only comes to morning coffee because we meet outside her office. Anyway, butter and microwaves are not the issues. The whole point of croissants is they are FRESH, not microwave-fresh!'

"Rory said the croissants were like her response to the minister's questions, 'Day Old.' Like the facts, 'same old.' She never asked for people's views or opinions. Medowcroft, said Rory, had made us into a propaganda machine for the minister, and ignored our responsibility to provide responsible assessment and courageous opinions on issues."

Misshaped buns and croissants, strewn among paper coffee cups and butter packages, burst on to Stapleton's notepad as he tried to keep pace with my narrative. I was in full flight and kept going.

"Cale said, 'Always the same eh, Rory? Bitching about the director; she's not all bad.'

"Rory said, 'Yeah, well how come she spends all her time on spelling and grammar style rather than the substantive content? Why do I bother with analysis?'

"Cale said, 'Analysis, ha ha! That's your problem, Rory. You analyze everything.'

"Before Rory could go off on Dudley and Cale,

Amy said, 'Well, I like crispy croissants.'

"I sensed Amy's blond comment might tip Rory over the edge, so I said, 'Come on, let's go.' That's what I remember, anyway."

Stapleton, his lips pursed and parted at the same time, as though brain, emotion, and instinct had jumbled together, looked incredulous when I ended my rendition of the coffee shop exchange. I waited. I didn't think the coffee shop exchange was particularly weird. Maybe the police had their own croissant issues, and I had touched a nerve. Another moment passed, and Stapleton came back with his typical succinctness.

"So, Rory had a tiff with Dudley and Cale over some buns. Why do you mention it?"

"Well, the croissant argument seemed to be a bit of a tipping point. Things had begun to change in March when Dudley and Cale obtained promotions. For their part, they began to adopt, espouse, and promote establishment views concerning policy development, priorities, and issues. In addition, they increasingly parroted every position and view Medowcroft and Kingsmore expressed, and they defended those positions with slavish devotion.

"Rory, already pissed because of their dubious promotions, responded to Dudley and Cale with thinly-veiled contempt and repeatedly challenged them on all aspects of their bureaucratic dogma. The more Rory pushed, the more Dudley and Cale retrenched.

"After the croissant incident, Dudley and Cale began frequenting Starbucks and took their coffee at different times. As I said, Dudley and Cale's promotions had gained them one foot on the executive ladder, and they didn't want to jeopardize such a gain to satisfy the need to make conversation over coffee.

"Rory, I, and some of those bit players I talked about earlier, remained loyal to Tim Horton's. A divide

Public Service

along the lines of sedition and group-think had been seeded."

"Really?" said Stapleton.

"Yes. The sedition on our part was by association with Rory. Our group-think was that Dudley and Cale were now executives in outlook, and could no longer be trusted with plain speaking discussions.

"For Dudley and Cale, Rory represented a threat to their career advancement, and his constant, aggressive challenges were seditious behaviour. Their group-think was their increased abandonment of constructive dialogue in favour of toeing the party line."

"You have painted an ugly picture of your office, Jeff. What did you think about things and how Rory was being treated?"

"Like I said, I've been in government for fifteen years. I gave up fighting the system about five years ago. In fact, I was a bit like Rory. I used to be idealistic, make suggestions, and have thoughts and views on things, but after working in five different departments, I realized I was wasting my time. The public service problems are endemic and systemic: senior management begets middle management, begets junior management, and begets senior analysts. Likeminded is the rule, risk aversion is the guide, and survival and promotion are the goals. Like a dynamo generating electricity, the more the dynamo turns, the more electricity it generates, and the faster it goes, the more it needs.

"Rory got the shitty end of the stick a lot of the time. I figured he would give up as so many others do. You know, do the time and take the pension. I never thought he would kill anyone. I mean, that's crazy."

Caught up in my own rhetoric, I had huffed and puffed a lot. I was trembling with energy, and Stapleton put down his pen and fixed me with a direct stare. When he spoke, my energy drained, and nervous foreboding rushed in.

"Well, Jeff, we haven't actually confirmed Rory killed anyone yet, including himself."

Another smiley face, this one large and unmissable, because the detective had drawn it upside down so that it was clear to me, filled a page of Stapleton's notepad. Bile burped in my gut. What the fuck was he up to? I coughed and snorted to cover my discomfort and uncertainty before forcing out a weak reply.

"Oh, I thought that was why you wanted to understand him."

"We want to understand everyone involved, Jeff."

"Mm. Okay."

Stapleton's face mimicked the smiley face, and he said, "Listen, Jeff, why don't we change things up a little? Much of what you have told me centres on Director Prudence Medowcroft. What can you tell me about her and Rory?"

Relieved to move on, I didn't miss a beat. Medowcroft had been a real bitch since the day she started at the secretariat. I had no problem recounting details of Medowcroft to the detective.

"I remember when Prudence Medowcroft started. She came from another security-related department and soon confirmed the reputation that had preceded her."

"What reputation?"

"Crap leader. Superior. Nitpicker. An all-round bitch."

"Oh. Did many people agree with her reputation?"

"Yes. People actually called to commiserate with us."

"How did she get hired in the secretariat with such a reputation?"

"Well, that would have been the purview of our illustrious Assistant Deputy Minister Rena Kingsmore. She hired the executives. In the last six years or so, she hired nine executives. Seven were complete disasters. Like Medowcroft, they had reputations for weak leadership, poor interpersonal skills, and were light on policy development skills. But Kingsmore still hired them."

Twenty-One
Rena Kingsmore - Alive

After thirty years as a federal government or associated agency employee, with no private sector, or non-governmental, work experience, Rena Kingsmore was the Assistant Deputy Minister of Canada's Inland Security Secretariat. She earned between one hundred and fifty and one hundred and seventy-five thousand dollars annually. Rena married for love at twenty-two. Three children soon followed. By thirty-five, comfort and security had replaced love. Shortly after her fortieth birthday, her youngest child left for university, and she was free to pursue her career with renewed ruthlessness. Now, age fifty-seven, she had reached the pinnacle of her career, and in two years, she would be able to retire with a maximum, index-linked pension. All she had to do was play the game and hang on.

Rena was a tall, full-figured woman, with big bones, wide hips, large feet, long legs and a long stride. A strong, straight nose dominated her wrinkled, hollow-cheeked face and orderly brown hair, full and thick, sat on wide shoulders: mannish. Unfeminine.

Despite her affluence, Rena Kingsmore was cheap, cheap like people with money often are. She screwed every penny from a purchase and avoided personal expense and maneuvered or bullied others into paying.

She was a condescending, vindictive grudge holder and a poor judge of character, who kept to the middle of the road and ignored problems for as long as possible. An intelligent but weak and unoriginal leader, able to grasp the big picture but unable to add to the canvas. No more than a policy parrot, who used her position and rhetoric to promulgate government views and stifle creative or inquisitive minds. Despised by minions, feared by direct reportees, and accommodated for mutual benefit by peers, Rena Kingsmore ran the secretariat with malice and indifference, only attempting to lead through professionalism or compassion for personal gain.

Even when Rena Kingsmore did attempt to provide some kind of team building leadership, she would fuck up the basics. For example, each summer she would host a barbecue for the staff at her home. Kingsmore lived in an exclusive neighbourhood, owned a smart house with a large yard, and a beautiful, south facing swimming pool. It sounded good, and it should have been, except for a few details, like BYOB, timing, speeches, and more recently, BYOM/V - Bring Your Own Meat/Veg.

BYOB stood for Bring Your Own Beverage (beverage, not beer, although beer was allowed). BYOB was not such a big deal. BYOB was a common requirement when large numbers of friends came together for an afternoon and evening of socializing.

But the staff party/barbecue only lasted for two hours, from one to three p.m., which made it unlikely to be a booze fest. Most of her employees thought that with her substantial income, she would pay for a few drinks, especially as only fifteen or so people attended. At two beers each, hell, at four beers each, Kingsmore might have spent one hundred and twenty dollars or approximately .0008 per cent of her annual salary.

In addition, the timing was poor: one to three p.m. was after lunch and before supper, which meant people who had snacked became uncomfortable because they weren't hungry at two p.m., and people who hadn't snacked became uncomfortable because they were starving by two p.m. Then, at three p.m., people returned to work. Also, the party was on a Friday, when everyone had Friday night plans.

Finally, Kingsmore always arrived between thirty and forty-five minutes late, stuck close to her lackeys, and made everyone squirm in the sun as she bludgeoned her way through an ill-prepared speech that presented a distorted reality of the previous year's results, office morale, and what we might accomplish in the coming year.

On top of all this, she didn't even do any of the organizing herself. She dispatched office minions, with government taxi chits, to purchase the burgers and buns and set things up at the house.

A recent enhancement of the annual party occurred when Kingsmore instituted a BYOM or V policy: Bring Your Own Meat or Veg, and sought a volunteer to bring buns. Her cup may run over, but don't worry, not a drop will spill on you!

Employee departure parties provide another testament to Kingsmore's leadership and team building capabilities, most notably the "two tier" celebration system: significant differences existed depending on where the person sat in the hierarchy, or more importantly, one's position on the "good employee" scale. Favourites, or departing employees with the potential to aid in the future, or with significant contacts, received well-timed, well-organized, well-provisioned affairs with everyone expected to attend. Decent wine, cheese, crackers, breads, pate, chilled soft drinks and an adequate speech, with well-worn and embellished anec-

Public Service

dotes, would be the norm.

Lesser mortals, or "bad employees," or those departing to a lateral position and with no perceived future value to Kingsmore or the group, received a different send-off: lackeys would be tasked at the last minute to organize "something" in the boardroom. Cheap wine, chips, occasional cakes or donuts, sparse or absent executive attendance, and awkward silence marked these events.

A few golden fuckups managed to overshadow even this obviously insulting and blatant disparity: one time, the departing employee received no invite. Another time, the departing employee had already booked off the leaving party day for a family event: Kingsmore cancelled the party and sent his card to him in the internal mail. Thanks for your service!

The best, though, was when Kingsmore forgot the name of the person who was leaving the secretariat. She had to be reminded right there in front of the person as she stumbled through another unprepared speech. The employee, not one of her favourites, had worked for her for three years. There are only twenty-five or so people in the group, and we pass each other every day and interact one-on-one at least once a week. Thanks for your service.

Demoralizing and insincere annual staff parties and leaving parties did enough damage, but the real and crucial deficiency in Kingsmore's management abilities was her success in hiring incompetent executives. Over a six-year period, Kingsmore hired nine executives: seven disasters and two good ones.

The seven were sycophants, narcissists, and incompetent. All had well-known reputations as poor leaders, with poor interpersonal skills, and for being unpleasant people. Yet Kingsmore hired them. Of the two good ones, Selena Bale and Emma Otherwell, Bale was so superior to Kingsmore that she soon exposed Kingsmore for the lousy leader she was. Bale lasted less than a year before she secured a significant promotion and got out of Dodge. Kingsmore didn't actually hire Otherwell. The minister forced Kingsmore to accept Otherwell. She too soon departed for greener pastures. Therefore, out of the eight executive recruitments Kingsmore did herself, one was good. That's about a 12.5 per cent success rate. A better rate than the .0008 per cent of her salary she might have spent on beverages for her staff.

#

During the summer, Kingsmore had purchased a hot tub. The hot tub had proved to be everything she had wanted. Everyone at in the secretariat had to suffer through stories about the tub and how pleased Kingsmore was with the latest addition to her backyard oasis. Since deciding which model to buy, Kingsmore had bombarded and bored her staff with zealot-like enthusiasm for all things hot tub, repeatedly displaying the ignorance of the well off, by an incapacity to understand why everyone did not have one. Weeks of hot tub stories had filtered down to even the lowliest employee, including too much detail on how Kingsmore spent her Sunday evenings. Kingsmore boasted how on Sunday evenings, she had the tub to herself because her husband curled, and her children were away at university. After supper, and after her husband had left, she would take a glass or two of chilled white wine, her iPod and iPod stereo, and bubble everything and everybody away at one hundred and three degrees Fahrenheit.

Kingsmore's pretentious description of her intended solitary hot tub forays had followed a summer of listening to how she had hunted since early spring for the best deal on a hot tub. In early August, she had found the perfect, extra-deep, six/seven person tub, with full lounge seat, hydrotherapy jets, and padded head and neck rests, for at least forty per cent less than the regular price. She followed the story of the hunt with tales of her ruthless negotiations with electricians and contractors until she had beaten them down to an acceptable price. These stories included how, after she had agreed to buy the hot tub, she refused to pay eight hundred dollars to have it craned over her house and into her backyard. Instead, she had insisted they bring it around to the back of the house via the adjacent green belt area at the rear of her property line, and pull aside, without cutting, a four-foot wide path through the dense cedar hedge at the bottom of her garden.

In addition, she had balked at the electrician's suggestion to install a GFCI plug socket about ten feet from the hot tub, in case she needed to use an electrical appliance like a radio or TV. She told people tartly how she had explained to the electrician that she wouldn't be watching TV in her hot tub, and if she wanted music she would bring her iPod dock and player outside as it had excellent batteries. Boastful stories of how she saved money on the "assisted cover and slip-proof steps" filled uninterested ears, reinforcing Kingsmore's reputation for being cheap and petty.

Twenty-Two

Interview - Room 5, Ottawa Police HQ

"Why did Kingsmore hire these people if they were no good?"

"Oh, you know, the usual reasons. Kingsmore attended university with two; she had worked in another government department way back when with another; to pay back a favour to some other assistant deputy minister, or a shortage of candidates who would want to work for her. Any combination of these could have been in play."

"You mentioned two exceptions."

"Yes, Selena Bale and Emma Otherwell. Everyone agreed Bale and Otherwell had merit and ability."

"What happened to them?"

"They hung around long enough to get the secretariat/PCO experience and then moved onward and upward in other departments."

"How did Rory get along with them?"

"Bale was there before Rory joined the secretariat. Otherwell got along with everyone."

"You started to tell me about Prudence Medowcroft. How did things go when she arrived? Did she live up to her reputation?"

Public Service

"Oh yeah, and then some. Her first leadership gem was to inform her staff that her office door would always be open. After some crude comments about open doors and how no one would put anything into it, an actual test of what Medowcroft promised soon occurred."

"What do you mean by a test?"

"To see if she meant what she said. Rory, eager to test the water and start on the right foot with a new boss, marched up to Medowcroft's door on the third or fourth day. Closed door. Rory asked Amy Hurley if Medowcroft had someone in the room. She said, no, Medowcroft didn't like interruptions, and he should make an appointment, or he could send her an email, unless he needed to see her urgently.

"'A fucking appointment! An email! What happened to the open-door policy?' ranted Rory when he returned to our shared space. I assured him Medowcroft had only begun three days ago and probably needed catch up time to concentrate. I was wrong, though. The door remained closed unless you had an appointment and even then, appointments with lowly analysts were restricted to five minutes sandwiched between other meetings."

"What did you think about the situation?"

"Suited me fine. Less face-time with public sector directors was the optimum situation unless you had a burning need to draw attention to your file or responsibilities. Unfortunately, in Rory's opinion, all his files needed executive awareness and decision-making, and Medowcroft's closed open-door policy did not facilitate Rory's perceived needs."

"Did the door remain closed to everyone or only Rory?"

"Everyone. I told Rory her door policy applied to everyone and not to let himself get wound up. Instead,

Rory became indignant on everyone's behalf, even Dudley and Cale. I suspected things would calm down in a few weeks as Medowcroft became more comfortable and confident with the files and processes. Not so, though. The 'open door' travesty paled next to the 'talk to the hand' incident. This didn't involve Rory, although his level of indignation at Medowcroft rose significantly. You want to hear about it?"

"You mean 'talk to the hand' as in that show *Martin* in the early 1990s?"

"Yes, that's right. Dogbert also used it in the *Dilbert* TV shows in 1999-2000. Listen, it's kinda funny if you don't take it too seriously. You see, the 'talk to the hand' incident involved one of the bit players I mentioned earlier. I know I said I wouldn't mention them, but William, never Bill or Billy, has to be mentioned because he was also involved in the Prue incident, which was a follow-up to the 'talk to the hand' incident.

"Prue. Who's Prue?"

"Just bear with me a minute and all will be revealed. The 'talk to the hand' incident involved William, a mature, thirty-year veteran of the bureaucracy, and as mild mannered and respectful as they come. He approached Medowcroft's uncharacteristically open door for a scheduled appointment."

"How do you know what happened?"

"William told the story many times. Also, Amy Hurley's cubicle is outside Medowcroft's office. She told people about the hand too. I think she had a thing for William."

"A thing?"

"I mean, like a father figure thing. Anyway, William stood in the doorway and coughed to obtain Medowcroft's attention and make her aware of his arrival as scheduled. In response, Medowcroft's head never lifted from the document on her desk. Her left arm lifted up and pointed toward William. At the horizontal mark, Medowcroft's hand, fingers pressed together, flipped up like the cover of an inverted cell phone and pointed at William. Taken aback, William, according to his story, moistened his mouth to speak, but stopped as the hand flitted right to left several times. Simultaneously, Medowcroft's chin dropped, as though she needed a firmer body stance to convey her message."

Stapleton's notes had turned into aimless spirals and interconnected circles, which I think represented my ramblings. I expected the detective might cut short my anecdotes, but he kept on doodling, and I kept on talking.

"Who knows what Medowcroft was thinking at the time? I'm sure she didn't realize William was the right vintage to remember the origin of the slang phrase 'talk to the hand,' and how using the hand was a contemptuous and obnoxious way to say one doesn't want to hear what the person has to say. Or, as William took it, 'She told me to shut up before I had even spoken.' William, mild mannered and a gentleman, was upset and shared his feelings with everyone. After that, any appointment with Medowcroft became conditional on the 'hand'"!

"Not the way to motivate staff."

"Yeah, no kidding."

"You mentioned Prue?"

"Prue, was short for Prudence. A few weeks after the hand incident, William was again the brunt of Medowcroft's acrid personality. Medowcroft, in a weak effort to be friendly, called William 'Billy.' What's the big deal? Well, there wasn't at first, except for William's stunned look and mild annoyance. But, encouraged by Medowcroft's familiarity or, in a rare moment of devilry, William called Medowcroft Prue.

"Medowcroft, like that skit from *Monty Python*

about the queen not being amused, responded in cold, clipped tones her name was Prudence. Never Prue. She did not want, or expect, any member of her staff, under any circumstances, to call her Prue. The rebuke, both personal and public, upset William. William never again initiated contact with Medowcroft.

"I'm mentioning the 'hand' and Prue, not because Rory was directly involved, but because he considered Medowcroft's behaviour very unprofessional. As he said to me, 'She's just fucking rude.'"

"Mm. Those incidents don't cast a good light on Medowcroft's nature and personality."

"I can tell you more about her if you want. She was quite the bitch."

"Okay. Background always helps. Do any of your recollections involve Rory?"

"Well, I told you about the day-old croissants and the staff meetings. There are a few more. One concerns Rory, and the others are more about the kind of person Medowcroft was."

"Start with the one that involves Rory."

"We had been asked by the minister's office to provide some indicators to measure our productivity and effectiveness during the last year. Medowcroft said we should count the number of briefing notes we had produced for the minister and the prime minister and how quickly we had produced them. The results would indicate our productivity.

"Rory scoffed, and said that counting briefing notes and the time taken to produce them might provide some measure of productivity, but it would not measure effectiveness."

"Did Rory propose something different?"

"Oh, yes. He wanted to conduct an analysis of all the briefing notes and figure out how often the minister or prime minister used the advice and opinions. 'That,'

Public Service

said Rory, 'would measure effectiveness.'"

"How did Medowcroft react?"

"She said it would be too difficult to measure and impossible to collect the data. Rory said the level of difficulty in collecting data shouldn't be the criteria for deciding what to measure. Rather, he said, what to measure depends on the quality of the results the measurement can provide. Anyway, we counted briefing notes and calculated the average time it took to produce them."

"Was Medowcroft happy with the results?"

"Oh, yes. The results were guaranteed."

"What do you mean?"

"The parameters for what would be counted, and the calculation for time taken to produce a briefing note, ensured the secretariat looked awesome."

"Were the numbers inaccurate?"

"Let's say wiggle room had been built into the numbers in case the minister asked for clarification. Anyhow, we never found out why the minister's office wanted the information or if he had asked any questions. I do know Rory was right. Counting briefing notes didn't measure effectiveness, but no one wanted effectiveness measured anyway. Medowcroft and Rory rubbed each other the wrong way all the time."

"You mentioned you had other examples of Medowcroft's personality."

"Yeah, little stuff. Like the day construction work on the road outside our building bothered Medowcroft. She told Amy Hurley to go outside and tell the workers to stop for a few hours because she couldn't concentrate with the noise, and she had an important note to prepare for the prime minister."

"Really? What happened?"

"Well, Amy did speak to the construction workers. She told us the workers laughed themselves silly and said that if her boss could dig up concrete quietly, she should come down and show them how to do it. Of course, the workers didn't stop; the noise actually got louder for a while. I half expected the story to make the local paper or radio or something. You know, 'Poor bureaucrat can't work due to noise.' Anyway, that's the kind of person Medowcroft was."

Tiredness sucked my innards. I had hardly slept for seven days, and all I wanted was to lie down and sleep before the detective caught me out. Fighting exhaustion, I went on the attack.

"Before you ask, I was home on Sunday night. I don't know anything about Rena Kingsmore's or Rory's death. My wife worked the ten-six night shift at the hospital. I stayed home with the kids. We had pasta with meatballs and an early night. Go ahead; you can jot that down on your pad as well."

My outburst threw the detective off course, and he mumbled a quick thank you and left the room with the Muddle. Grateful to be alone, I walked, stretched, and tried to hide my fear from the cameras that were recording every twitch and expression. I wasn't sure I could keep this up much longer.

Twenty-Three
Rena Kingsmore - Dead

By the second Sunday in October, Kingsmore had perfected her hot tub routine. With average evening temperatures around four Celsius and many clear, star-filled nights, Kingsmore loved how steam rose gently from the tub, to pull tension from her body and mind. She had reason to be tense. Four of her staff had died during the last week. Incredible, and to someone who had spent three decades in the intelligence world, somewhat suspicious. However, no matter how she pushed, or whom she called, all the evidence, at least the preliminary evidence, pointed to either bizarre accidents, in the cases of Cale Lamkin and Amy Hurley, or simply a tragic accident, in the case of Dudley Hobbs. Prudence Medowcroft, of course, had killed herself. Not a great shock but a surprise nonetheless. Still, their deaths were unsettling. Not only because she had to replace them, and quickly, but they had generally been "good soldiers," as her father used to say of bureaucrats who knew how to do as they were told.

Well, Hobbs and Lamkin had been good soldiers. There was never any problem with them conforming. Their promotions to senior analysts had been a good decision, and they had stepped up to the role nicely. Analysts who understood and were willing to play the game made life much more bearable. Kingsmore reflected on Hobbs. She conceded he was weak and malleable and chuckled at the fact his usefulness stemmed for those very characteristics. She could always count on Hobbs to write a briefing note that didn't say anything. A skill that armed her with the right information to avoid saying anything that might rock the boat, while at the same time appearing to know what was going on. Hobbs was a perfect backroom man. He would be hard to replace simply because of his blandness.

Cale Lamkin was similar yet different. Physically, Lamkin was a stud. She had, more than once, imagined him naked and aroused in the hot tub with her. Each time she had hosted those interminable staff parties at her home, she always hoped Lamkin would dive into the pool. Like Hobbs, Lamkin had been a good soldier. Unlike Hobbs, his good soldier characteristics stemmed from years of obedience in scouts, cadets, and more recently, as an army reservist. He could also be relied on to volunteer. Whatever needed doing, he would be the first to offer, and one could be sure the product would conform to expectations. No trouble with Lamkin, that was for sure. She would miss Lamkin in the flesh, but she could still have him in her dreams.

Amy Hurley. Well, she had been a pretty thing. Not too bright, but she had kept the older misogynistic bastards happy, particularly Sherwood Rosborough. He left little doubt concerning his views on the right place for women: attached to his pecker. Unfortunately, his extensive "old boy" connections made it impossible to get rid of him, which is why she had facilitated and schemed to place Amy and Sherwood in as much proximity to each other as possible, and supported his suggestions to promote Amy. Had Amy not blown herself up, it was only a matter of time before the old goat would have gotten himself in a compromising situation with her. One that Kingsmore would have had no difficulty in exploiting: another promotion for Amy would have ensured her cooperation. Now Hurley was dead, and she would have to find another slut to tempt the old bastard.

Poor Prudence, such a lonely woman, and according to rumour, never had a man either. Just her and her cats. She had been a passable employee. At least she turned out to be a good buffer between herself and the workers. Almost like a guard dog, keeping riffraff away, except, of course, for Hobbs and Lamkin, whom she could count on to keep her in the loop on the general pulse of the office. Well, Prudence hadn't been at all popular. No one would miss her. Nonetheless, hanging oneself was a bit drastic. Half naked too, grimaced Kingsmore to herself as she took another sip of chilled Pinot Grigio.

If dying staff hadn't been enough, that idiot navy man caught selling secrets to the Russians had gotten everyone in a spin. How the hell was she supposed to know what the inland security implications were for Canada? Inland security, she had explained to the minister, was her job, not naval affairs. God, ministers were stupid sometimes.

Anyway, tonight was Sunday. Roger, her dour but reliable husband, had gone curling, the kids were at university, and cool air and clear sky served to accentuate the heat and comfort of her decadent hot tub. In keeping with her rhetoric, Kingsmore sipped more wine and mentally willed her thoughts of death and deception to float away with the rising steam. Music, specifically *The Celts*, by Enya, drifted through the steam from her iPod, placed five feet away on a small table. In a moment of brilliance, at least according to her, she had placed the remote control inside a Ziploc bag. This way she could control the music without getting out of the tub. Another of her brilliant ideas had been to buy wine in tetra packs instead of glass bottles, thus keeping a supply close by. Another good idea had been to turn off the motion detector light.

The Celts soft string instruments and light bell sounds seeped inoffensively across Kingsmore's patio, just managing to breach the dense cedar hedges at the bottom of her garden without suffering too much distortion, except for the place where the hedges had needed to be manhandled to allow passage of the hot tub delivery two months earlier. While the disturbed hedges were indeed growing back, and the green wire and string used by Kingsmore's husband was guiding the hedges in the right direction and formation, sound from the iPod met significantly less resistance. So much less that, a person, with a little patience and wriggling, could easily enter into Kingsmore's sanctuary undetected.

#

Close to midnight, Kingsmore's husband, Ted, returned home from his curling game. Ted played with the Ottawa Recreational Club curling team, and they had easily beaten a team from the East Ottawa Sports Centre. Despite arthritis in his hands, which made it difficult for him to hold and guide the rock, Ted was an excellent player.

Bright lights and open curtains greeted Ted as he pulled on to the driveway. Ted entered the house through the garage and went directly to the adjacent kitchen. Confused by the sight of an electrical cord snaking from a kitchen receptacle through the open patio door, Ted followed the cord out through the door, down the patio steps, and on toward the open and steaming hot tub.

911 responses were quick but not quick enough.

Public Service

Kingsmore, curled fetus-like in her precious hot tub, was dead before they arrived. The presence of wine and an electrical cord steered responders to shake their heads and speculate about the stupidity of people and another life cut short by a preventable accident.

Paramedics and Ted had wanted to remove Kingsmore from the tub, but a police officer, despite the "accident consensus," told them to leave Kingsmore in place until the homicide inspector arrived.

Twenty-Four
Interview - Room 5, Ottawa Police HQ

I guessed that about three hours had passed since I had arrived at Ottawa Police Headquarters, and the interview room had not gotten warmer or more comfortable. My stories and anecdotes about Medowcroft and Rory seemed to stimulate Detective Stapleton, and he and mannequin Muddle left to check on something about half an hour ago.

My gut churned with apprehension, and gravity tugged my eyelids. The breakfast sandwich and coffee consumed, weariness, brought on by my nocturnal activities and the pressure to maintain the right tone and consistent story line with Detective Stapleton concerning Rory's persona, pulled my head to the table. I slept and dreamed; shadow and light, steam and water, road and lake, life and death, gas and fire: all jumbled without order and competed for attention.

"Mr. Parsons. Mr. Parsons. Are you all right?"

In my unconscious mind, I had achieved order. Words had formed and escaped my lips. I peered through pressed eyelashes at Detective Stapleton and mannequin Muddle. Stapleton studied me intently; Muddle hovered, animated.

"Er, yes. I'm fine, thanks. Why?"

"You groaned and mumbled about people threatening your family and your way of life. What's going on? Is everything all right, Mr. Parsons?"

"Yes, yes, just a jumbled up dream or something. I'm fine."

Detective Stapleton and Sergeant Muddle swapped telepathic insights. Neither spoke. They were good, but so was I.

Fresh Tim Horton's coffee, courtesy of the unknown police officer outside the room, waited on the table. I used the process of adding cream and milk to gather my thoughts and seize the initiative.

"Before you ask, detective, I can't remember Rory being bothered by anything in June. June is a crazy month. The government wants to get legislation passed before ministers break for the summer. I had my head down most of the time. I passed Rory in the hallway and heard him tap on his keyboard or talk on the phone. June is always a mad dash for the finish line before we can all switch off for July and most of August. You know, like teachers. So anyway, I can't think of anything."

Detective Stapleton remained silent, no doubt reflecting some more on my subconscious outburst a few moments earlier.

"All right, Jeff. You mentioned coffee and cake mornings when you described how Dudley and Cale started to go to Starbucks instead of Tim Horton's. Why don't you tell me more about coffee and cake?"

Oh, God, coffee and cake, I thought he might have forgotten about that.

"Yeah, okay, morning coffee and cake."

Memories of when I came to Canada, and how I had thought coffee and cake were like an institution in public and private entities, flirted in my head: like tea and biscuits used to be in England, I suppose. Not so much now since the explosion of coffee shops enabled people to get out of the building and away from their sterile cubicles and offices. The memory faded, and I said, "Every Thursday morning at ten a.m., in the general area outside Medowcroft's office, we gathered for coffee and cake. Each person, according to a schedule and standards established through peer pressure, would take a turn to bring cake. Wholesome, motivating discourse occurred as people nibbled and drank."

Detective Stapleton raised his eyebrow a millimetre or two. I interpreted the movement as a signal of skepticism. He was right.

"Well, not quite. Not everybody came. Often people had meetings to attend, or deadlines to meet, which sometimes trumped time for cake and coffee. On average, sixty per cent of our office, or about fifteen people, turned out each Thursday morning. The others would stop by throughout the day to suck up any leftovers. These fifteen or so people would subdivide into small groups: management, in with the management crowd, and the ones who mostly came for the cake and coffee, and preferred to keep any conversation more private."

"Rory attended these?"

"Yes. Rory always attended. And he invariably provided more upscale cake and treats."

"What do you mean?"

"Remember when I told you about Medowcroft's day-old stale croissants?"

"Mm. Yes. Did other people bring stale cake also?"

"Yes. Cake contribution spanned a wide spectrum of effort. Medowcroft's day-old croissants represented one end, along with a last minute purchase of a box of Tim Horton's donuts. On the other end, some people baked the cake or cookies themselves."

"What did Rory do? Did he bake?"

"No. He brought cakes from high-end bakeries. They were always fresh."

"Okay. So there was no problem with Rory's contribution?"

"No, not at all. Rory's problem stemmed from the conversations. Unfortunately, coffee and cake allowed Rory an opportunity to interact with management, and even more unfortunate, he pursued the opportunity aggressively. Ridiculous maybe, but it usually played out like this: as soon as someone mentioned a government security policy, Rory would seize on the discussion and expound on his opinion of all government security policies."

"What were his opinions?"

"He would go on about how these policies were uncoordinated, over- or under-funded, driven by myopic political motives, failed to address root causes, pandered to allies' priorities, were based on poorly quantified threats, and rarely included realistic follow-up and evaluation processes."

"How did people react?"

"Not well. The analysts and management responsible for these policies were the ones eating cake. Rory's perspectives and opinions didn't endear him to either."

While I described the Thursday morning coffee and cake, Stapleton drew pictures on his notepad. Cupcakes, muffins, and a large sponge cake, surrounded by mugs with little swirls coming from the top to convey heat, crowded each other on a plain desk. Stick figured people, all the same height and shape, and clumped in groups of two or three, surrounded the desk. Initials, attached to individual stick figures by straight or bent arrows, indicated who attended. Circles appeared to coral the groups of two or three, and more arrows connected some of the circles to other circles. Away from the circled groups, Stapleton had drawn a lone stick figure. Its head, formed with a question mark, seemed to observe the others.

Stapleton's pen hung over the question mark, poised to add letters or words. Distracted by the detective's art, I stopped talking and waited for him to add the letters that would identify the figure with the question mark for a head. My silence disrupted the rhythm of the room and interrupted Stapleton's thought and deduction process. The detective, now aware of my scrutiny, halted his pen, flipped over a fresh page to cover his drawing, and said with vigilance, "I expect people didn't enjoy listening to Rory's critiques."

I don't know what I had expected the detective to write over the questioned marked stick figure, but unease rippled my spine. I hesitated as I tried to recall the detective's drawing to figure out whose initials needed adding.

"Jeff, Rory's critiques?" prompted Stapleton.

"Yes, right, hold on. Criticizing security policy wasn't the real issue: the real issue was no one engaged him or debated him. They listened, and when he had finished, they carried on with their own discussions. As though his interjection had become an expected and predictable intrusion to be tolerated but not acknowledged. Being ignored burned Rory deeply. Especially because Rory was neither entirely right nor entirely wrong. I mean, realistically, all government policies contain at least one, and more often several, of the problems Rory mentioned. The issue was how Rory labelled everything the same way. He seemed unable, or unwilling, to consider, concede, or evaluate the nuances all policies contain. On the other hand, no one, including myself, made much effort to help him develop a more balanced, or at least informed, opinion. Thus, he was labelled as a malcontent who could not be reasoned with."

"A malcontent who could not be reasoned with. Who called Rory a malcontent? How do you know? Did you actually overhear someone call Rory a malcontent, or was that your impression?"

"Well, I don't want to say. It won't sound right."

I paused. Stapleton leaned in and said, "What do you mean?"

"I'm responsible. I used the word malcontent."

"What? I thought you were friends with Rory. Why would you call him malcontent?"

"Yes, we are... I mean, were friends. Look, I've had enough of this. Rory was a good person, and you're making me say things that make him look horrible. Rory wouldn't hurt anyone. I don't believe this shit about Rory killing everyone and then doing himself in. I want to go home now. I am tired of this room, of you, your questions and of Muddle staring at me as though I'm a criminal! My wife and kids will be worried, and my wife needs to rest because she has another shift tonight. I don't want to help you anymore. I'm going home."

I stood up. The detective stood. Muddle came off the wall. We formed a rigid triangle and stared at each other. Stapleton defused the tension.

"Okay, Jeff. I'm sorry," said Stapleton. "I guess I've gotten caught up in the investigation. Six people are dead and there are many unanswered questions. It's not my intention to make you say things to put Rory in a bad light. I only want the truth, as you understand it. Because you were closest to Rory, I thought you would be the best person to establish a foundation or reference point for whatever anyone else has to say about Rory. Your insight and knowledge of Rory and the secretariat is invaluable and really is vital to my understanding of what was going on and how and why this tragedy occurred."

Indecisive, I shuffled my feet a little and studied the floor.

"Mr. Parsons, Jeff, I would like to apologize and ask you to please stay. We can move to another room if you like. Maybe take a break?"

"What about my wife and kids? I should call them. Tell them what's going on."

"I can take care of that, Jeff. An officer is with your family. I can have her updated on the situation, and she could explain directly to your wife. I think we are almost done now."

We stared at each other. I wanted to go. I needed to stay.

"I can leave if I want to, right? I mean, I'm not under arrest or anything. I don't need a lawyer, do I?"

Stapleton smiled wide and opened his hands like a priest inviting a confession.

"No, no, Jeff. I mean, yes, you can leave any time you want. No, you're not under arrest. I can't say whether you need a lawyer, though. That's your right, but you haven't done anything wrong, have you?"

The detective's direct question about my not having done anything unnerved me. I began to worry about how much longer I could maintain my composure. I swallowed bile and decided to see it through to the end.

"Yes, that's right, I haven't done anything. Okay. I'll stay for another hour, but after that, I'm going home. And I want someone to tell my wife what's going on, all right?"

Stapleton thanked me for agreeing to stay and instructed Muddle to have my wife contacted.

We both returned to our uncomfortable seats, and Stapleton gently nudged me back to our conversation.

"Malcontent?"

"The word malcontent slipped out one day at the tail end of coffee and cake. Rory had done a real num-

Public Service

ber on a government security policy and…"

"Which policy?"

"I can't tell you which one unless I get clearance to do so."

"Okay, so Rory said things about a security policy. What did he say?"

"Oh, the need for a policy had been identified five years ago and since then three different assistant deputy ministers had been appointed to get a policy going. Millions of dollars spent to establish a task force but nothing concrete achieved. The policy submitted to the secretariat from the department had actually been developed by a self-serving consultant who stood to benefit from the recommendations. Rory also said the policy was flawed because it didn't address a key security weakness."

"Sounds serious. Was he right?"

"I don't know. I'm not an expert on that particular security file."

"Did Rory have expertise on the file?"

"No. He said people who were experts had told him what to look for in the policy proposal."

"Who in the secretariat had responsibility for the file?"

"Dudley Hobbs. It was one of those slow-moving files I mentioned earlier."

"How did you come to label Rory as a malcontent?"

"I didn't label Rory."

"I thought you said you did."

"I did. I mean, I supplied the word. Cale hung the label, not me. Look, after Rory left, Dudley and Cale were talking about Rory's comments and were struggling to find a word to describe Rory. They said he was always bellyaching, complaining, and unhappy. I wasn't part of the discussion, but the word malcontent popped into my head and I said it out loud. Cale seized on the word immediately and said malcontent was the perfect term to describe Rory.

"A few days later, Dudley and Cale referred to Rory as a malcontent several times. It became their sort of pet name for him. I think they probably told Medowcroft. That would be the kind of thing they would do."

"Did Rory know they called him a malcontent?"

"Yes. He told me someone from another department informed him Cale had referred to him as a malcontent at a party or something."

"I expect Rory was upset?"

"Actually, no. He said Cale had given him a compliment."

"A compliment?"

"Yes. I don't remember the exact details, but Rory explained how the Malcontents were a faction of gentlemen in the Fifth French War of Religion in 1500 and something. They had opposed the policy of Henry of Valois, or someone like that, who had become king under the name Henry III and allied himself to the Huguenots. The main goal of the Malcontents was to oppose the absolutist ambitions of the king. Rory said he was opposed to the absolutist nature of the management in the secretariat and government in general, and if Cale thought calling him a malcontent was an insult, it just emphasized Cale's ignorance. You know what's funny?"

"What?"

"I thought the Malcontents were a group of Transformers."

"Did you tell Rory?"

"Mm. No."

In the silence, Stapleton drew a passable American Hasbro Transformer and topped it with an ancient

Public Service

crown. I was beginning to believe Stapleton had serious issues when, without warning, the door opened. A uniformed officer, cell phone in hand, moved to Stapleton and whispered in the detective's ear. Stapleton nodded, and the officer placed the cell phone on the table before leaving. Stapleton picked up the phone and said with some compassion: "Jeff, your wife called the station and wants you to call her. I understand it has something to do with your son Ryan." He handed me the phone as he and Muddle made to leave the room.

"We will give you some privacy."

I dialled as fast as I could. Guilt, for what I had caused in March when I had left Ryan at the gym and taken his insulin shots with me, caught in my throat. Anne answered on the first ring.

"Anne, it's me, Jeff. What's wrong? What's happened to Ryan? Is he all right? Where are you?"

"Jeff, Jeff, it's okay. Ryan is fine. I mean, it's not serious. He's not in any danger."

Confused, I hesitated. Anne beat me to my question about why she needed to talk to me. Her explanation chilled me.

"Jeff, Ryan is upset because he can't stop thinking about a dream he had last night."

"What? You need to talk to me now about a dream Ryan had last night. I don't understand."

"Jeff, last night, while I was at work, and you were home, Ryan dreamed that he woke around 2 a.m. and that he was alone."

"What do you mean alone?"

"Ryan said he felt sick, and he called for you, but you didn't come. He called Michael as well, but he didn't come. When no one came, Ryan went to the bathroom and was sick in the toilet."

"I don't understand. I mean, I didn't hear Ryan calling, or I would have gone to him. You said Michael.

173

Didn't he hear Ryan either?"

"Yes. Michael said he was dead asleep and heard nothing."

"Well, I don't know. I guess it really was just a bad dream."

"I know, Jeff. That's what I told Ryan, but the strange thing is there is vomit on the toilet seat and on the bathroom floor."

"Well, I guess Ryan must have woken up at some point then."

"Yes, but why would he think he was alone, and why didn't you and Michael hear him? You are both light sleepers. You two always wake up if Ryan has a problem in the night. It doesn't make sense, Jeff."

It made sense to me. I wasn't home, and Michael, because of what I had put in the boys' supper that night, was unconscious. Being home with the kids while Anne worked was my alibi. I tried to think.

"Jeff?"

"Yes, yes, I don't understand either. Maybe Ryan just thinks he called out. We should reassure him that we never leave him alone at night, and one of us is always there. Probably all the business this morning with the police has upset him, and he is a bit worried and confused. Tell Ryan I will be home soon, and we can talk about it then."

"Okay, Jeff, you are probably right. I will calm him down. Jeff, how long will you be? What do the police want anyway? The officer with us hasn't told us much of anything."

"The police want me to tell them about Rory O'Grady and stuff about work, that's all. I'm almost done here."

"Come home soon, Jeff.

"Jeff."

"Yes."

Public Service

"One other thing, the police have been asking me about where you were and what time you came home on Friday and Saturday. Why are they asking, Jeff?"

"They want to know where everyone was when people died. Apparently, everyone at work is a suspect in the deaths."

"What? I thought the deaths were all accidents. Why do they need to know where people were?"

"I know it doesn't make any sense. They seem to think the deaths might not have been accidents. Just answer their questions. It's all right."

"Okay, Jeff."

"What about Sunday night, Jeff?"

"What do you mean?"

"Well, I told them that you were home because I worked the night shift. Should I tell them about Ryan's dream?"

I wanted to scream no. Don't tell them a fucking thing. I had to be careful, though. Anne was smart, and I couldn't afford her to have any doubts that I was home on Sunday night and that I had nothing to hide. I couldn't imagine how the police might form questions about Ryan's Sunday night sleep, so I took a small risk and said, "If it comes up you can, but I don't think the police would be interested in the dreams of a ten year old."

"You're right, Jeff. Hurry home, okay? I love you."

"I love you too, Anne."

I put the phone on the table, and Muddle and Stapleton entered the room. Muddle moved forward, nodded and said: "Is everything all right at home, Mr. Parsons?"

"Yes, all good, thanks. Just a question about logistics, and when I will be home as Anne, my wife, has to work later today."

Body heat, generated by tension and fear, pushed sweat out of my pores. Had Stapleton and Muddle listened in on the call?

Twenty-Five
Rory O'Grady - Alive

Rory O'Grady lived in Old Barrhaven, one of many Ottawa suburbs that sprawl south, east, and west of the city's compact downtown business and entertainment area. Despite pedantic contempt by city folk for imagined deprivations and bland conformity, Ottawa's suburbs housed more than ninety per cent of Ottawa's nine hundred and fifty thousand inhabitants. Barrhaven, located about seventeen kilometres southwest of Ottawa, has a population of over eighty-five thousand comprised of middle-income families, first-home buyers, and a large but declining bedroom community.

Originally seeded with a modest, two hundred acre housing development in the 1960s, Barrhaven's commuter community grew with the fortunes of Canada's capital city and the ever-expanding public service. In the 1990s, big box stores, high-tech companies, and new schools provided the jobs, infrastructure, and amenities to spur more generic grid patterned townhouse and strip plaza developments until its character became reflected in the derisory tag "Bore-haven," a term used superiorly by non-urbanites, and ironically by urbanites from "better suburbs."

Nestled within the westernmost area of Barrhaven,

and as the site of the original 1960s housing development, Old Barrhaven had not succumbed to modern development designs or infill pressures. As such, it had retained the charm and elegance of well-established beauty and grace with wide streets, old trees, and small houses on large lots.

In January 1994, about four months after receiving his first Government of Canada paycheque, Rory obtained a mortgage from the Toronto Dominion Bank and purchased a small, three bedroom bungalow on one of Old Barrhaven's oversized lots. Determined to own instead of rent, as every generation of O'Gradys before him had hoped to do, but had never succeeded, Rory had raced to pay down the mortgage. Rory was proud of his mortgage-free Old Barrhaven house but not "house proud." An air of neglect permeated the exterior and interior, as Rory had focused on ownership before maintenance.

A large, one hundred and twenty by two hundred and fifteen lot, mature trees, fire pit, and distance from neighbours, had attracted Rory to 212 Shauna Street. The brick exterior, single car garage, three bedrooms and a basement recreation room, two bathrooms and hardwood floors, sparked thoughts of a family: a subject Rory's mother constantly raised at every opportunity as she boasted how his brothers had all given her grandchildren, and she practically accused Rory of being a bad Catholic.

Rory hated that remark and wondered if his mother thought he used contraceptives or did unnatural things. Rory hadn't done anything unnatural. In fact, Rory hadn't done much of anything that could result in grandchildren. Oh, he had tried, especially at university where it seemed everyone had sex. During the first three weeks of Rory's first year, Davey Ferris, one of the many freshmen who lived on the same floor as

Public Service

Rory in the "on campus" student accommodations, claimed to have shagged four girls. Most other guys claimed at least one fuck and many others two or more.

Rory also hated how his lack of sexual success became a frequent discussion topic for fellow students Davey, Colin, and Marc, with whom he had become friends. Discussion of Rory's sexual failure often included backhanded compliments such as, "Look at you, man. Six foot something, built like a wall, decent looking. Okay, you're not a movie star or anything, but you look all right. Christ, if Marc can get laid, you should be able to."

Marc, a small, potbellied, glasses wearing nerd, who guys thought would be the last person to get laid, had frequent sexual success. At the time, neither Rory nor many other guys recognized that Marc was funny, a little shy, and didn't get completely pissed or stoned out of his head all the time: attributes many girls, though not always the prettiest, seemed to like. Hence, Marc was often "taken" to bed by girls.

Rory had *GQ Magazine* features, but he wasn't considered funny, shy, or sympathetic. Constantly on the alert for a real or imagined slight or insult, and quick to anger and confront, Rory repelled rather than attracted women. Even girls initially drawn by his physical presence would soon back off after a few short verbal exchanges.

Friends often said to Rory, "You have to calm down, Rory. Not everyone is against the Irish. No one gives a fuck where you are from. People just want to have a good time. If you just smiled and nodded instead of arguing all the time, girls would want to fuck you. No problem."

It wasn't just the Irish thing, though. Rory hated the arrogant kids who had money: those whose parents paid for everything. He hated them for wearing designer clothes, having cell phones, cars, and laptops. He also hated all those people who had shit on him while growing up in Cabbagetown. Of course, Rory did eventually lose his virginity, but even when he did, he couldn't boast about it.

On a typical Saturday night, by nine p.m., Rory and his three friends had achieved the desired buzz, and they headed downtown to cruise the local bars and clubs in search of flesh, conflict, more alcohol or all three.

Buoyed by drugs and alcohol, they decided to strut their stuff at the Madison Avenue Pub. The Madison, located near the Spadina Street subway, opened in 1983 as a one-room pub at the bottom of Madison Avenue. Since then, the pub has been a staple of the university students' drinking and socializing scene, and has grown into a huge, sprawling watering hole with six pubs and five multilevel patios spread through numbers 14, 16, and 18 Madison Avenue.

The Madison, in addition to regular Canadian brews, also touted a wide range of imported European beers, and in the early 1990s it was a favourite destination for students who considered themselves real beer drinkers. In Rory's case, that meant Guinness. The availability of imported European beers also attracted a slightly older, post-university crowd, who frequented the bar to relive their less restrained days.

On the Saturday night that Rory and friends entered the Madison, a group of six female University of Toronto alumni, circa 1976, had already spent three hours celebrating their fifteen-year reunion. Four of the six had already been to the alter, and two of them had subsequently divorced. One was a happy lesbian, and the sixth was a single, well-worn but attractive, self-destructive, alcoholic man-hunter.

The two groups intersected at one of the pub's six

Public Service

pool tables. Men circled women and women flirted. By midnight, the happy lesbian and the two married women, sensing the scent of unwanted sex in the air, left for home. The two divorcees teased Davey, Colin, and Marc about whom they would take home with them. In the end, after receiving much attention and plenty of drinks, the divorcees settled for more mature company and left with two men from a similar era, who had watched the evening's rituals with amusement from comfortable bar stools.

Rory, though, had struck gold. Encouraged by Davey's introduction of Rory, the blond, skinny woman said her name was Moira, and that her grandparents had come from Ireland. At the time, none of the boys noticed the smiles or smirks of "Moira's" friends at this introduction, nor did they notice the few times "Moira's" friends had called her Millie.

As the alcohol lubrication increased, Rory and Moira fawned and fondled each other to the point of indecency until Moira led a stumbling but cocky Rory out and away from the Madison. Shouts of encouragement from Davey and Marc rang in Rory's ears as he followed Moira eagerly and expectantly. Faced with an emptying bar, and experiencing the conflicting needs for food and sex, Davey, Colin, and Marc headed for the strip joints where plastic food and silicone implants would provide expensive and inadequate satisfaction of both needs.

Rory didn't remember much about what happened until Davey and the others, who had stumbled back to Davey's pad for a toke around four thirty a.m., found him sprawled on the sofa. When they woke him, they gawked at the deep scratches on Rory's face and neck, and the congealed blood on his knuckles and shirt. Rory never explained the details except to say that the woman's name was Millie, not Moira, she wasn't Irish, and that she had laughed after they had fucked and said she liked a bit of the Irish in the morning. Rory said he had given her a bit of fucking Irish all right, and that she wouldn't call herself Moira again.

Few women sought Rory out for sexual pleasure. The few women who craved his physical attributes above all else could ignore Rory's persecuted personality for so long, until like men with blonds, they took their pleasure and moved on.

After repeated bruising, by one-way, shallow liaisons, Rory had substituted disproportioned, silicone-implanted women of pornographic magazines for the flesh, blood, and pain of reality: masturbation over exploitation.

Twenty-Six
Interview - Room 5, Ottawa Police HQ

My description of Thursday morning coffee and cake, as well as my threat to leave, had put me back in control. I sipped coffee and kept the pace going. I wanted to stop helping with inquiries as soon as possible. I needed sleep. Sleep without anyone observing, or listening, to my uncontrollable subconscious.

Deep lines creased Detective Stapleton's forehead, as though an imminent Sherlock Holmes-like deduction was seeking a way out. Concerned, I needed to break his thought, so I said, "I know, July and August, right?"

Stapleton's forehead smoothed, and he murmured to me, "Mm, yes, but you said July and August are slow because parliament is closed for the summer."

"Yes, I did. Things are slow from a policy perspective, but if something security-related happens, things can be hectic."

"Did anything happen last summer?"

"Not in Canada. Security and terrorist issues and events in Afghanistan, Syria, Israel and Gaza, and others I am not able to mention, did concern the government because of Canadian victims. Anyway, we focus on inland security, so we didn't have too much direct engagement in those issues."

"What about Rory? How was his July and August?"

"Bad. He got worked up about his performance review, and he argued with Medowcroft about how she edited his work."

"Did he get a bad review?"

"No. He didn't get any review. He didn't want one."

"I don't understand. What was the problem?"

"Two things happened: first, a chance occurrence, second, a self-destructive action by Rory."

When I suggested Rory might have been self-destructive, Detective Stapleton's eyebrow lifted clear off the eye socket, and he asked what I meant by that.

"Do you know much about Federal Government Performance Reviews, Detective Stapleton?"

"No, but I suppose they work as they do anywhere else. A person's performance is measured against goals, targets, or something. I expect it's the same in government."

"Mm. Yes and no. Here are the basics. Once a year, managers in the public service prepare written reports summarizing the performance of employees they supervise. They discuss the report with the employee and provide him or her with a copy of the final report. The report includes information about the employee's potential, training and development needs, future assignments, and other career-related information. The performance report is assessed against objectives previously agreed on between the manager and the employee. Basic performance review theory."

"Okay, seems straightforward. What happened?"

"First, I should tell you about the chance occurrence because I think it might have led Rory to the self-destructive thing I mentioned. By chance, Rory obtained a copy of the performance reviews for Dudley Hobbs, Cale Lamkin, and me."

"How did he get a copy? Aren't they confidential?"

"Yes, but a reality in offices in general, and our office in particular, are that things get left lying around. Ironically, Amy Hurley provided Rory with the performance reviews, which supported his assertion that Amy obtained promotions by her horizontal capabilities rather than office management expertise.

"Recycling was the culprit. More accurately, the act of recycling as practised by Amy. She accidentally photocopied the three performance reviews on A4-sized paper instead of legal-sized paper the first time. Instead of shredding the unwanted copies, she tossed them in the recycling box.

"Rory claimed he looked in the recycling box for scrap paper, but I'd seen him root around in the recycling almost every time he passed the box.

"Anyhow, he had the copies and became apoplectic as he read the performance reviews for Dudley and Cale, which indicated they were exceptional employees. 'Fucking exceptional.' Three times, I heard Rory say exceptional before he grunted and said, 'Completely Satisfactory. Not bad.' Apparently, this last comment had been in relation to my performance review.

"Rory mumbled 'fucking exceptional' for several weeks, and used the word exceptional numerous times in staff meetings whenever an opportunity linked with Dudley or Cale arose. I don't think anyone except me noticed the connection to the performance review language, and I think the lack of response to the word exceptional only irritated Rory more.

"Not the best thing for Rory to have gotten hold of, considering his thoughts about Hobbs's and Lamkin's promotions in March. What did he say about your performance review? Did it bother you that he had seen your review?" Stapleton asked.

"No, I wasn't bothered. I don't believe performance reviews mean anything anyway."

"Why?"

"A couple of reasons: First, let's consider the ratings and the people and groups rated. In the government, only one per cent of employees achieve an outstanding evaluation, about sixteen per cent get superior, and more than sixty per cent get fully satisfactory. Twenty per cent get satisfactory and only one per cent get unsatisfactory."

Stapleton appeared perplexed and said, "I don't understand."

"Look, I might believe only one per cent are outstanding, but I can't accept only one per cent are unsatisfactory. Simple observation proves that wrong. However, the bigger issue for me is how more than ninety-five per cent fit in the satisfactory to superior rating scale. It's like election statistics in Cuba or China: not credible. Claiming ninety-five per cent of employees are anything, except maybe on the payroll, is bullshit. Second, and on the same theme, when about ninety-seven per cent of federal government executives, or managers, receive performance pay bonuses, you have to question the credibility of performance reviews. Besides, I've accepted that I don't fit the public service mould well. I have probably already reached, or exceeded, the highest level I could achieve, so Rory peeking at my performance review didn't cause me a problem."

Stapleton's perplexed expression changed to an amused half-smile.

"You're quite the cynic, Jeff."

"If that's what recounting facts makes me."

"Okay. So Rory had Hobbs's and Lamkin's performance reviews and wasn't happy about them. Am I right?"

"Yes."

"What about, what did you call it, his self-destructive action?"

"Oh, his refusal to participate in the process, or the process our boss, Medowcroft, wanted to follow. As I said, performance reviews should measure performance in relation to the goals set between the manager and the employee at the beginning of the year. Problem was, Medowcroft had never sat down and discussed and agreed upon performance goals with Rory. In fact, she hadn't set performance goals with anyone. Therefore, she told us all to write down what our goals would have been had they been set at the beginning of the year, and then outline how we had achieved them."

Stapleton, who was scratching barely legible notes, interrupted my flow and said, "Just a moment, Jeff. You're going too quickly."

I waited for Stapleton's pen to stop, and then I continued.

"Medowcroft would then review and approve, or not approve. In practise, the approve aspect would be a matter of degrees of approval. This after-the-fact goal setting is common in government. It's part of the business model. As I said before, this practice would go a long way to explain how ninety-seven per cent of government executives receive their annual performance bonuses!

"Well, Rory would have none of it. He said setting performance goals at the end of the year was ethically wrong, and that it was even more so to report on them. He went further, to me at least, and said retroactive goal setting was fraudulent."

Stapleton, his interest piqued, asked, "Fraudulent? What did you say?"

"Yes, I said fraudulent, detective. For me, the entire process was bullshit anyway. I explained my position to go with the flow as non-compliance could do more harm than good. I advised Rory to consider what he had done last year, turn his actions into goal statements, and report his success at achieving the goals. Although, had I been smarter earlier in my government career, I would have realized how adopting an aggressive, proactive approach to performance reviews and padding, embellishing, and emphasizing goals and achievements could make a person appear good. In addition, as management in the government changed constantly, a performance review would likely be the only official document concerning what one had done in any given year, irrespective of its accuracy or truth. Of course, if you buy into the retroactive approach, a kind of symbiotic codependency with the system is established, and the reviews would continue to develop and get better and better. Employee, boss, and department all look good. Everyone's a winner. However, I didn't consider performance reviews that way. Too late now.

"Anyway, Rory refused to play the retroactive game for Medowcroft. Said he wouldn't compromise his ethics, or maybe he was too stubborn for his own good."

I sat back, as far as the rigid steel of the chair would allow, and waited for Stapleton's reaction.

"Let's review this," said Stapleton. "Hobbs and Lamkin both receive outstanding performance reviews, which Rory, based on his opinions of them, does not feel they deserve. Then Rory refuses to go along with the practice of retroactive performance reviews and ends up with no review at all. I expect Rory held Medowcroft responsible?"

"Oh, yeah. He never shut up about her. Anyway, things got worse because after he refused to accept the performance review process, Medowcroft kept reviewing Rory's work and making him do rewrites."

"Was Rory's work bad?"

"No. Medowcroft edited Rory's work for style rather than substance. Rory hated it."

My mouth was dry. I asked Stapleton for some water, and Muddle left to fetch and carry while Stapleton flexed his fingers and wrists. I was almost done, just September to go. While I waited for water, I thought about Philip Bergon and the day it had all started.

Twenty-Seven

Jeff Parsons
The Beginning

I had been in the government for fifteen years and with the secretariat for six. Six years in the same position convinced me my zenith within government had come and gone: a view shared by the current management. With blame equally apportioned on both sides, I believed management and I had reached an unstated agreement that if I met the basic requirements of the position, didn't ruffle any feathers, and followed instructions, I could expect a long, if uneventful, tenure with the secretariat and the public service. In essence, conform, don't rock the boat, do as you are told, and you could keep your seat on the government gravy train. I wouldn't ride in the club car, or even first class, but my seat on the train would be secure, and I could ride undisturbed until my retirement in 2025.

My role in the secretariat was benign: I focused on policy development for inland security response and mitigation, rather than the more intense and sensitive inland security issues of prevention, intelligence, coordination and engagement.

Pedantic work that usually required preparation of two or three briefing notes per month, with most of the content recycled from previous notes. Slow and unimaginative policy development created a light, day-to-day workload. This enabled multiple trips out of the office for personal activities such as shopping, doctor and dental appointments, dry cleaning, car maintenance, gym visits, squash games, and on occasion, afternoon matinees at the nearby cinema.

The arrangement suited me: secure and undemanding employment had enabled me to lead a quiet, comfortable life, which provided security for my two young children and a modest income to complement my wife's similar income as a nurse at the Ottawa Hospital. I also counted on keeping the generous public service health care plan that had become so important in helping manage and pay for Ryan's Type 1 diabetes. I fully expected to continue my unremarkable, public service-supported life for many years. Many times I had calculated how little would have to change upon my retirement thanks to the generous public service pension plan. I had never been an outstanding or even an above average employee, but I was reliable, dependable, honest and willing to go along with anything the management wanted. I was a good enough soldier; or so I had thought.

Philip Bergon, like me, had also been a long serving, good enough soldier. He had provided the secretariat with general office support service for twelve years and had never, to my knowledge, said or done a bad thing to anyone. Soon after my arrival in the secretariat, we recognized each other's stripes: average, reliable government employees who put up with a lot and didn't cause problems. This recognition soon developed into a quiet understanding that we could and should look out for one another.

For my part, I would occasionally send him on fictitious errands to allow him to leave work early to beat the traffic to an Ottawa Senators NHL hockey game. Other times, I might cover for Philip if he was late or deliver and collect stuff if he had too much to do, as I had plenty of free time. For his part, because he had access to management email accounts, calendars, and minutes of meetings, Philip would give me a heads-up on where management would be and what they had said in meetings related to my files. He didn't give me any confidential or personal information, only stuff to keep me ahead of the curve and on the ball. Over the years, we proved our mutual trust and enjoyed the accrued benefits.

In the February 2012 Budget, the government announced a Deficit Reduction Action Plan, or DRAP. Every government department had to reduce operating costs by ten per cent by the end of fiscal year 2012/13. Recent events, such as kidnappings of foreign nationals in Nigeria, tensions related to the Syrian conflict, Canada's ongoing engagement in Afghanistan, and several unannounced terrorist threats against Canada and Canadian nationals ensured national security remained a hot political topic, and the focus of international and national politics. As such, the impact of the cuts on the secretariat would be minimal.

Smug and safe with this assessment, we paid little attention to how, or even if, the cuts might affect our "critically important" group. The only discussion around the coffee shop centred on how the cuts would affect the poor bastards in other departments.

Assured by this assessment, and confident my "good enough" soldier contribution to the secretariat would keep me safe from any cuts, however unlikely, the email handed to me on March 2 by Philip Bergon destroyed my confidence with fatal consequences.

The email was a printed copy of a terse email exchange between Rena Kingsmore and Prudence

Medowcroft. The email discussed how they could manipulate impending government cuts to achieve their own staffing aims.

February 29, 2012
From: Rena Kingsmore
To: Prudence Medowcroft
Subject: DRAP Ten Per Cent Budget Cut
Re: Our Discussion

Prudence, do you have any ideas?
Yes, the easiest way to find money is to cut salary dollars.
Whom do you have in mind?
Irish.

Of course, but that's not enough. What about Parsons? How are his files moving?

His files are slow. We can have somebody else take them over. I don't think we will miss him much.

That's about two hundred and thirty thousand dollars. We need another one hundred thousand dollars if we are going to promote Hobbs and Lamkin, and give them French training. And we will need to promote Hurley also. I'll tell you why later.

What about Bergon? That would save another seventy-five thousand dollars. We could also cut back on training for everyone else.

Okay. Let's plan that way. Have them out by the end of the year, Prudence.

Before or after Christmas, Rena?

I don't care. Whatever works best for you...

And remember, the story is we have to do this because of the government's DRAP cuts.

Understood.
Yes.

The cold indifference to the lives of their employees did not surprise me. Even the callous reference to a pre- or post-Christmas termination didn't rattle me. Rory being the first candidate for the chop had always been a certainty as Medowcroft hated him. Getting rid of Philip, while certainly insensitive, kind of made sense as Philip only had two years to retirement and some kind of attrition deal would be available. Advanced plans to promote and train Hobbs and Lamkin were in step with the system and of no real concern. Even Hurley's reward for "services rendered" didn't rile me.

What did propel anger and rage into my head, what fueled an intense desire to obliterate Kingsmore and Medowcroft, was the intention to break our unspoken contract. I had kept my side of the deal. I was a good soldier, damn it. I deserved my seat on the government gravy train.

Several times I read the email; each re-read compounded and magnified my fury and indignation. My vision blurred. Bloodied images of Kingsmore and Medowcroft melded together as I wrung and crushed the email and threw it across the room. I sweated and seethed. Then I retrieved and un-crumpled the email. I read it again and found more malice and deceit hidden in the words:

<u>And remember, the story is we have to do this because of the government's DRAP cuts.</u>

"The story is." DRAP and government cuts had not come to the secretariat. The need for a ten per cent budget cut did not apply to us. Kingsmore and Medowcroft intended to use the cuts as an excuse to terminate Rory, Philip, and me to find money to train and promote Hobbs, Lamkin, and Hurley. Vicious and destructive words bounced in my skull.

Kingsmore and Medowcroft's plans would destroy my current life, compromise my pension and retirement, threaten the security and health of my children and my home, so they could reward and promote their sycophant lackeys and painted whore. That was not acceptable. It would not happen.

#

During the weekend, I applied my mid-level analytical skills to the problem. Fifteen years of experience and observation had taught me I could not beat the system. The power rested with management. No appeal, no counter-proposal, no shenanigans unsupported by management would have any impact. Finding another position in government during a time of deficit reduction would be impossible. In fact, once Kingsmore and Medowcroft got me out of government, the likelihood of regaining entry at fifty years of age was minimal. If I was "let go," I might never find alternative employment. Not to mention, employment suited to my family and me.

I was angry, angry enough to kill. I had long understood the "going postal" syndrome and how disaffected employees slaughtered co-workers and bosses after downsizing or workplace harassment. After the bloody fantasies had played themselves out several times over, I realized that no matter how satisfying a bloodletting might be, the consequences for myself and my family would not be worth it: I would be in prison, or dead, and my family would be destitute or worse.

As the weekend wore on, the battle between anger and analysis yielded two concrete conclusions: First, I would not permit Kingsmore and Medowcroft to implement their plan. Second, the only way to prevent them was to remove them from the decision-making process. Further analysis determined the only way to remove them was to kill them. Without fully realizing the implications of my analytical conclusions, I returned to work on Monday a lot calmer than I had been the previous Friday. Philip didn't come in on Monday.

Which was a good thing, because I might have told him not worry about the email, and as events turned out, it would be much better for Philip if he was never able to recall my giving him any such assurance.

By late May, repeated analysis confirmed I would have to kill Kingsmore and Medowcroft. Like many other would-be murderers, I had the problem of how to do it without capture. All my efforts to plan the deaths of Kingsmore and Medowcroft had centred on two clichéd problems: first, how to be in two places at the same time, and second, how to ensure someone else paid for the crime.

I had considered many crime thriller standards. I could be at home watching a show I had previously recorded. I could drug my wife, so she wouldn't wake up when I sneaked out in the night. I could even risk leaving my young children asleep at home while my wife worked her shift. Maybe I could set up some kind of automated computer search function to show me surfing the Net from home while I was out and about killing people. I even considered asking my wife outright to be complicit in the crimes. These amateurish plans were the backbone of pulp fiction crime, and no protagonist had ever gotten away with murder based on those alibis. I needed something better, and I needed someone else. Rory provided the answer to the second problem.

Rory did not have friends; he had acquaintances. Even though I had shared steaks, beers, and joints with Rory at his home, I would never be more than an acquaintance-plus. Our shared views about government, management in general, and the secretariat in particular, formed the basis of our acquaintance-plus relationship. We agreed the hiring system was corrupt, and promotions were political, strategic, self-serving and had more to do with cronyism than ability and merit. Weak policy

Public Service

work, overspending, disingenuous motives, short-sightedness, old boys and women's clubs, bias, and all the things against which Rory railed, I had witnessed in spades. However, we had one fundamental difference of opinion: I understood the impossibility of changing things and the futility of raging against the machine.

#

During a steak and beer Friday at Rory's house in early June, the first glimpse of a plan appeared. Rory and I had left work around four forty-five and arrived at his place by five-thirty p.m. We hadn't said much on the way, and Rory appeared more irritable than usual. The steak sizzled half-cooked, and I had started a second beer when Rory turned and pointed the BBQ fork at me and said, "Those fuckers Hobbs and Lamkin are pissing me off. Ever since Medowcroft gave them their fucking promotions, they think they are better than I am. I'm sick of listening to them say the same shit as Kingsmore and Medowcroft."

Rory often had outbursts about management and employees, and I nodded and sipped more beer. He had bitched and complained about the Hobbs and Lamkin promotions since March.

I asked Rory what had gotten into him. I told him promotions were old news, and he should let it go and relax.

"I can't," said Rory. "Did you hear them at Tim Horton's the other day? Defending that bitch Medowcroft and her stale croissants?"

"Rory, it's just croissants. Who gives a fuck?"

"You know it's not just fucking croissants, Jeff. They support and defend everything she and the other bitch Kingsmore do or say, no matter how fucking stupid or useless. Sometimes I just want to beat the shit out of them. All of them. Everyone in the fucking office."

"I hope present company is excluded."

"Yeah, yeah. Just getting wound up. It must be the Irish in me. Want another beer?"

When the screen door to Rory's house clattered shut behind him as he went to fetch more beer, multiple ideas slammed into my thoughts. I bet if I told Rory about the email between Kingsmore and Medowcroft and their plan to get rid of him, he would be fit to kill them too. Maybe we could do it together. Give each other an alibi. What if I gave him the ideas and he did the killings?

"What are you thinking about?" said Rory as a brown, sweaty beer bottle hung at the end of Rory's extended arm and dangled in front of my face.

"Oh, nothing. Just waiting for my steak."

"It'll be ready in five. I'll just get the salad. Don't bother getting up!"

I looked hard at Rory's back as he went into the house again. Could he become a trusted accomplice? Would he be able to keep the contents of the email to himself, or would he get even more wound up and confront Kingsmore and Medowcroft with the information? Rory was a hothead and capable of violence, but could he wait, plan, and be calm? The crash of a dish and a string of expletives from the kitchen gave me my answer: Rory was too volatile to trust with something that might put me in prison for the rest of my life. On the other hand, Rory might be exactly what I needed.

#

Being fifty years old and brought up in the three TV channel era of the BBC/ITV broadcast monopoly in England, I had seen more than my share of Film Noir movies. Classics such as *The Maltese Falcon, Murder*

My Sweet, and *Touch of Evil* came to mind, as a possible role for Rory took shape in my mind. Protagonist characters and themes of the Film Noir movie era included alienation, disillusionment, disenchantment, pessimism, ambiguity, moral corruption, desperation and paranoia. Rory, in the secretariat context, contained all these things. A key component of a Film Noir movie was the fall guy: someone to take the blame for the murder or the crime. That's what I needed, a fall guy. And poor, disillusioned, brooding, pessimistic, violent and paranoid Rory suddenly seemed a perfect candidate.

Ten ounce, medium-well done, strip sirloin steak and store-bought, Caesar salad slipped down my throat with ease. Cool, amber Beau's Beer from a nearby regional brewery accompanied the steak and salad intermittently until a soft burp conveyed my satisfaction and gratitude to Rory. Well fed, and with a solution to my problem, I grinned.

"What are you so pleased about?" said Rory as he pushed the last of his own steak into his mouth.

"Oh, just that it was an excellent steak as usual, Rory. I was thinking how well our little dessert will go down as well."

"You brought some, then?"

"Of course. Here, pass me the barbecue lighter."

In addition to our shared office location, employment, and general contempt for the government, we also shared an unhealthy habit we both picked up during our university years: a little weed constituted my contribution to our Friday steak and beer get-together. One for me, as I had to drive home later, several for Rory. For some reason, Rory didn't like to roll joints and insisted I do all the rolling. Mostly, I left him with three or four for the weekend. Sometimes he asked for more.

I had been to Rory's house after work on Fridays a

few times the previous year, toward the end of summer and into the early fall. He invited me back again in early March, which was a bit cold for a barbecue, but I liked the opportunity for a beer and a joint, and while I loved my kids very much, I welcomed the chance to avoid the odd end-of-week tiredness.

Twice a month seemed to be the routine. We would arrive after work around five forty-five p.m. Steak, beer, and a joint would last until about eight-thirty, and I would be home for nine. Our Friday ritual seemed to suit both of us: a simple, uncomplicated relationship anchored by a few common interests and bound by the illicit nature of our shared mind-altering indulgence.

One curious and, as it turned out, beneficial, at least to me, aspect of our Friday nights was we never told anyone at work about them. On my part, I deliberately kept private and work life separate, and I rarely associated with colleagues outside of work.

While I think Rory shared the same desire for privacy, he was also somewhat uncomfortable with the fact I was one of those "fucking Brits." I asked him once in a half-joking way how he put up with sharing a meal with a Brit. He said, a bit less than half-jokingly, even beggars like him needed company. Plus, he said, even though I was a "fucking Brit," I was still just a lowly immigrant.

#

On Friday, March 2, 2012, the dispassionate email correspondence between Kingsmore and Medowcroft had led me to take my first step toward becoming a murderer. On the second Friday in June, while sharing steak and beer with Rory, I identified and decided on a viable fall guy and took my second step.

Public Service

Next, I needed an alibi. Several of them. I revisited my original list and decided three key factors determined my options: my wife worked shifts, I had young children at home, and six people had to die in seven days. Difficult but not impossible.

Twenty-Eight
Interview - Room 5, Ottawa Police HQ

"Okay, Jeff, let's get to September."
"Do we have to? I'm pretty tired."

Tired was an understatement. With only two hours sleep, my head bobbed every time Detective Stapleton paused for a silent treatment moment. The room had also gotten warmer. My throat needed moisture, and my head needed a pillow.

"I understand, Jeff. We're all tired. We could resume tomorrow, but it would be a big help to the investigation if you told us about September now to help us keep the thread of things. You have assisted us a lot already, and we're getting a good idea of Rory and what made him tick. Also, the forensic teams will be done at the O'Grady house and office later tonight. If we complete your interview today, we might be able to put things together sooner. Of course, if nothing happened in September, we could end right away. Did anything happen, Jeff?"

I thought about what I had said so far. Had I told enough? Would more be too much? How far should I go? I didn't want to overdo it. I needed to stick with things others would corroborate. I wanted to leave, but

Public Service

I also needed to stay. Catch 22.

"Okay. I guess so, but I'm not doing Rory any favours. What will people think when they find out what I've been saying about him? I mean, it's not a pretty picture, is it?"

"Jeff, as long as you tell the truth, what does it matter? At this point, what people think about your comments about Rory isn't the most important thing. Six people, including Rory, are dead. That's what's important. Now what happened in September?"

"All right, all right, but listen, I'm the messenger here. I'm not making this up, right?"

"September, Jeff. Please."

"Okay. Two things happened. The annual summer staff party at Rena Kingsmore's house and an incident with Prudence Medowcroft about language training."

"September is a bit late for a summer party. Why don't you start with the staff party?"

"Yeah, the party was later than usual because of the hot tub."

"Hot tub? What about the hot tub?"

"Summer staff parties are held at Rena Kingsmore's house. During the summer, Kingsmore had bored the shit out of everyone with monologues about the hot tub she had ordered for the staff party. She went on and on about how she had gotten the best price, the best delivery deal, and a whole list of features the tub had. Anyway, for all her boasting, the tub delivery was repeatedly delayed and wasn't installed until the end of August. Since she had bragged about how the tub would be great for the staff party, she kept delaying the event. That's how the summer party ended up being in September - or early fall."

Stapleton, tapping his pen tip on the three dimensional hot tub he had drawn on his notepad, said, "You didn't like the idea of a hot tub? Sounds to me like

Kingsmore wanted something nice for the staff. What's wrong with that?"

"Hmm. Listen, detective, you need to understand the parties before you judge me. People kissed up and kicked down; hung with the in and out crowd; ooh-ed and ah-ed at the garden and pool, and ate and drank the food they had brought before returning to the office."

"Sounds like a typical staff party. What was the problem, Jeff?"

"First thing, there is very little 'party' in the staff party. Mostly the party is an opportunity for Rena Kingsmore to show off how much she has compared to everyone else: the big house in an expensive neighbourhood, the swimming pool, the hot tub, her Mercedes XL7Q. During the party, she would pontificate about her home, and this or that new something or other she had gotten. Everyone, except her lackeys, Medowcroft, Lamkin, Hobbs, and, of course, horny old Rosborough, and a couple of others went because they had to. I've been to a bunch of these so-called summer staff parties; no one ever used the swimming pool, and no one would soak in the hot tub. You looked but didn't touch: ooh and ah, but don't use."

Stapleton seemed unimpressed and a little irritated with my story.

"So, Jeff, you're saying the parties were more of an obligation than celebration and weren't much fun. I understand. I've been to a few myself, but how does the staff party relate to Rory? Did something happen?"

"Er, yes. The fact that Rory went to the party at all is what happened. In the four years he had worked at the secretariat, he never attended a summer staff party. He barely even went to the parties organized for staff who were leaving the secretariat. Usually, he responded to the email invite with a terse, 'I already have a commitment,' which he never did."

Public Service

"How do you know?"

"Rory told me. He said no way he would legitimize Kingsmore as being some kind of popular leader by attending a facade."

"Eh? What do you think Rory meant by a façade?"

"Rory said when people went to staff parties because they believed they had to, rather than because they wanted to, the whole thing was a facade. Worse, according to Rory, Kingsmore boasted to other management about the wonderful staff parties at her home and how her staff loved them. Rory said obligatory attendance only served to legitimize and support Kingsmore. Rory wanted none of it and said we were hypocrites for going."

"Everyone was a hypocrite?"

"Yes, detective. Rory said even Kingsmore supporters only went to score points with her and keep on her good side. The rest went to try to stay off, or less on, her bad side. Rory called half of them sycophants and the others slaves."

"Harsh words, Jeff. Are those your words or Rory's?"

"Rory's words. He had strong opinions. Which is why people were surprised, even shocked, when Rory showed up at the staff party. Actually, Rory's appearance was even more bewildering considering the previous few months and the stuff about promotions. Anyway, like I said, Rory surprised everyone."

"Did Rory say why he had come? Did you ask him?"

I paused, undecided about my next comment. How much should I say?

"Shit, yes, I asked him, and yes, he told me, but I don't feel right saying this considering…"

"Considering what?" asked Stapleton, his tone becoming a little aggressive for some reason.

"You know, how Kingsmore died."

"Come on, Jeff. Remember, it's about the truth, not about leaving things out to save someone's feelings. Why did Rory go to the staff party?"

"Oh, fuck. He said he had come for the hot tub."

"What?"

"For the fucking hot tub. He said he might get one at his house, and thought he would take a peek at Kingsmore's and maybe get a few tips from her on installation and costs. That kind of thing."

"What did you think?"

"Well, he had never mentioned getting a hot tub before. The only time he talked about hot tubs was to scoff or shake his head when he heard Kingsmore prattle on about getting one. So, I didn't believe him. I thought he was being sarcastic and taking the piss out of Kingsmore."

"How did the others react when Rory showed up?"

"Surprised. You know, taken off guard, not having time to react or anything. Except Medowcroft, of course. She scowled and then cracked a thin smile. But mostly Rory's presence was handled like, er, you know, one of the office morning cake and coffees I told you about."

"You mean 'tolerated'?"

"Yes."

"So, Rory shows up at the staff party unexpected and out of character, and told you he came to look at the hot tub and ask Kingsmore for tips about getting one. Is that right?"

"Yes."

"Well," said Stapleton, "did Rory ask Kingsmore about the tub?"

"Oh, yes, he did. In fact, they had a long discussion. Well, not exactly a discussion, more like a one-sided conversation where Rory listened as she enumerated every minute detail of the tub, its purchase, how the tub was brought in through the hedge, and how she loved to soak on Sunday nights with a glass of wine when her husband was out curling and…"

"Did you say Kingsmore told Rory about her Sunday nights?"

"Oh, shit. Yes, she told Rory, but lots of people heard about her Sunday night soak too."

"It's okay, Jeff. Muddle interviewed your colleague Philip, and he recounted how Kingsmore talked about her Sunday night soaks. How long did Rory stay?"

"About half an hour. He poked and prodded the tub, listened to Kingsmore blab on about the tub's features, took a walk around the yard, said nice things about the yard and left."

"Did you get the impression his visit to the party had upset him?"

"No. Not at all. The opposite. Rory seemed kinda calm."

"Now, the party took place in mid-September. Did you and Rory ever talk about his unexpected visit after the party? At the office or coffee shop?"

"Oh, for sure. I asked him the next day. I couldn't wait to ask him, to be honest. He said he had been thinking about how I dealt with things, and he had begun to understand it was no use fighting the system. 'It is what it is,' he said. I figured Rory had finally started to chill out, and I told him so."

"And how did Rory respond to your suggestion he was chilling out, as you put it?"

"He said, 'Yes, I am chilled these days.'"

Detective Stapleton combined silence and a raised eyebrow, and I faltered under the pressure.

"What?" I said. Had I gone too far, I wondered.

"Oh, nothing, Jeff. Just thinking."

Bullshit. I didn't believe the detective. Oh, he was

thinking all right, but what about? Had I said something out of sequence or mentioned a detail I shouldn't have known? Stapleton stretched and craned his neck to exchange more unspoken thoughts with Sergeant Muddle. Christ, I was tired. I hadn't gotten home until almost four a.m., and my head pounded with fatigue, dehydration, and caffeine. Distracted by a desperate over-analysis of what I had told Stapleton, I jumped when he touched my hand and said, "Are you all right, Jeff? You look as though you want to tell me something."

"Yes, yes, you're right. I do. I guess I'm tired of it all now and…"

"Go ahead, Jeff. Take your time."

I stared past the detective, through the sergeant, and into the wall. I held my breath and focused on an imaginary speck of mortar deep with the wall. Hubris. His versus mine. My vision reversed out of the wall, back through Muddle, and settled on Stapleton. He had almost gotten me. The clever bastard. But not clever enough.

"Oh, yeah," I said, "I have to tell you about Rory and language training."

Twenty-Nine
Jeff Parsons
Murders 1, 2, and 3

Morning murders had not been a problem. I left for work at irregular times depending on my mood, the workload, my wife's need for sleep following a night shift, and my kids' schedule. On Monday, to meet Cale by the river, I had to leave home earlier than usual, but not nearly enough to stick in anyone's memory or arouse suspicion. Lamkin's posted running schedule and route placed him by the bend in the river between seven forty-five and seven fifty-five a.m. His running route passed within three kilometres of my home. I left home at seven-twenty a.m., and arrived at the river at seven thirty-five a.m.

Previous reconnaissance of the gravel path had shown ongoing maintenance work, and various stretches of the path were under construction. I found a desired construction spot and changed the position of the orange hazard cones to direct path users closer to the water's edge rather than toward the safer, landside of the path. Lamkin was a rule follower. If the cones said go left, then left he would go.

I didn't have to wait long. Lamkin, decked out in all his ridiculous gear, slowed as he approached the loose gravel and large drainage pipe and assessed his options: ignore the orange cones and go left over the turned gravel or follow the cones and go right on the grass by the river's edge. He chose right, riverside. I charged directly into Cale, wrapped my arms around his middle, and pinned his left arm against his body. Cale, startled and hindered by his mist-covered Ray Ban sunglasses, shouted at me.

"Rory? What the fuck? What the fuck?"

The momentum of my charge and impact propelled Cale toward the riverbank. Unable to grip the damp grass with his high-tech running shoes, and caught off guard and off balance by the sudden assault, Cale teetered on the precipice above the dark water six feet below. With his left arm trapped, and unable to reach with his right, Cale could not grasp me. For a microsecond, Cale hung helpless in the air before he plunged into the river. I held my breath as the cold water closed over his head. Then he bobbed up, and his head snapped to attention.

I watched water rush into Cale's mouth, nostrils, eyes and ears. I smiled at the memory of how I had overheard Lamkin tell Amy one day that his true reason for not swimming for exercise was that he could not swim. A shortcoming Amy said he had been embarrassed about but had never conquered.

Cale's head bobbed some more, and I watched the fear crush Cale's mind and indecision confuse his reactions. His backpack, filled with Monday's forty-pound weights, and extra towels and clothes for the week ahead, quickly absorbed river water. Cinched and secured electronic equipment challenged his panicked hands and fingers. Lightweight running shoes, with sealed air bubble heels, floated upward as the sodden backpack inverted Cale's body and pulled him backward and head down into the calm water.

Public Service

I stared with satisfaction as the last air bubbles broke the surface. Then I bent down and picked up the Ray Bans that had fallen from Cale's face. Pocketing the sunglasses, I moved the orange cones marking the temporary trail back to their original position on the shore side of the gravel trail. After a visual pan of the area, and a long stare at the river, I straightened my Rory look-a-like hat and walked calmly away. No trace, save a faint impression of an expensive running shoe on the damp grass by the river's edge, remained of Cale Lamkin.

Lamkin had hit the water at seven fifty-four. By eight- fifteen, I had parked my car at the office and squished myself beside other workers into the elevator for a short ride to the first floor to grab a generic coffee from the no-name sandwich shop that provided bland food to those too lazy to forage farther afield. As I sipped my coffee, I thought how Lamkin had been so scared I didn't even have to push him that hard. The best part, the part I remembered the most vividly, was the moment of angry realization in his eyes as he lost his struggle with gravity, weight, and water. When he knew all his exercising, all his cardio work, all his gym time, would not prevent the power of physics from doing its work. I have relived his fear-filled eyes, pulsating neck muscles, and gritted teeth as he succumbed to the serene Rideau River's still water. I think I will buy my own pair of Ray Bans sunglasses, and visit the river and gaze at the spot where Lamkin's last bubble of air squeezed from his lungs and pricked the surface. Who the fuck runs in sunglasses at seven-thirty in the morning anyway?

#

Dudley Hobbs's death also presented few problems. Hobbs lived on Bishop Street just east of downtown Ottawa. I first visited Hobbs's street in July. I stood in the shade of beautiful Maple trees and observed Hobbs secure his worn, brown briefcase to the black steel rack over the rear wheel of his bike before giving a curt nod to his frumpy wife. Every day, Hobbs blathered on about his beloved bicycle, and I relished the idea of linking his death with the bicycle. Two additional visits provided me with enough information to formulate a plan.

First, Hobbs rode without a helmet. Second, for some inexplicable reason and, I thought, quite out of character, Hobbs always crossed Millwood Road directly where his own street intersected with Millwood, instead of crossing a little farther east at the light-controlled crossing. Sure, it was out of his way, but Millwood, during morning and evening rush hours, was a heavily trafficked road. Third, Hobbs's proficiency at bike riding equalled that of a five or six year old. Had his bike been equipped with stabilizers, they would not have gone unused. An unsteady, helmet-less cyclist who habitually crossed a busy road made my decision rather easy. I would run him down. The trick, or challenge, was to have the hit and run attributed to Rory instead of me.

Several weeks passed before the idea of borrowing Rory's car to transport IKEA furniture cemented itself. Once I had decided on using Rory's car, it took about a week to work out a route that avoided traffic cameras in the immediate vicinity of the supposed accident. Farther away was fine, because I wanted Rory's car connected to the accident but not too quickly. In addition to avoiding traffic cameras, I had also spread mud on the license plate to slightly distort, but not hide, all the details. Enough, I hoped, to slow down the search for the vehicle but not enough to discount Rory's car either. I didn't want the police to get to Rory's house until I had finished with the others, and, of course, finished with Rory.

The other problem was timing. Being a tardy bastard, Hobbs could only be relied on to cross Millwood Road between eight-thirty and nine a.m. Millwood Road was busy; I couldn't park and wait for Hobbs without drawing lots of attention and probably creating traffic backup. The solution was perhaps risky but effective, and yielded an unexpected bonus: a simple iPhone security camera remote-viewing application allowed me to set up a live view of Hobbs's street from two tiny battery operated cameras attached to those majestic Maple trees. One camera, attached to a tree opposite Hobbs's house, pointed directly at his driveway while the second, placed on a tree about fifty feet before the Bishop/Millwood intersection, showed the intersection, the road, and the public cycle path on the other side of Millwood. When Hobbs passed the second camera, I estimated I would have about ten seconds before Hobbs approached Millwood, slowed, and then started to cross the road. The cameras had been risky because I had to install and retrieve them without arousing suspicion.

Installation, done during the night, had been easy. Retrieval, which I hadn't done, would have to wait. Originally, I planned to place the cameras at Rory's house along with the other incriminating evidence, but time, police, and neighbourhood activity, had limited my opportunities to retrieve the cameras. The unexpected benefit was I had a pretty decent video of Hobbs's last bicycle ride, my perfectly timed impact, Hobbs's flight and impact into that majestic Maple tree, and until the battery ran out, a good view of the emergency response and police presence.

The video showed how both front and rear wheels cleared the curb by several feet when the weight and momentum of the black, three thousand and eighty-four kilogram, four-by-four vehicle, travelling at one hundred and fourteen kilometres per hour, nudged almost imperceptibly into the rear tire of Dudley's bicycle. Bicycle and cyclist parted ways in mid-air. The English Roadster continued across the sidewalk until it fell contorted on the public pathway. Dudley was less fortunate. He splattered against the stout trunk of the hundred-year-old Maple tree. I heard in a news report that Dudley's wife had, with unwitting irony, mentioned how the preservation of the old Maple tree had been a factor in deciding where to locate the pedestrian crossing.

After the initial impact, Dudley slithered to the base of the tree on his own blood and excrement. Watching the video, I imagined how his lungs might have failed to inflate against the pressure of his crushed rib cage, his confused thoughts about the black car's proximity, and his decision to cross the road battled for rightness. My camera captured his broken briefcase, its contents strewn around. Near Dudley's body, out of reach, brown, viscous liquid oozed onto golden leaves as globules of Sunday's leftover gravy defied the designer's claims and escaped from the spill-proof container.

I loved that video and wondered how well it would do on YouTube. Perhaps it would out-view the "Gangnam Style" video. Another thing about the video: it made up somewhat for Hobbs's death not being a bit more hands-on because when I had accelerated toward Dudley, I relished the expected impact. Instead, I felt disappointed at the lack of physical sensation when the car's front left bumper struck the rear wheel of the bicycle. I had wanted more than a slight bump and almost no sound. Momentarily unfulfilled, I tugged down on my flat cap and brought the car back within the speed limit. Two hundred metres on, and a right turn off Millwood and onto a side street, I drove sedately into a quiet suburb with lots of stop-signed intersections but no traffic lights. Thirty minutes later, after a careful cross-city drive, I squeezed the car back into Rory's untidy, single car garage and switched into my own nondescript sedan and drove to work. On the way, I stopped at Pennzoil on the corner of Bank and Riverside for a quick drive thru oil change. I commented to the technician I had come by earlier, but there had been a lineup and I had gone for coffee. He had agreed and said between seven and nine in the morning was always the busiest time. I arrived at ten-fifteen, and, as I had previously told colleagues, explained I had taken my car in for an oil change. No one gave my lateness a second thought. Two down, four to go.

#

Evening murders were more difficult than morning murders. I figured I would have to risk two nights with weak alibis but not three consecutive nights. I chose Friday and Amy Hurley's death as the night I would risk my first weak alibi. I often went out after work on Friday nights; to Rory's for a steak, beer, and joint; or to meet some friends from my soccer team. Usually, though, I arrived home by ten p.m., which would not accommodate my plans for Amy.

The night I killed Amy, I followed her for a while and watched as she and her friends flaunted their sex to desperate men: cougars devouring cocks. By eleven forty-five, Amy and company had already consumed a bunch of martinis. I was confident that either alone, or with company, Amy would return home in an intoxicated state.

Weeks earlier, I had cruised by Amy's house a few times to scope out possibilities. The first good sign had been its location on the edge of town on a large lot, back from the road and far away from the neighbours. The second helpful thing had been the large, gas cylinders stacked against the side of the house, which suggested the house used gas for heating and cooking. I called the house a few days before Friday, pretending I was ready to deliver their quarterly replacement gas cylinder. Amy's mother told me they had gotten gas the week before and didn't need any. Another factor that worked in my favour was that Amy had sort of adopted Philip as a father figure and had told him a lot about her family and growing up. Philip, well intentioned in that he wanted to soften people's opinion of Amy because of her hard life, had told parts of Amy's story to others, including me.

The key details were that her mother was a complete ho: a dope smoking, booze hound that, at forty-something, looked sixty and brought home any stray who would fuck her. Being thorough, and because I like to check things, I followed Amy's mother one Saturday night and confirmed everything Amy, via Philip, had said.

A cab had picked Amy's mother up at eight and taken her to a roadhouse bar on Rural Route 4, just east of Ottawa. Motorcycles, pickup trucks, and old beater cars revealed the clientele, as did the Bud, Blue, and Canadian beer signs that illuminated the potholed parking lot. Guessing she would be in the bar until closing, I left to avoid sticking in someone's memory. I returned around one a.m., and sure enough, there was Amy's mother and a denim- and leather-clad man half-dragging each other to his motorcycle. I watched, fascinated as the man defied my expectations and managed to start and ride his motorcycle out of the parking lot and off into the night with Amy's mother clinging desperately to his body from behind. I followed them as

Public Service

far as Amy's house and watched long enough to see them head inside. Twice more, I observed Amy's mother venture into the night, and was convinced her predatory habits and reputation would be instrumental in the way in which any inquiry into her and Amy's death might go.

After leaving Amy and her friends to their night out, I joined a few of my soccer friends at the Manx Pub for a couple of hours to strengthen my alibi. Around ten-thirty, I left my friends and drove to Amy's house. I parked a few blocks away, walked nonchalantly up Amy's driveway, and positioned myself in the centre of some overgrown bushes adjacent to the driveway and opposite the front door.

Around twelve-thirty, the roar of a motorcycle announced the homecoming of Amy's mother. The bike skidded to a stop, and Amy's mother and her heavily tattooed and bearded trophy stumbled into the house. Lights illuminated the living room. Through the window, I grimaced in disgust at the spectacle of physical intimacy reduced to animal baseness. Before the motorcycle engine had cooled, the tattooed man exited the front door, hitched his pants, and secured his belt. Amy's mother, naked and distraught, followed. She stood soiled and drunk in the driveway and pleaded without success for the biker to stay. Satisfied, man and bike departed. She screamed obscenities before going inside and slamming, but not locking, the front door. Through the windows, I followed the mother's shaky hand as she lit reefer after reefer until she staggered to her bedroom.

I waited for ten minutes and entered the house. I conducted a brief reconnaissance of the house layout before stepping into the mother's bedroom. I stood over Amy's mother. I had wanted to kill her there and then. Painfully. Mercilessly. Amy hadn't had a chance.

Her mother had made Amy what she had become, and she deserved punishment. Fortunately, for her mother, a battered and bruised corpse would have compromised my desire for an initial accidental death theory.

I left the mother snoring like a pig and crept to the third of the three bedrooms. The room, smaller than the other two, seemed to house all the things Amy's mother intended to sell, repair, or give away. I waited.

#

My watch, illuminated by a push of a button, indicated one thirty-five a.m. Car headlights pierced the window, and engine sounds pushed through the walls. A Blue Line taxi stopped. Amy got out and slammed the door. She hurried through the front door, and I heard the lock engage. Water ran from a tap, smoke from a cigarette polluted air, and a toilet flushed. Amy's feet sounded in the hallway, a brief pause by her mother's door, and on into her bedroom. Zip, rustle, clothes off. Squeak, bump, and pillow punch, bed.

Moments later, I perspired as husky murmurs fed my involuntary imagination. A final sigh sounded success, and fighting a sexual urge, I stepped into the hallway and moved to Amy's partially open bedroom door. Through the crack, the sight of Amy's jeans, thong, bra, and shirt stirred my groin painfully. Oh, I had wanted to. I could have. But, besides making me a hypocrite, there would be the problem of physical evidence, no matter how careful I might be. Resolved, I stuck to my plan, entered the room, and pocketed Amy's discarded thong.

With one long look at Amy's vulnerability, I left Amy's room and entered her mother's room. I made sure her cigarettes and lighter were within easy sight and reach, and closed all the windows in the bedroom. I checked windows throughout the rest of the house and, when I was satisfied the house was as airtight as a 1970s house could be, I went to the kitchen.

Confident there was plenty of gas, I opened but did not light the largest of the gas rings on the cooker. Gas, lighter than air, bled from the stove. The low hiss soothed my nerves, and I smiled in anticipation.

Unrestricted by open doors, the gas hugged the ceiling and meandered from kitchen to living room and on down the hallway to bedrooms and bathroom. Unpressurized, the gas mixed and mingled with the home's stale air, silent and unassuming.

Initially, I'd had mixed emotions about killing Amy. True, she wasn't very good at her job, but death was a bit "overkill" for incompetence, especially as her increased incompetence resulted from promotions she had received for skills and services that were not in her job description. It was also true that I had never actually seen or heard about Amy fucking any of the bosses at work. Until earlier, when I had taken the picture of her dry humping Sherwood Rosborough, the director general, in the office before she left work to meet up with her sex-mad friend Debbie and the other two women. Even with the evidence of her sexual relations with Rosborough, and probably others if her friend Debbie was any indication, I might have spared her. After all, she was only using her assets. Unfortunately, in addition to Kingsmore's email to Medowcroft about getting rid of Rory, Philip, and me, the email had mentioned how the department needed money to promote Amy. I had no doubt, especially after witnessing her little erotica session with Rosborough, that he had asked Kingsmore to find a way to reward Amy and ensure her continued sexual favours. If the cost of Amy's promotions did not come from my salary dollars, I wouldn't have cared who, or how often, she fucked people in the office. I guess Amy, like her mother, was collateral damage.

I wished I could have stayed for the explosion, but it was already two-thirty, and I needed to get home and complete my alibi.

While I followed and observed Amy and her friends flaunting and teasing their way around town, I had called my wife shortly before ten p.m. to say I would be a bit later than usual. Anne, who had already worked a ten to six shift, said she was tired and would head to bed. In the morning, when she asked if I'd had a good time and when did I get home, I said around eleven-thirty p.m. Anne is a sound sleeper and hadn't stirred when I had actually crept into bed at three thirty a.m. Not perfect but good enough.

Thirty

Interview - Room 5, Ottawa Police HQ

"In theory, all federal government employees in Ottawa can access French language training. In practice, access to effective language training is at the discretion of the management. In Rory's case, Prudence Medowcroft held the power to grant or deny language training."

"Why is language training so important?"

"Language training is essential for anyone who aspires to hold a management position in government. Proficiency in both English and French is required, despite the reality that ninety-nine per cent of government business in Ottawa occurs in English.

"Anyway, the point is, or was, I guess, Rory functioned well in French but not well enough to obtain the required minimum C, B, C level needed for all government executive or management positions. Rory had C, B, B, and needed about six to eight weeks of training to improve his written French before being tested."

"How do you know Rory needed only six to eight weeks?"

"He told me. I don't know where he got the numbers from though."

"Go on, please."

"Rory had asked Medowcroft for French training for the past two years. While Rory did not get approval, several other people, including me, did receive some French training. I think he asked Medowcroft every three months about training. He told me he even offered to take half-pay to help offset the cost. I can't say if he did, but offering to take reduced pay would be the kind of fresh idea he would think of."

"Rory must have been very keen to obtain French if he was willing to forgo his pay."

"Yes, I guess so."

"Anyway, Medowcroft never agreed to send Rory on French. She cited lack of money, or too many people away, or 'big files' coming to the secretariat. She always had a reason to say no."

"How did Rory react?"

"He didn't like the reasons. He was skeptical about their truth, but he grudgingly accepted Medowcroft's story as long as no one less deserving got French training. I have been thinking about what you asked me earlier. When you asked me before if any one thing might have pushed Rory over the edge, well, language training might have."

"You think so?"

"Yes. Not so much Medowcroft's refusal to allow Rory access to language training but more who would get the training. I remember Rory's view changed in September when he learned Dudley Hobbs and Cale Lamkin would each get six months' language training in 2013."

Stapleton was thoughtful for a moment and said, "Mm. Based on Rory's opinion of Hobbs and Lamkin, I can understand why he might have been upset."

I doubted the detective understood. French language is essential to obtaining a promotion in the public service. I put him right.

"No, you can't. Listen. Hobbs and Lamkin were both promoted to senior policy analysts in March, right? The next promotion option is a move up to the first EX level. As I told you, a person needs bilingual English/French certification for EX positions. From Rory's perspective, Hobbs and Lamkin were being positioned to move to the EX ranks. Rory had been pissed off enough about the promotions in March, but when he heard about their French language training, he became angry. Now that I think about it, Rory muttered, 'No way Hobbs and Lamkin should get French before I do.'"

"Are you sure, Jeff? It's important. When did he say that?"

"I don't remember exactly but probably in early or mid-September. No, wait, yes, it was the first week of September. I remember because Kingsmore had the summer staff party at her house on the Friday of the first week instead of in July or August as usual. She wanted her fucking hot tub in place first. Rory said it the week after the staff party."

"You're sure Rory said that no way Hobbs and Lamkin would get French before he did?"

"Yes."

"What do you think he meant?"

"I'm not sure, but he did talk with Medowcroft and Kingsmore about languages training."

"How do you know?"

"He told me. Well, more like he vented to me. He told me Medowcroft gave him all the usual lines about budget, timing, and priorities, and fobbed him off with a vague statement that perhaps after Hobbs and Lamkin there might be a chance for him."

"I guess he wasn't surprised."

"No, but he was fucking mad at what happened

with Kingsmore. After Medowcroft blew Rory off, he cornered Kingsmore in the elevator and asked her for a meeting to discuss language training. According to Rory, Kingsmore agreed and told him to make an appointment with her executive assistant. The next day, Medowcroft called Rory to her office and laid into him about who his manager was, who made decisions about training, and that he was not to bother Kingsmore with his petty complaints. Furthermore, she said he should forget language training until he learned his place."

"Why didn't you mention these events when I first asked you if you knew of things that might have upset Rory?"

"Mm, you asked for something that would make him crazy enough to murder. Yes, he was pissed off and ranted on about it for a day or two, but then he stopped. He stopped complaining about everything. In fact, he became quiet and relaxed. I remember asking him if he had won the lottery or if he was getting laid or something."

"What did he say?"

"No, no lottery win, no sex-crazed chick. He told me he realized I had been right about the system, and he had decided to 'go with the flow.' He planned to concentrate on enjoying life outside work rather than getting all worked up about things he had no control over.

"That's why I didn't think about telling you initially. I mean, yes, he was fucking mad at first, but the language thing seemed to calm him down. Like a Zen moment when you realize a truth or something and accept the way things are. Anyhow, I thought of Rory's calmness as the end of his being upset rather than pushing him over the edge. Makes sense, right?"

Stapleton turned to exchange a glance with Muddle. They appeared to reach some kind of conclusion. Back toward me Stapleton wearily said, "I guess you've never taken a psychology course, Mr. Parsons?"

"Eh?"

Thirty-One

Jeff Parsons Murders 4 and 5

On Saturday evening, I needed to be out from seven to eleven p.m. Prudence Medowcroft would be home alone as usual, and four hours would allow plenty of time to drive, and canoe, to and from Rorke's Drift. My alibi plan wasn't great. I drove to the Athletic Club and swiped my membership card in at seven p.m. The club did not require members to swipe out, so the best I had was an arrival time at the gym. If I needed more, because four hours at a gym would not be credible, I planned to say I had stayed at the gym until nine o'clock, then, wound up and stimulated from my workout, I had taken a walk by the river.

I left the Athletic Club a few minutes after I swiped my entry car. Before I set off for Medowcroft's place, I took the kitten I had purchased from Pet Smart in the morning out of the trunk and placed it on the passenger seat. The kitten had nestled itself contentedly in an old shoebox, and I comforted it with gentle strokes as I drove toward Rorke's Drift. New leather gloves and coiled rope lay innocent on the rear seat.

Four hundred metres west of Rorke's Drift, I pulled into the parking lot of the public beach. Night had arrived, and the lot was deserted. I donned my flat cap, put on the new leather gloves, gathered up the kitten and rope and walked to the point where the beach gave way to brush and rock. I clambered through the brush and over the rocks for about fifty feet until I came to the place where I had stashed my small, dark coloured canoe. My gentle paddle strokes propelled the canoe across calm water, prompting the kitten to turn around and around as it kneaded itself a bed in the centre of the still-coiled rope. I beached the canoe on the narrow stretch of weed-covered sand that marked the beginning of Medowcroft's one hundred and seventy-five foot waterfront property. Confident of the cat's continuing slumber, I walked to the rear of Rorke's Drift.

A mature Maple tree, left in place to provide soothing natural shade during the summer, stood about thirty feet from the cottage. At night, the tree cast long moon shadows to the edge of double glazed glass patio doors and windows. Hidden in shadow, I observed Medowcroft dexterously roll a joint. Although the discovery, during my summer reconnaissance, of Medowcroft's drug use had surprised me, and reaffirmed my opinion of her as a hypocrite, I smiled at the thought of how drug use would make my objective so much easier.

For an hour, in between watching Medowcroft open a second bottle of wine and roll another joint, I collected the kitten and rope from the canoe. After removing the flat cap, and placing the cat inside to keep it warm and asleep, I uncoiled the rope and threw one end over a sturdy branch of the Maple tree I had stood under while observing Medowcroft's relaxation routine. I grasped the thrown end and pulled on the rope until the pre-made noose at the other end hung about three feet above the ground. Satisfied with the height of the rope, I expanded the noose until confident it would slip easily over anything the diameter of a basketball. Then I secured the non-noose end of the rope under a rock and pulled up the overhanging slack until the noose rubbed up against the underside of the branch. After checking to ensure the dim evening light concealed the rope, I took one of the six black, wrought-iron patio chairs and placed it out of sight behind the Maple tree.

A quick glance at the window showed Medowcroft still seated and relaxed in her leather chair. She had placed her feet on the ottoman, and her silk robe had fallen to the side, providing an unwanted view. How different from Amy Hurley, I thought, and grimaced at the contrast of the two women's flesh. Assured of Medowcroft's inactivity, I withdrew a small, bright red Swiss Army knife and a leather cat leash from my pocket.

The kitten was still asleep when I tightened the leash on its neck. It mewed in protest as chill night air replaced the warm comfort of the flat cap. My knife blade caught the moonlight, twinkling as it passed through the leather of the leash into the soft, moist ground directly under the hidden noose. Restrained by the leash, and limited to a one-foot radius by the knife, the kitten pawed the ground and tugged at the leash. Frustrated, cold, and hungry because I had not fed the cat, the kitten mewed and snorted.

Inside the cottage, sensitive cat ears pricked and rotated as the kitten's distressed calls seeped in through the night air. I threw a small rock at the kitten, and the impact knocked the kitten sideways, prompting louder and more frantic cries. Drawn by instinct to the pleading cries of one of their own, the house cats scratched at the patio door, adding their own cries to those of the kitten.

The baying of distressed cats was probably the only

sound that could have penetrated Medowcroft's alcohol- and drug-compromised consciousness. Medowcroft ripped away from whatever dream fantasy she was lost in, opened her eyes, and searched for the cause and source of the sounds. Shock spread over her face, as she slowly comprehended the sight of her cats pawing frantically at the patio door. Concern and confusion replaced shock, and she quickly rose from her chair to comfort them.

Through the patio window, I interpreted her wine stained lips as she mouthed questions to the agitated cats.

"What is it, kitties? Is there a storm? What's out there?"

Responding to the cats, Medowcroft flicked the light switch by the patio door. Bright light flooded the patio and a fifty by thirty foot swath of her backyard property.

An easily read "Oh, my God" burst from her mouth as the bright patio light revealed my distraught kitten flailing and tugging on its leash.

Without bothering to put on her slippers, or question how or why a kitten had suddenly appeared, Medowcroft opened the patio door and rushed out to rescue the kitten. Her own cats followed. Halfway to the kitten, she noticed the red leather leash.

"Oh, you poor thing. How did you get lost?" asked Medowcroft with genuine emotion.

The kitten's plaintive cries spurred Medowcroft on, and she fell to her knees to scoop and comfort the cat.

Obscured by shadow and tree, I watched Medowcroft's emotions unfold as she released compassion and love for six ounces of primitive feline. Pathetic. I wondered when she had last expressed such compassion for a human. I kicked the rock holding the rope in place. Rope and noose dropped from the underside of the branch, and stopped behind Medowcroft's now kneeling form.

Medowcroft brought the cat to her bosom and cooed as she rubbed her chin on its tiny head. The motion made the leather cat leash taut until human strength loosened the knife and the leash broke free. Puzzled by the knife, Medowcroft kneeled upright. Her eyes widened and darted as though uneasiness that something wasn't quite right had begun to break through her drugged, alcoholic, and emotional haze.

Too late. Unseen, I darted from the shadows to her left and grabbed her shoulder from behind. I pushed my right knee into her back between the shoulder blades, forcing her shoulders and head back. I yanked down on the rope and slipped it easily over her head. Mid-scream, I pulled the rope taut and felt the coarse, rough material tear at her throat.

I pulled the rope up far enough to force Medowcroft to her toes. Then I played out enough rope to reach the wrought-iron chair behind the tree. I dragged the chair to Medowcroft and placed it next to her tautly stretched and swaying body. With the chair in place, I pulled on the rope, and made Medowcroft climb on the chair. Her robe fell open exposing a mass of unkempt pubic hair, drawn breasts, and slack abdominal skin. I moved to the front and pushed the end of the rope into her hands. She mistook the gesture for assistance, and Medowcroft grasped and tugged at the rope, unwittingly depositing skin and DNA.

When I snatched the rope from her hands, she looked at me and croaked out a dry, ragged, "You!"

Excited as recognition lit up her eyes, I tugged the rope roughly until Medowcroft stood on the tips of her toes; an inch separated her from death. I tied the rope off on the trunk of the tree and stood back to enjoy Medowcroft's cats as they fawned over and consoled the distraught kitten, unaware of the plight of their mistress two feet above their heads.

Medowcroft had never exercised. Loose muscle and slack skin attached to brittle, calcium deficient bones could not combat gravity. Feet, toes, and calf muscles fought ineffectually to relieve the pressure of the rough rope on her neck. Oxygen depletion confused her limbs. A leg flailed, and the chair tipped over. A final contortion forced a last breath into her lungs.

The cats, startled by the tumbling chair, fled for the safety of the cottage, indifferent to their mistress's ignominious end.

Medowcroft's limp body swayed and twisted in the slight breeze that rolled up to Rorke's Drift from Lake Phillip, and moonlight shimmered against her silk gown. Satisfied with the outcome, pleased with my plan, and comforted by the closeness of her death, I tugged my flat cap on my head. I consulted my watch: nine forty-five p.m. Good, I would be home in time for Soccer Central at eleven p.m. Content, I collected my knife and tossed it into the lake as I paddled back to the public beach.

When I arrived home, my wife had nodded off on the sofa. I waited until I had changed into pajamas and gotten a beer before I woke her. By then it was just before eleven, and I said I had been home around nine-fifty. Anne couldn't remember when she had fallen asleep, so my arrival time home was established at nine-fifty, which if needed, would support my claim to have taken a short walk by the river after my gym workout. Again, not perfect but, I hoped, good enough.

#

I had needed more time and a better alibi for Rena Kingsmore on Sunday night and Rory on Monday morning. Kingsmore usually slid into her hot tub between nine-thirty and nine forty-five. She would lounge for about forty-five minutes, which meant I had to be in her backyard at ten o'clock. I could deal with Rory after Kingsmore, but as soon as possible as I needed to be home well before sunrise.

The key to Sunday night and Monday morning was that my wife had to work a ten p.m. to six a.m. shift. The timing was tight because the hospital was close to our home, and she didn't leave the house until just before her shift.

The second issue was our children. They would be in bed by nine forty-five, but rare as it was, I couldn't risk them waking up to an empty house. At the least, they would be scared to wakefulness until someone came home, or at worst, they might call their mom at the hospital or me. They would not forget either outcome, and it would be impossible to explain.

Dealing with my children's potential wakefulness was the most difficult and risky part of my entire plan. Not only was I anxious about the usual perils of kids left alone at home like a fire or a burglar, I also had to worry about Ryan's diabetes. Back in March, because of my inattentiveness, Ryan suffered a serious hypoglycemia episode that put him in hospital. I wrestled with my need for an alibi and my need to ensure their safety for weeks. The solution finally came from the same sleeping pills I used on Rory. I made the kids pasta and meatballs for supper that night, and crushed several sleeping pills into the kids' meatballs. With Ryan stuffed with pasta and meatballs, I was a little less concerned he might have any problems. Even so, Ryan and Michael's safety remained on my mind the entire night. My wife and I had leftover curried chicken, which the kids didn't like.

The kids became groggy around seven-thirty and were in bed by eight p.m. My wife, supported by me, commented that maybe the kids had too many activities if they were falling asleep by seven-thirty. Anne actually left for work earlier than usual because it was her turn to pick up a box of Tim Horton's coffee and a box of donuts for the other nurses on the night shift.

I left home at nine thirty-five and had no difficulty threading my way through the cedar hedges at the rear of Kingsmore's backyard in time to hear the soothing sound of Enya drift seductively from Kingsmore's iPod. Kingsmore's head lay back on the much-touted padded head and neck rests. I stood motionless and peered through the steam swirling about the head of my prey.

Tonight was my third nocturnal visit to Rena Kingsmore's backyard oasis. Two previous Sunday night visits had been enough to confirm Kingsmore's evening habits, as well as determine where I would find the needed equipment and how I would deploy the equipment for the desired outcome.

On both visits, Kingsmore's exit and entry point when using the hot tub had been the patio door, which led to the kitchen and breakfast nook area, rather than the back door proper, which led to the laundry room and garage. The advantage of the patio door, I assumed, had to do with accessing wine, and the fact that light from the kitchen, while providing enough to see the step and ground, was not intrusive to anyone enjoying the hot tub. The fact Kingsmore faced away from the patio door and light also supported my assumption.

Her second habit was to turn off the motion detector lights on the patio. I knew many people who did this to prevent on/off lights from spoiling the ambiance. I had also made note of the make and model of her iPod dock and speaker system. A Logitech X15S 4. The speaker was both the strength and weakness of my plan. Thinking of the potential weakness, I fingered the

AC power cord in my pocket. An anonymous cash purchase three weeks earlier from Best Buy. While using this purchased cord might compromise the initial conclusions about what happened to Kingsmore, the result would be the same.

The most vital observation and discovery, though, had been the presence of a fifty-foot coil of electrical extension cable, wound and hung on a hook, right next to the patio door. Farther along, about thirteen feet, an external GFIC plug socket poked out from the wall. The plug socket was difficult to see and reach in the dark, a fact I hoped the investigators would note.

Another Enya tune wafted across the garden as I stuck to the shadows and made for the patio door. In time with a musical high note, and with eyes locked on the back of Kingsmore's head, I reached the patio door and stepped quickly through. My plan allowed only the briefest of moments to locate and retrieve Kingsmore's own AC power cord. I followed my instinct. The power cord lay on the kitchen counter, still plugged into the outlet: the most convenient and logical place to charge the system for outdoor use.

Grasping the power cord, I exited though the patio door and glanced at Kingsmore's still reclining form. Reaching to my left, I unhooked the fifty-foot electrical cable and stepped back into the house. Inside, I inserted the extension cord into the house receptacle and attached the AC iPod power cord to the extension. Back outside, I uncoiled the cord as I walked toward the hot tub, pushing my flat cap up with my wrist.

As usual, the iPod speaker sat on a small, white metal table near the hot tub. I picked up the speaker and inserted the power cord into the AC jack. The speaker's power must have been low because the surge in power from the AC boosted the volume, and Kingsmore shifted in her seat.

Back light from the kitchen, and swirling steam from the hot tub, obscured my dark human form standing next to the hot tub. Floating about mid-chest height, I held Kingsmore's iPod speaker system and listened to the gently soothing tones of Nora Jones's "Come Away with Me," one my own favourite relaxation songs.

I waited, tasting the moment. Kingsmore's eyes opened. Fear scrunched her features as she peered above the sound and into the place where my face should be. I could see her throat tense in preparation for a scream. I turned toward the light cast from the kitchen, chasing the shadow away to reveal my smiling face.

Recognition and confusion suspended her scream.

"Jeff. What the hell is going on? What are you doing here?"

"Hello, Rena. How's the water?"

"Never mind the damn water! I asked you what the fuck you are doing in my backyard. Get the hell out of here before I call my husband."

"Whoa there, Rena. I've just come to say goodbye."

Kingsmore remained seated in the hot tub, and I suspected she was reluctant to stand and reveal her bikini clad body to me. Perhaps sensing her vulnerability, especially as she knew Roger wasn't home to respond to her call, Kingsmore opted for dialogue.

"Goodbye. What do you mean goodbye? Where are you going?"

Instead of responding, I let my eyes absorb her fear and uncertainty. Her thick brown hair had become lank from moisture, and her head looked shrunken and insignificant. Between chin and breast, blue-purple veins showed through sagging, tallow-like skin.

Strengthened by fear, Kingsmore's voice rose and

cut at me.

"Get the fuck out of here, Jeff. Whatever it is you think you're doing, you've made a big mistake coming here. Now fuck off!"

I stepped closer to the hot tub, and Kingsmore recoiled into her corner seat.

"I'm not the one going, Rena. You are."

"Get out. Get out. You're going to be fired for this on Monday."

"Oh, I don't think so, Rena. You won't be firing anyone on Monday."

"Put my fucking iPod down and get out! My husband is here, and I'm going to call the police."

I leaned over the side of the hot tub and said, "Listen, Rena, we both know your husband curls on Sunday night. Remember you told everyone about your Sunday nights? How you relax, all alone, with your music, wine, and hot tub? Now you shut the fuck up and listen to me."

She cowered at my change in tone and aggressive posture.

"I wonder, Rena, would you be so rude if I were Cale Lamkin, or would you be asking me to get in the tub with you? Everyone knows how you drool over him. Of course, he's dead now, so you will have to let go of that little fantasy."

Rena's eyes swivelled left and right. Her weight shifted as she maneuvered her feet and arms for leverage.

"Stay where you are, Rena. You can get out in a minute, but first you're going to sit there and listen to me."

I waited while Rena calculated her limited options. She remained seated but tensed and ready to attempt flight.

"Tell me, Rena. Lamkin is dead, Hobbs dead,

Medowcroft dead, and poor Amy too. Surely someone like you, who spends all her time surrounded by analysis of suspicious events and coincidences, must have wondered about the death of four of your employees in just a few days."

"What do you know about their deaths? They were accidents, regrettable, but just accidents."

"Regrettable. Accidents? Are you so sure, Rena?"

"What do you mean?"

"Do you really believe hard-bodied, super fit, wonder boy Cale Lamkin would fall into the river while running to work? Did you think Dudley Hobbs fell from his bike in an accident? Christ, the impact flung him fifty feet into a tree! What about Amy Hurley's accident? Leaving the gas on and blowing herself up. How cliché is that? Of course, you probably didn't give Amy much thought. You had no regrets about her death, eh? And Medowcroft, I bet..."

"What, what are you saying? Get away from me. Get away from me."

Kingsmore's hands were knuckle white as she gripped the sides of the tub, and she had drawn her feet up and braced them on the bottom.

"What I am saying, my dear Rena, is that accidents do happen but not in fours and not in the space of six days."

"Oh, my God. You. You killed them. Get away from me. Get away. Help! Somebody, help!"

She lunged to get out of the tub, but even fear-induced adrenalin could not overcome age, wine, and relaxation. Instead of launching herself out of the tub, she slipped and her body flailed backward.

"As I said, Rena, I came to say goodbye. I'm going now, but before I go, here is your music."

I tossed the iPod speaker as Kingsmore's falling body hit the hot tub shell. With nothing else to grasp, she caught the iPod and provided the alternating current its naturally determined and imperative route to the ground.

According to the websites I had consulted, the AC current would flow through her body, her heart would skip and cardiac arrhythmias would begin. Kingsmore screamed as the shock of the electrical current triggered nerves and brain signals. Water entered her gaping mouth and choked off her screams as she slid down into the centre of her extra-deep hot tub and curled into a fetal position to sway in the gently circulating water.

With Kingsmore's body simmering nicely at one hundred and four degrees Fahrenheit in her hot tub, I pointed my car east and headed toward Barrhaven and Rory O'Grady's suburban home.

Thirty-Two
Interview - Room 5, Ottawa Police HQ

"Let's backtrack, Jeff. When you mentioned Kingsmore's summer staff party, you said something about 'her fucking hot tub.' Why did you say 'fucking hot tub'?"

"Kingsmore had been going on about hot tubs all summer. How awesome they were for relaxation and stress reduction. How she couldn't wait to get one despite how much they cost. Like I said, she delayed the summer staff party at her house to show off her hot tub. Then when we got to the party, she had the tub open and running but only to look at. No one was expected to get in the tub, except maybe Cale Lamkin, of course."

"Lamkin. Why?"

"Oh, pretty much everyone thought Kingsmore had the eye for Lamkin. I mean, he is… sorry, was a good looking guy."

"Did Rory think so too?"

"Yes. I mean probably. I have no proof or anything, just the way she looked and drooled at him in meetings or in the corridor. I never noticed. The girls, mostly Amy Hurley, stoked the rumours."

"Did Rory ever say anything about Lamkin and Kingsmore?"

"No, not directly. He considered them part of the wider problem of government cronyism and moral corruption."

Stapleton had nudged his watch as he gathered his detective wares from the table and the black-on-silver roman numerals faced toward me. I followed the movement of second, small, and big hands as they synchronized on twelve noon. Eight seconds after the synchronization, a ping sounded from my pocket: email.

The ping signalled a message from the dead. Recklessness welled inside me. I beat it down.

Stapleton, alerted by the ping, said, "You can check your email if you want. We are done here. Perhaps your wife is trying to contact you. You can tell her you will be home soon."

Recklessness resurged. What should I do? Refusing to check my email would appear unnatural. I had been taken from home by the police at seven in the morning and cooped up for hours. I knew who had sent the email and why. I could not check my email and pretend I hadn't seen the name in the 'From' section. Shit, ten more minutes and I would have been on my way home, and another recipient of the email could have told Detective Stapleton. Caught without an option, I retrieved my BlackBerry and opened Outlook.

Stapleton regarded me expectantly. I thought irrationally he also knew who had sent me an email and why.

"Your wife, I expect."

I entered my password and made a show of opening the inbox and read the 'From.'

I reeled back and shouted, "What the fuck is this? Holy shit. Rory!"

"What?" said Stapleton and Muddle together as

Public Service

they moved toward me.

"From Rory, the email is from Rory. I thought you said he was dead!"

Detective Stapleton held his open hand to me and asked for my BlackBerry. I gave it to him.

"Do you mind if I open the email, Jeff?"

"Um, sure."

Stapleton held the BlackBerry at arm's length to match the small buttons and print to his eyesight. He toggled the centre ball and pressed a button. He read slowly. His eyebrows rose and fell. Muddle craned over the detective's shoulder.

Seconds dragged.

Stapleton's face expanded and contorted as his eager eyes swept left to right to devour the words. Appropriately, I butted into the detective's thoughts.

"What is it? What does it say? How the fuck did he send an email to me? What's going on? This is crazy."

Stapleton's eyebrows came down, and Muddle's neck sank back on to its spine. Their composure restored.

Stapleton, almost regretfully, said, "It appears, Jeff, that Rory had sent a confession via email."

I pasted a mask of disbelief on my face.

"Why to me?" I asked.

"Not only to you, Jeff. Rory sent the email to everyone in the secretariat, as well as several newspapers and TV stations."

"Wow! Um, can I see the email?"

Muddle and Stapleton exchanged a glance before Stapleton said, "Yes. Actually, Jeff, perhaps you might tell us what you think about the email."

"Okay."

I took the BlackBerry from Stapleton. I didn't read the words. I counted off forty seconds in my head and added another fifteen to be sure I took the right amount of time to read one hundred and fifty words.

"I don't know what to say. What do you want?"

"You're familiar with Rory's writing. Would you say the email was written by Rory?"

"Er, yeah, I guess so. The message is a bit terse and to the point like he writes. But, I'm no expert. I…"

"That's all right, Jeff. Thanks."

Sergeant Muddle coughed and said, "Sir."

Detective Stapleton gave me a mindful stare and said, "Well, thank you, Mr. Parsons. You have been very helpful. I know it has been hard telling us about Rory. You can go home, and get some rest."

"Yeah, okay. I feel like a heel. I don't care about the email. Rory wasn't a bad person. People just shit on him a lot."

Stiff from the hard steel chair and exhausted from the tension of the last four hours, I staggered from the room and retraced my way down, up and through sterile corridors until I stood shivering on the edge of the parking lot. I stared at the water, cold and dirty, that filled the potholes. An unmarked police car halted in front of me, and a man hopped from the passenger seat and opened the rear door for me. Tired and numb, I entered the car without comment. As the car pulled smoothly away, my eyelids fell, and I was suddenly in my own car heading to commit one last crime.

Thirty-Three
Rory O'Grady - Dead

The illuminated colon that separated hours and minutes on the digital clock in my three-year-old sedan blinked between eleven and thirty-one. A bright quarter moon illuminated the dark, unlit side roads that linked Ottawa's semi-rural hinterland. I had driven the route several times before on the way back from Rory's house after one of our Friday steak, beer, and joint nights. Less direct than going north to Highway 416, east to my side of Ottawa, and then south again to my own little piece of suburbia. During the longer but quieter route, my thoughts drifted to Rory.

Rory had taken my advice. I wasn't surprised. He had done so all summer. When I suggested he take a week off work and do nothing but discover the benefits of "herbal meditation and relaxation," he agreed without hesitation. He had been even more agreeable when I offered to supply good Western Canadian Blue Grass weed and roll enough joints to last him the week. "Hell," I said, "if you get ahead, I can come by with more joints. No problem."

Not only did I roll a week's worth of joints, I packaged and labelled them by day, Saturday through to a week Sunday. Eight days' worth. Four a day is what Rory wanted: breakfast, lunch, dinner, and a nightcap.

He told me he planned to stock up on Guinness, steaks, and movies, take the phone off the hook, the battery out of his BlackBerry, shut himself away from the world, and figure out what he was going to do with his life. Just as I had suggested he should.

When I gave Rory the joints on Friday night for his week of meditation and self-discovery, we agreed that I would collect his car on Tuesday night, supposedly to collect new beds for my kids from IKEA on Wednesday morning, and return the car before noon. Rory, joints in hand, said, "Sure, Jeff, no problem. I won't be driving anywhere. Just park it in the garage when you're done."

On Wednesday morning, after I had used Rory's car to kill Hobbs instead of collecting beds from IKEA, I parked in his garage as instructed. I kept the keys, though. I hadn't wanted Rory driving anywhere for the next few days. Rory driving wouldn't have been safe. Besides, Rory's house keys were also on the key ring.

With little traffic and hitting green traffic lights, I was making good time across the city. Another ten minutes and I would reach the outskirts of Barrhaven. Five more and I would be at Rory's house.

This night had been a long time coming. Back in early June, when I had first thought of how Rory might help me get rid of Rena Kingsmore and Prudence Medowcroft, and ensure I did not become a victim of their planned "budget" cuts, I had been unsure I could go through with it. Now, with Hobbs, Lamkin, Hurley, Medowcroft, and less than an hour ago, Kingsmore, all taken care of, I wondered what the fuss had been about.

I hadn't wanted to admit it at first, but killing Lamkin had been, well, it had been fun. I liked to plan, analyze, and prepare, and I was gratified my plan had worked so well. No, killing Lamkin had been more than fun: it had been deeply satisfying. Like Rory, I hadn't liked Lamkin much anyway. A loud-mouthed, boastful fucker. Ironic, perhaps, that his boastful nature had made it easy for me to kill him.

I have to admit it was a bit of luck, or maybe fate, when Lamkin told everyone in the office he would have a hectic weekend of athletic activities and that he would be exhausted on Monday. Maybe that was why it was so easy to push him into the river. Anyhow, despite all his macho bravado, Lamkin was scared shitless when I jumped out at him on the trail by the river. Oh, how I enjoyed the helplessness in his eyes as the river sucked him down.

Even better was Cale's belief that I was Rory. It's amazing what props can induce. When I first purchased a flat cap, like the one Rory always wore, from the Scottish and Irish store on Robertson Road in West Ottawa, I only intended to wear the cap while I killed Cale to provide any potential witnesses a distinctive detail to tell the police and point suspicion at Rory. Cale's assumption that flat cap equaled Rory gave me the idea to wear the cap for all the murders. Thanks to Cale, sightings of a flat or odd-looking cap, or hat, featured in several initial witness accounts of the driver who knocked Hobbs off his bike and later in the recollection of people who had seen a man lurking around Prudence Medowcroft's cottage and Amy Hurley's house: good circumstantial evidence that Rory had been involved.

#

Shauna Street approached on my left. I slowed and allowed the car to coast into the turn. I feathered the accelerator to roll down the street and onto Rory's driveway. Another light touch on the accelerator, and I came to a stop in front of Rory's garage.

Rory's fixation with paying off his mortgage at the

expense of house maintenance worked in my favour: the motion lights over the garage door hadn't worked for years, and I tucked my bland sedan into the shadows cast by the house.

Before opening my door, I reached up and slid the dome light button to "off." The door swung open. I sat, unmoving, and listened as erratic clicks and clacks of contracting automobile materials blended with night sounds of insects, swaying trees, and the hum of distant traffic.

Between the edge of the open door, and the steel support of the car's body, the front of Rory's house zoomed into focus as though viewed through an adjusted camera lens. I hadn't seen the front of Rory's house at night. Previous visits had me arriving in late afternoon or early evening light. My nighttime departures had always been away from the house. Now, with Rory's house tightly framed by the space between car door and car body, I noticed how neglected the house had become. Cracked windows, peeling door and trim paint, eroded grout, askew porch light fixture and debris-filled gutters, combined to pull the house into the ground as though trying to hide its embarrassment. The condition of the house reminded me of the garage door; I would have to be careful to minimize any squeaks as I opened it. Fortunately, the door wasn't automated, so I would be able to ease it up gradually.

I reached for a new pair of gloves. They fit tight. I balled and flexed my hands to stretch the leather: The sixth pair in seven days. I wondered if I might set some kind of record. Had any other person killed six people in seven days with six pairs of gloves? Maybe I should have made it six deaths in six days with six pairs of gloves. Six, six, six, that would be something for psychologists to debate.

With my gloves loosened, I picked up the shoebox

that had held the kitten so snug on Saturday night when I drove to Medowcroft's ridiculously named cottage, Rorke's Drift. What a pretentious, lying bitch Medowcroft turned out to be. Medowcroft had proclaimed to everyone how the cottage had been named Rorke's Drift by her great-great-grandfather, who had participated in the British Army's 1879 defence of Rorke's Drift mission station in Africa during the Anglo-Zulu war. What a crock! The battle of Rorke's Drift, along with the 1854 Charge of the Light Brigade at the Battle of Balaclava, was one of the best-documented military events of the British Imperial era. I found no record of anyone surnamed Medowcroft in the public documents and records. Medowcroft's parents had been government busybodies in African Commonwealth countries for forty years, and the Rorke's Drift connection was likely a product of romanticized delusion at best or plain outright lies at worst. Pathetic.

At the end, when Medowcroft's body stopped writhing and hung limp and flaccid, with her precious cats fawning beneath her feet over the little kitten, before they scurried to the warmth of the cottage, I had felt no pity. During the four years she had been in the secretariat, she had inflicted nothing but misery on her staff. Medowcroft was a vain, selfish, and insecure woman who built her own fragile self-worth by demeaning others. She abused staff through neglect and criticism: She was devoid of empathy and sincerity, concerned only with maintaining an upward-facing facade as she sought promotion to ever-higher positions of authority to which she believed she was entitled.

Like Lamkin, Medowcroft had provided the means and opportunity for me to kill her. Often had she announced how precious and sacrosanct her Saturdays were. We all knew she turned off her BlackBerry on

Saturday nights and Sunday mornings and blamed the non-reception on various aspects of the weather in the Gatineau hills. Medowcroft also crowed about the isolated beauty and tranquility of Rorke's Drift. How she would provision herself with meats, cheeses, and breads and a little wine. "Only a little, mind you, of the good stuff."

Then the fucking cats, three of them. "Poor things, left all alone during the week. They so look forward to the weekend with me." Pathetic.

I checked out her place several times during the summer. Plenty of people took evening canoe trips on the lake, many carrying binoculars to watch birds and other people; I was just another person enjoying a summer evening. My first canoe visit provided a general idea of the shoreline and the position of the house. I cross-referenced the layout with a Google Maps' image, and on my second visit, I pulled the canoe up on shore and stashed it in the lakeside brush.

Medowcroft's property had plenty of trees, and I had no difficulty finding a place to conceal myself while I studied the cottage through binoculars. I grimaced as Medowcroft flitted about in her silk robe and soft slippers, eating, reading, drinking, and playing with her cats. And something new! Medowcroft was a closet smoker. I had never seen her smoke, and she never smelled of cigarettes. I started to extend Medowcroft credit for having the discipline not to smoke at work until scrutiny showed the scale of her hypocrisy: Unless I was very much mistaken, which, given my own habit, I knew I wasn't, Medowcroft eagerly sucked back on a joint! Well, well, that little tidbit of insight would help a lot. All together, Medowcroft presented an unattractive and unappealing sight.

When I had observed Medowcroft's doting behaviour toward her cats, the idea of luring her outside with a lost kitten crept into my thoughts. What to do with Medowcroft once I had her outside didn't occur to me until several weeks later, when I overheard Medowcroft respond to Rena Kingsmore ruminating out loud on the subject of what to do with captured or alleged terrorists: "What's the point of capturing them anyway? It takes ten years and millions of dollars to prosecute them. Then we suffer years more of appeals and negative publicity. In my grandfather's day, in Africa, they hanged anyone suspected of plotting against queen and country. No fuss, no cost, and no appeals. That's what we should do with them. Hang them and let them rot."

I recalled thinking, "Thanks, Prudence; you have finally given me some excellent guidance."

#

Along with the shoebox, I took a small, black cotton bag from the passenger seat and eased out of my car. I stepped toward the original 1960s garage door. Divided into six equal panels by decorative vertical and horizontal plywood strips, the wooden door had seen better times. Flaked paint gave evidence of previous painting, and popped nail heads and a corroded handle confirmed the dating estimate. I knew the door was heavy, and I braced myself to lift it open. I hadn't locked it the previous Wednesday morning when I had returned Rory's car, and as expected, Rory had not had the presence of mind to lock it between then and now. Aged rollers, dry with dust and long absent any lubricant, squeaked and groaned during the door's partial accent. I only needed to raise it enough for me to crawl under and gain access. Once in, I pulled the shoebox and black bag inside, lowered the door, and cranked the lock that pushed the horizontal metal bar into the metal roller frame. The door, a little off centre, had to be pulled down hard and jiggled until the metal bar snapped into place.

I stood in the dark. The garage door, like the door connecting the garage to the main house, was windowless. I made my way around the side of the car toward the connecting door and felt for the light switch. Unconcerned with light seepage from the dim sixty watt bulb, I turned on the light and waited. There was no sound of human movement. Mesmerized by the swirl of dust particles disturbed by the influx of cool air sucked in when I opened the garage door, I waited a little longer.

Rory's black, four-by-four, SUV resembled a caged bull in the tight confines of the single car garage, except dust, rather than sweat, covered the car. The SUV was powerful, much more than my modest sedan. When I had picked up Rory's car on Tuesday evening, for my fictitious IKEA furniture run on Wednesday morning, I had taken the car for a spin to get used to the acceleration and handling. Several times, I had gone from standing to one hundred kilometres in about nine seconds and three hundred feet; about half the distance and time I had calculated I would need to intercept Dudley Hobbs on Millwood Road.

I stepped past the blue and black recycling bins and edged my way around to the front of the brooding bull. There it was. I hadn't expected it not to be there, but I liked to check things. Left of centre, about a third of the way down on the front bumper, or two-thirds up depending on how you looked at it, a clear scuffmark. The mark was not enough to scrape the paint down to the plastic but enough to expose the base grey/black primer underneath the hard finish. The limited damage to Rory's car had surprised me a little, but then I suppose the impact of plastic on the rubber of an inflated tire wouldn't make much of a mark. In any case, small as the scuffmark was, no doubt forensic analysis would

Public Service

find the required traces of rubber from the rear wheel of Hobbs's pretentious English Roadster bicycle.

Christ, that bicycle. Hobbs was a complete and utter twat. I don't mean twat in the sense of the vulgar term for vagina, pussy, vulva or clitoris. I mean in the sense of a contemptible and stupid person. An idiot. Even if killing Hobbs hadn't been necessary to flesh out the framing of Rory, I might have killed him anyway. Dudley was a tardy hypocrite, who survived and excelled because luck had matched his abilities and personality with favourable files and management: slow-moving, single-issue files, and myopic management sustained by sycophancy. I also hated his packed lunches.

Satisfied and reassured by the scuffmark on the front of Rory's bumper, I inched my way farther around the car until I reached the point where a half dozen rusted nails protruded from the wall in no particular pattern or order. Each nail supported a typical household implement: rake, spade, broom, hose, electrical cord and on the last nail, a soiled jacket topped with a baseball cap and flanked by a gardening glove jutting out of each pocket. Past the assembled implements, hanging on the only real hook on the wall, was the tool I wanted: a short, steel chopping hoe used to break ice from the driveway. I had noticed it during earlier visits to Rory's and had double-checked to ensure it was there on Wednesday when I had returned Rory's car.

I lay down beside Rory's car and pushed the steel ice chopper under. I wedged the chopper between the exhaust pipe and the car's under-body directly in front of the catalytic converter. Several wiggles and leverages later, the exhaust pipe detached from the catalytic converter. Now the car's emissions would contain as much carbon monoxide as possible, especially during the first few minutes when the engine was cold and the combustion process less efficient.

Breaking the exhaust system pipe wasn't strictly necessary; however, I wanted to speed up the process of carbon monoxide poisoning and removing the catalytic converter from the exhaust system would do just that. Besides, it was a simple and quick job, and its removal would indicate a degree of premeditated planning, which would, I assumed, add to the conclusions surrounding Rory's death. Also, I liked to be sure of things.

At first, I left the ice chopper on the floor under the car. Then, mischievously, I placed it neatly back on the hook. I wondered if the investigating detective would wrack his brains trying to figure out why a man intent on killing himself would take the time to replace the ice chopper on the hook. I could almost hear him asking someone, "Why not just leave it on the floor under the car?"

I worked my way back around the car to the door that led from the garage into a small alcove and then on into Rory's kitchen. Before trying the door handle, I bet myself the door would be unlocked. I was wrong. No problem, though. I hadn't returned Rory's car keys on Wednesday as we had discussed. Instead, I had kept them in anticipation of this night. Anyway, Rory wasn't going anywhere, and the worst that could happen would be he would call me to ask about them. He didn't, though. His house keys were attached to the car keys, and I unlocked the door.

I opened the door a sliver and listened for sounds of life. Pungent air escaped the confines of the house and stabbed at my body through the narrow opening. Light and sound clawed through the thick air. With lips pressed together, I swallowed involuntarily, not wanting feel, smell, and sight translated into taste. Through the alcove, I could see and sense the kitchen. Pushing the

Public Service

door farther open, I heard pizza boxes crumpling between the door and the wall. Empty beer bottles lay and stood around, like disillusioned soldiers after a battle. Bile crept up my throat, and for a moment, I imagined I might find Rory already dead. Perhaps I had gone too far with the thirty-two joints I had so kindly prepared for him. Well, if that was the case, there would be less work to do, and, I thought angrily, less enjoyment too.

The joints I prepared for Rory had an extra ingredient: Doxylamine Succinate, which is the active ingredient in Donormyl, a prescription strength sleeping pill available online or over the phone. I experimented on myself for a few weeks until I established that two twenty-five milligram tablets crushed into a fine powder and rolled up with marijuana made me incredibly sleepy, and as claimed by the manufacturer, kept me asleep for between five and seven hours.

Rory's eight-day supply of four daily, pre-rolled joints contained ever-increasing amounts of Donormyl. Days one through three contained one twenty-five milligram pill in each joint; days four through seven contained two twenty-five milligram pills and today, day eight, each joint had three pills each. If Rory was awake, I was going to sue Donormyl for false advertising!

I escaped the pizza boxes and beer cans and moved slowly into the kitchen proper. On every surface, dirty plates, cups, and utensils competed for space with empty food containers: evidence of drug induced binge eating and an absence of any desire to clean up.

Stronger light and louder sound flooded over me as I approached the door-less entrance that connected the kitchen to the dining room on the left and the living room on the right. TV light back lit my frame as I peered into the dining room, casting my shadow the full length of the room and up onto the far wall.

Rory told me one time that he had only served one

meal in the dining room in the eighteen years he had owned the house. That had been in the summer of 1994, five months after he had first purchased the house, when his mom, dad, and brothers made their one and only visit to Barrhaven. Since then, the dining room had become a dumping ground for everything from out-of-fashion shoes and clothes, discarded sports equipment, broken but fixable electronics, and read, to-be-read, or never-will-be-read magazines, books, and newspapers.

In the far corner, a hardly-used upright piano, a testament to Rory's unfulfilled desire, gathered dust and cobwebs. More discarded takeout and delivery food containers lay between, on, and around Rory's eclectic collection.

I turned on my shadow to face the living room. My eyes fixed on the fifty-inch Samsung HDTV that dominated the overfilled room. On the screen, I recognized Daniel Day-Lewis, portraying the terrifying gang lord Bill "The Butcher" Cutting in a scene from the movie *Gangs of New York*. Cutting was leading a gang of native-born Americans opposed to the waves of immigrants coming into the city in New York's Five Points district. I watched the brutal action unfold as Butcher's gang fought a group of Irish immigrants in mortal combat. After the Irish immigrants lost the fight, Leonardo DiCaprio, cast as a downtrodden Irish immigrant, vowed revenge.

The movie reminded me of how Rory had planned to "soak himself in Irish" by watching the top ten Irish movies during his weeklong vacation. Strewn on the floor were the DVD boxes and disks for the other movies. *In America, In the Name of the Father, My Left Foot,* and *The Commitments* suggested Rory's weeklong marijuana- and alcohol-clouded viewing would have been an emotional roller coaster of Irish struggles.

Rory told me several times how he had connected with his true Irish identity during a visit to Dublin in early February 1996. Rory had been two years into his job as a junior political affairs officer in the Western European section, when he travelled to Dublin. During his working trip, Rory had driven to Belfast in Northern Ireland where the stark Republican-Loyalist conflict nurtured his Irishness and awakened him to the roots of Irish discrimination and persecution. Rory also visited Free Derry Corner in the Bog side neighbourhood of Derry, Northern Ireland. He had stood before the famous Republican mural that announced, "You Are Now Entering Free Derry," at the same time as the Irish Republican Army detonated a truck bomb at the Canary Wharf office development in the Docklands area of London, England, killing two, wounding thirty-nine, and causing millions of dollars in damage.

Rory, who couldn't stop talking when he was high, said he had found a cause and had become a secret IRA supporter and financial contributor. Rory lamented that he had been too late. In 1998, after the signing of The Good Friday Agreement, the IRA abandoned its bloody crusade and entered the mainstream political process leaving Rory more disillusioned, impotent, and angry. Now, Rory's only connection with the IRA was a stack of propaganda leaflets, several faded T-shirts, and a worn copy of the *IRA Green Book: An Introduction to the Irish Republican Army's Way of Life,* a terrorism manual, and a distilled presentation of the mission and psychology of the Irish Republican Army.

A less radical, and more publicly acceptable, symbol of Rory's Irish nationalism was his compulsive wearing of a tweed flat cap. Rory said that a flat cap represented the downtrodden working class and returned from Ireland with five caps. His favourite, and most often worn, was a traditional black and white, two tweed woven cap. Rory never left home without it.

Leaving the baby-faced DiCaprio to vow revenge on behalf of the downtrodden Irish, I focused on the human form slouched unconscious on the worn La-Z-Boy chair.

Rory's lean, six foot, well-built, and well-proportioned body occupied the entire length of the fully extended La-Z-Boy chair. Uncombed, red hair wandered over his head. Facial skin, slack in sleep, and obscured by week-old stubble, bunched on his left side in unison with his tilted head as it rested against the side of the chair. An off-white T-shirt with the slogan "Irish Canadian by Birth, Irish Republican by Choice" printed on the front covered his torso while his faded jeans ended at bare feet. Assorted food and beverages had attached themselves, as multi-shaped stains on both garments, and an unbelted belt lay draped across one chair arm. Socks, grey and rolled up, sat on the carpet beneath his feet.

Mismatched side tables squatted like dwarf-sized sentries on either side of the La-Z-Boy. The left side sentry stood guard armed with assorted cans and bottles. On the right, his companion struggled for dignity under the weight of overflowing ashtrays, matches, lighters, and pornographic magazines. Radiating out from the chair in an imperfect semicircle, more cans, bottles, magazines, and the ubiquitous prepared food containers told their own silent story.

Erratic TV light intermittently illuminated the room, casting irregular and distorted shadows. Dated furniture, much of it purchased second-hand, cowered in the unnatural light. Above the unlighted fireplace, a large, frame-less mirror doubled the drabness. Left of the TV, an imitation leather footstool, made redundant by the extendable footrest of the La-Z-Boy, waited for attention. Treading between the debris, I made my way

Public Service

to the footstool. I sat and stared at Rory. I hoped he had enjoyed his last terrestrial week.

I placed the shoebox at my feet and lifted the small, black bag to my knees. Melodramatically, I closed my eyes and reached into the bag. Even through my gloved hand, my finger sensed a soft fabric. Erotic signals sped to my mind and groin. I knew what my finger had found in the bag. I grasped and withdrew it hungrily. How could such a flimsy article of clothing induce such emotion? I brought the fabric to my nostrils and inhaled. Scent released as I played the fabric through my fingers, and I was back in the hallway outside Amy's partially open bedroom door. I was reluctant to relinquish her thong.

I withdrew Amy's thong from my nose and lamented an unused opportunity for intimacy. Rory's assorted porn magazines, tossed haphazardly about him, provided the needed repository for Amy's thong. I selected the nearest one, a well-thumbed copy of an old British, soft-core magazine, *Fiesta*, and flipped through the pages until I found a photograph of a generic, small breasted, slim, blond woman who resembled Amy. Resisting an unwanted urge, I slipped Amy's thong between the crumpled pages and tossed the magazine back on the floor.

My back ached from perching on the edge of the footstool. I stood to stretch. My movement caused one of those imperceptible changes in the atmospheric balance in the room, and Rory's subconscious, alerted by my standing, sent a warning message to his brain. Rory stirred, but the warning signal had been insufficient to overcome his drug induced slumber. Good. I didn't want Rory awake yet.

Stretched, I re-sat. From the black bag, I took out Lamkin's Ray Ban sunglasses, a Jacuzzi hot tub user manual, a pencil, sleeping pills, cigarette papers, a small bag of weed, and some spliff rolling paraphernalia. I had taken the manual from Club Spas, a hot tub store located just outside of Barrhaven on Hunt Club Road East. The store wasn't directly on Rory's daily commute, but it would not take a huge leap to conclude how Rory might have passed the store many times. I had folded and creased the manual open at the page that provided advice to those hot tub owners who possessed no common sense, thus protecting the manufacturer from such people.

On the page, large bold letters proclaimed the dangers of using any electrical equipment in or near the hot tub. Multiple red and black signs conveyed the same message in pictures and symbols; even the illiterate could have no recourse. A sub-section addressed the use of music players and radios, and stated, "If they must be used, then they should be a minimum of ten feet from the hot tub and battery operated. If a device needed an electrical supply, the supply must include a GFCI safety plug socket installed by a certified electrician. Under no circumstances should an electrical device powered from an electrical plus socket be within reach of the hot tub."

I drew a heavy, black pencil circle around the electrical warning section and underlined the warning related to music players and radios. The pencil, which I had taken from Rory's desk at work, and which contained plenty of his fingerprints and DNA, I threw on the floor.

My own hot tub had cost ten thousand, one hundred and ninety-nine dollars plus tax. Bringing appropriate AC electrical current to the hot tub cost an additional one thousand, three hundred dollars. Two additional electrical modifications, capping off a "within reach" electrical plug socket and relocation of a "within reach" patio light fixture, cost another one hundred and

Public Service

seventy dollars. Jason, the electrician, told me several times how important it was to keep household AC electrical current away from the hot tub. "You'll never believe how often I see people run extension cords out to the hot tub to plug in an iPod or radio. It's crazy. I don't think they understand how dangerous it is."

"What if the cord is plugged into a GFI socket?" I asked.

"Even then, it's not one hundred per cent safe. GFIs can fail, especially if not installed correctly. The only safe way is to keep electricity away from the tub. That's why most tubs now come with built-in connections for IPods and integral radios."

My hot tub had a connection for an iPod but no radio. Kingsmore's had neither, which was curious, considering her tub was a six to seven person tub. Audio capacity is standard on larger six to seven person tubs. I hadn't understood why Kingsmore's hot tub had no built in audio capacity until Amy Hurley revealed in a snide remark how pissed off the hot tub supplier had been with Kingsmore. Tired of Kingsmore's nitpicking, badgering, and endless penny pinching negotiations, he had told Kingsmore the audio module circuit boards for iPod and radio were not included in the model she had chosen. If she wanted them, it would cost her. Of course, Kingsmore balked at the suggestion and claimed audio had been included. According to Hurley, Kingsmore said she didn't care anyway and would simply use her own iPod.

Twice I had visited Kingsmore's backyard on Sunday nights to look for possible ways to kill her. The decision to kill her in the hot tub had been easy. During the annual staff party at her house, Kingsmore's pretentious and overbearing monologue about her fucking wonderful hot tub lit the idea of poetic irony in my mind. How perfect would it be if she died in her fucking hot tub? After that little epiphany, the rest was easy. During my two nocturnal Sunday night visits, Kingsmore provided sufficient material to work with.

My final visit to Kingsmore's, only two hours earlier, had been a real pleasure. I had never gotten such satisfaction out of my own hot tub as I did hers.

Poetic irony. I loved it. I turned the hot tub manual over in my hand once more and thought what a good idea it had been for me to convince Rory to attend this year's staff party. Once he had attended, I figured it would be easy for me to emphasize Rory's interest in Kingsmore's hot tub. He actually had been interested but not because he planned to get one for himself. No, Rory was just mocking Kingsmore, but who was going to contradict me?

With the hot tub manual prepared and the sunglasses in hand, I placed the cigarette papers, bag of weed, and sleeping pill bottle on the side table next to Rory's chair. I opened the papers, weed, and sleeping pill bottle, and spread bits of each on and around the table and ensured some spilled onto the floor.

I looked at Rory and contemplated my next move. I had all the pieces in place, but I wanted to get Rory's DNA and fingerprints on the manual, sunglasses, and the shoebox. I hadn't thought this part through and needed a plan. I sat listening to Rory's light snoring during the infrequent action lulls in the *Gangs of New York* movie, waiting for inspiration. I tapped the shoebox with my feet and mulled.

Shoebox, feet, cats, Medowcroft. That's where my mulling led me. I had time, so I let my thoughts return to Medowcroft. God, I had enjoyed killing that bitch. Oh, Kingsmore had been fun too, but Medowcroft had been delicious. Lamkin, Hobbs, and Hurley had been good also but not quite so delicious. What was different? I mulled a little more. Lamkin had been first. Really, I just pushed him into the river. Hobbs next. Hit and run. Then Hurley. Mmm. I had lingered a little, watching Hurley. More personal, she had been. Kingsmore? I had talked to her, taunted her a little. Seen and felt her fear. Medowcroft? I had looked in her eyes also. I had seen her comprehension: watched her life fade. Time and contact. Knowing they know. Mmm. My gaze had drifted to the pornographic magazines on the floor by Rory's feet, and I had become aroused. Did the flawless flesh and perfectly curved body of the spread-eagled women in the magazine stimulate my arousal? Or had thoughts of killing and death aroused me?

Rory snorted, my arousal departed, and a solution appeared. Simple, really. When the time came to wake Rory, I would place the sunglasses on his face, the manual in his hands, and the shoebox on his lap. During the waking process, Rory would take off the sunglasses, hold the manual, and move the box. Perhaps, with a little prompting, I would be able to get Rory to hold the pill bottle, weed, and papers. That was my plan, but first, I had one more preparation to take care of.

From my inside jacket pocket, I withdrew a folded sheet of paper. Double-spaced, size sixteen font letters covered three-quarters of the page. Roughly one hundred and eighty words. The text had taken more than two weeks to produce, not because the words presented any great literary accomplishment but because the text had to reflect Rory's style. Obtaining samples of Rory's style had been easy enough.

Every briefing note he had written was available on the office shared drive. More importantly, Rory had a habit of keeping all his draft-briefing notes as well, which included his own stylistic errors. The challenge was to keep the text meaningful with a minimum number of words, short enough to type as a BlackBerry composed email, and ensure my deliberate errors were believable Rory errors. Part of me thought the email was too much, but the idea of tidying things up and letting Rory have the "last word" kind of appealed to me. I unfolded the paper and read:

To: Canadian Inland Security Secretariat Mail Group; PCO Media Mail Group
Subject: My Public Service
   The Canadian Public Service is diseased. Too many public servants provide for themselves before the citizens they serve.
   I joined the public service to serve. I was proud, motivated, and sincere.
   However, inside the public service, I discovered a self-propagating, self-defeating machine, mired in bias and cronyism. A service led by narcissists and sycophants: a cadre of people motivated by personal gain, unaccountable, out of touch, insular, ignorant and self-important.
   I tried to serve, but I couldn't. They were too strong, too many.
   In the Canadian Inland Security Secretariat, I discovered a microcosm of the public service. Rena Kingsmore, Prudence Medowcroft, Cale Lamkin, Dudley Hobbs and Amy Hurley epitomized the diseased bureaucracy.
   I couldn't beat them, join them, or change them. Then I understood. My greatest public service would be to cleanse the public service of this microcosm.
   Therefore, I killed them.
   I hope you understand. I hope you like my public service.
   Rory O'Grady
   A true public servant

Satisfied with my composition, I looked for Rory's BlackBerry. The BlackBerry lay next to the DVD disks on the floor, switched off. I hesitated before switching the BlackBerry on because I knew as soon I turned it on, the buzzing of unread emails would start. I walked back to the garage and turned the phone on. Sure enough, a backlog of email arrived, and the notification buzz sounded for almost two minutes. When the email delivery ended, I entered Rory's password: "Ruaidri1166." Rory had told me over beers and joints how his password was based on Ruaidri Ua Conchobair, the last high king of Ireland, and how he had been named after him. Establishing Rory's password hadn't taken long: a little research on dates, knowledge of password uppercase, lowercase and number, requirements, and trying a few different combinations whenever Rory left his BlackBerry unattended, had been relatively easy.

I opened up Outlook and clicked New Email. In the main text area, I typed Rory's one hundred and seventy-five-word confession. In the Subject box, I typed, "My Public Service." In the Mail To address box, I entered the "CISS Mail Groups All" and "PCO Media Mail Group" address. Then I saved it to the Draft folder and placed the BlackBerry on the dashboard of Rory's car.

Re-entering the house, I moved quickly to the living room. Time had passed. It was now two twenty-five a.m., and I wanted to be home by four a.m. I would need some sleep to get me through the coming days. Rory had not moved. I stood next to Rory and watched him for a few moments. More irony struck me as I thought of an Englishman using Rory as a fall guy. I picked up Lamkin's sunglasses and placed them on Rory's face, tucking them onto his ears. The hot tub manual I placed in his left hand and pressed fingers and palms onto the pages. Imperfect, I knew, but enough when added to all the other evidence. The shoebox I placed on his lap, then wedged it under the right forearm and hand. As expected, these movements and handling began to penetrate Rory's consciousness.

Reluctantly, Rory's body began to articulate. Head lolled left and right as dry eyeballs sought focus through fluttering eyelids. Mouth and throat worked in unison to moisten tongue and lips. Nostrils stretched in search of oxygen. His lips parted, and a swollen, spittle tipped tongue ventured timidly out to taste the world.

"Rory. Rory. It's me, Jeff. How are you feeling? I got your message. I've come to take you to the dentist."

"Jeff, Jeff. Oh, shit, man. Thanks for coming, man. Where are we going?"

"To the dentist. Remember, you said I have to come and take you today."

"Rory, take off your sunglasses."

"Okay."

"Here, let me help you up."

"Where are we going again? I'm so tired. Do we have to?"

"I know you're tired, Rory. Look, you can sleep in the car. I'll drive, all right?"

"Okay. Yeah. Thanks, Jeff."

In a sudden lucid moment, Rory bolted upright.

"I don't have any socks or shoes on, Jeff."

"It's okay, Rory. I put some in the car. You can put them on after we get there."

Rory was heavy, and he stank. Seven days of dope, booze, fast food and limited hygiene had made their mark. Rory was pliable and malleable.

I steered Rory to the garage.

Rory complained he was cold and asked why we were going out.

I told Rory to get in the car and that I would turn the heat to warm him.

I guided Rory gently into the backseat.

"Hey, Jeff, why am I in the back?"

Public Service

"Ah, Rory. Just rest a little. Pretend I'm your chauffeur!"

I closed the door and moved around and into the driver's seat.

I looked back at Rory.

Rory Michael Ethan O'Grady wasn't really the enemy. In fact, Rory was one of the twenty per cent of public servants who cared about his responsibilities and duties: a good employee, by my reckoning. Rory had sought change for the better. Sure, he had a bitter and cynical streak and a huge chip on his shoulder about the plight of the Irish. I knew about his IRA sympathies, and I never understood how he reconciled his job in national security with his support of an avowed terrorist organization that sought change through violence. Rory also had a temper, and alluded on one drunken occasion to committing a violent crime or two in his past. Rory wasn't my best friend. I doubted he was anyone's best friend. Rory did not do warm and fuzzy. He did angry and oppressed. Unlike the others, I had broken bread with Rory, drank his beer, sat by his hearth and edged into his confidence.

Although Rory's name derived from royalty, he didn't look kingly. My own name had Teutonic origins and originated from one of three Old German names, meaning district, traveller, or peaceful pledge. Apparently, a Geoffrey Plantagenet was the father of King Henry II, and a Geoffrey Chaucer wrote *The Canterbury Tales*. Well, I hadn't fathered a king, or written any revered literature, so I guess bestowing a name on a child gives no assurance of the adult to follow. Then again, hadn't the majority of kings died ignominious and violent deaths, often at the hands of their most trusted allies? Perhaps Rory was dying a king's death after all!

I didn't like these thoughts. Rory had allowed himself to be manipulated. Rory deserved to die. Not because he threatened my job, or my family life, or because he was a part of the diseased public service: Rory deserved to die because he had been weak.

I turned the key, and the engine coughed noisily to life. Rory stirred, and the un-muffled roar from the exhaust aroused a faint suspicion. I needn't have worried, though. Rory slept. Exhaust fumes clouded the garage. I grasped Rory's BlackBerry and called up the Draft email folder. I clicked on the message I had prepared, opened it, and scrolled to the Send Delay function. I set the send time for noon. I reached back and took Rory's hand. I placed the BlackBerry in his hand and with his thumb pressed Send.

The fumes had accumulated. I felt dizzy. I stumbled to the back of the car and lifted the garage door. I rolled out under the door and pulled it down behind me. I lay, breathing heavily for several moments. The same night sounds of insects, lightly swaying trees, and the hum of distant traffic soothed my head as oxygen gained the upper hand over the carbon monoxide. Close. I almost ended up dying with Rory.

I got to my knees and leaned on the garage door for support. I waited a few seconds and then pushed off. Unsteady, I walked to my car and fell into the driver's seat.

I sat quiet and still. The digital clock on the dashboard had progressed to three-fourteen a.m. I drew deep breaths and stared at the garage. Faint, white grey wafts of hot exhaust fumes leaked from the side and top of the door. The buzz, the cumulative high from Lamkin, Hobbs, Hurley, and then Medowcroft and Kingsmore, and finally Rory, charged into my veins, my mind, and my soul. I felt fulfilled. Giddy and lightheaded, I turned the ignition, shifted the transmission to drive, and pulled gently away from 212 Shanua

Street.

When I arrived home at three-forty a.m., the kids were asleep, and I slipped into bed undetected. At six-thirty a.m., the sound of urgent police sirens, polite doorbell chimes, and pounding fists punctured my unconsciousness.

Epilogue

Philip Bergon
A Loose End

"Hi, Jeff, it's Philip."

"Hi, Philip, it's great to hear from you. How is retirement?"

"Really good thanks, Jeff. Lots of time for the grandkids, time at the cottage, and my wife and I have booked a cruse in Europe. How are things with you?"

"Things are a bit difficult, to be honest, Philip, even though everyone has been supportive and nice. I even got promoted, and will be able to complete my French language training soon, but I feel guilty about, you know, benefiting from what happened."

"You shouldn't feel guilty, Jeff. What Rory did had nothing to do with you. You're as much a victim as anyone else."

"Yeah, that's what others say as well. Still, it's not easy. How about you, Philip? How do you manage?"

"Well, that's kind of why I am calling. I have been doing quite well. After a month or so, thoughts of the deaths mostly fade away, but that detective, you know Stapleton, keeps coming to ask questions. Every time he asks me, the thoughts return and I end up back at square one. Does he bother you with questions, Jeff?"

Public Service

"Actually, no. I haven't heard from him for about three months. What does he want? What kind of questions has he been asking?"

"Well, that's the other reason I called. He seems to want to know more about you than Rory. I mean, he always starts by asking about Rory but then the questions drift to things about you."

"Mm, that's odd. What kind of questions?"

"Mostly he asks about your relationship with Rory. You know, how well you knew him, how much you hung out together, how often, stuff like that."

"I told him all that. I mean, it's no secret. It's too bad he has to keep asking you the same things and dragging up the memories for you. Maybe you should tell him to stop. Maybe ask your lawyer to keep him away."

"Yes, you're right, Jeff, and that's what I was about to do today, but then all the detective's questions finally triggered something that might explain why Rory killed everyone."

"Really, Philip, what?"

"The email, Jeff."

"Email. What email, Philip?"

"You know, the one between Kingsmore and Medowcroft when they discussed getting rid of Rory, and you, and me, to save money and use the money for Hobbs and Lamkin and poor Amy."

"Oh yeah, I remember that now."

"The thing is, Jeff; did you ever show it to Rory or tell him about it? I mean, if Rory knew about the plans to lay him off and use the money for the others, I bet that would have driven him crazy. You know Rory really hated Hobbs and Lamkin, and I thought the email might be the kind of thing Detective Stapleton would want to know about."

"Christ, Philip, you are right. I guess with all the

269

stress and worry, I forgot about that. Yes, I did tell Rory about it over a beer at his house, but you know he wasn't all that mad about it. Now you've made me remember, I recall that Rory just shrugged and didn't seem bothered, which was weird, I guess."

"That is strange. I would have expected Rory to rant and rave about it."

"Yeah, me too. Hey, Philip, have you told Stapleton about this yet?"

"No, not yet, I only remembered the email this morning. I thought I had better call you first and check my memory was right and if you had told Rory about it. I have to pick the grandkids up at noon and watch them until Friday while my son and his wife go to a concert in Toronto. I'll give Stapleton a call later today after the kids leave."

"Hey, Philip, I'm not busy. I could call Stapleton for you and explain the email. I mean, he will probably want to know all about when I told Rory and how he reacted and all that. I can save you having to explain the email, and I can tell him about how I told Rory. You should focus on your grandkids and not think about murders and death and all that while you are with them. I can do it, and I can ask Stapleton to give you a call next Monday after the kids are gone."

"Yeah, thanks, that would help a lot, Jeff. Tell Stapleton to call Monday but not too early. I'll be exhausted after having the kids for the weekend."

"Okay, Philip, no problem. Oh, Philip, what are you going to do with the kids on the weekend?"

"We're going to the cottage. The kids love the lake and the boat. On Sunday afternoon, my wife, Kate, is taking the kids to Almont for a festival, so I will have the place to myself for a few hours, and I will be able to get a little quiet fishing in."

Ah, that's the life, Philip. Have a great weekend,

and don't worry about the email and Detective Stapleton. I will take care of everything."

#

Since Philip's fatal boating accident, life has been good, better than ever. In six days, parliament will recess until September, and I can settle back and relax for the summer. The evidence against Rory was overwhelming, and as he could not speak in his own defence, Rory was quickly condemned as a despicable and deranged murderer who sought to counter his impotent and unfulfilled life with drugs and alcohol. The media added to Rory's character assassination by playing up Rory's IRA sympathies, and based on his possession of the *IRA Green Book*, portrayed Rory as an expert on death and suggested he may have been an international terrorist. The media attempted to pull me into their circus, but I stayed clear and issued only one statement: "I can't understand how it all happened, and my heart goes out to those who lost loved ones."

In January, without a competition, I received an acting senior policy analyst position. In October, I begin French language training until I reach the required proficiency to make my acting position permanent. I didn't really want a promotion, but the new assistant deputy minister of the secretariat insisted I accept. I think he wanted to give me something for surviving Rory's slaughter.

The new boss appears to be part of the ten per cent good management, and he is trying to create a positive and productive environment. Of course, the secretariat also gained a new director, to replace Medowcroft, and three new policy analysts to replace Hobbs, Lamkin, and O'Grady. Regrettably, the new director, plucked from the backwaters of the Department of the Environment, is no better than

Medowcroft. The new analysts, one senior and two junior, are firmly in the ninety per cent bad worker camp. They fawn, supplicant, flatter and play the game. They do not impress me.

Detective Stapleton visited me several times after my initial "help with inquiries" session in room 5 at Ottawa Police Headquarters. Each time, he asked open-ended questions about my relationship with Rory, especially concerning drugs, the secretariat, and how was it that I had no inkling of what Rory planned to do? The detective employed his eyebrow, silence, and speculative hypothesis in an attempt to draw me out. The detective had an itch, but I didn't help him scratch. Eventually, the detective scratched his itch, gave up, or moved on to another crime. Either way, he stopped coming by the early spring.

When I say life is good, I mean my job, pension, and family are all secure, I am not in prison, and everyone believes Rory committed the murders: all in line with my original objectives. In that sense, I achieved everything I set out to do. Yet, an unintended consequence of my actions has taken root in my essence. I have tasted the power to allow life or deliver death. I cannot cleanse my palate, nor banish the desire for more. I study public servants and assign them to an arbitrary scale of life or death. In my head, I formulate meticulous plans to cull the unworthy and clear the way for more deserving and virtuous people.

The federal public service employs more than a quarter of a million people. Based on employee performance reports, one per cent of employees rate as unsatisfactory, and one per cent rate as exceptional. However, as performance reports are often fraudulent, which of the two one per cents are more unworthy?

Public Service

During the quiet summer months, I will study and analyze these two "one per cents." Then I will decide which of the unworthy will satisfy my appetite and fill my desire.

After fifteen years in the federal government, I am finally enjoying public service.

<<<<>>>>

Made in the USA
San Bernardino, CA
26 March 2017